HARRAP'S

Agatha Raisin and the Vicious Vet

M.C. BEATON

First published in the UK by Constable, an imprint of the Little Brown Book group, in 2002.

Pour les notes en marge du texte :
© Larousse, 2020
21, rue du Montparnasse
75283 Paris CEDEX 06

HARRAP's® est une marque de Larousse SAS
www.harrap.com

ISBN 978 2 81 870709 8

About the author

M.C. BEATON was born in Glasgow in 1936. She was the author of both the Agatha Raisin and Hamish Macbeth series, as well as numerous Regency[1] romances. Her Agatha Raisin books were turned into a TV series on Sky[2].

She lived in Paris and in a Cotswold village that is very much like Agatha's beloved[3] Carsely. She died in December 2019.

1. de l'époque de la Régence britannique [début du XIXe s.]

2. [chaîne de télévision par satellite]

3. cher

DIRECTION DE LA PUBLICATION : Carine Girac-Marinier

NOTES EN MARGE : Étienne Leyris

RÉVISION DES NOTES : Marianne Mouchot

RELECTURE : F. Le Dantec

INFORMATIQUE ÉDITORIALE ET MISE EN PAGES :
Philippe Cazabet, Sharareh Maljaei, Marie-Noëlle Tilliette

CONCEPTION GRAPHIQUE : Uli Meindl

FABRICATION : Rebecca Dubois

Mot de l'Éditeur

Vous aimeriez lire en langue originale, mais le vocabulaire, les expressions figurées ou la syntaxe vous arrêtent parfois ?

Cette collection est faite pour vous !

Vous trouverez en effet, en note dans la marge, une traduction de certains mots et expressions qui vous permettra d'avancer facilement dans votre lecture.

Nous n'avons pas cherché à vous donner une traduction littéraire de l'ouvrage et nous nous sommes parfois écartés du sens littéral pour vous fournir le sens qui convient le mieux à l'histoire. Aussi les mots sont-ils traduits dans le contexte du texte original.

Les expressions figées anglaises sont, bien entendu, rendues par une expression équivalente en français.

Les allusions à des réalités culturelles du monde anglo-saxon sont expliquées également dans la marge, pour vous aider à mieux comprendre la trame de l'histoire.

Vous aurez ainsi, en regard du texte original, tout le savoir-faire d'un dictionnaire rien que pour vous et adapté à ce livre !

Notre objectif est de vous mener jusqu'au mot FIN en vous donnant les clés nécessaires à la compréhension du récit.

Laissez-vous gagner par l'angoisse, l'humour et le suspense qui règnent chez les maîtres de la littérature anglo-saxonne.

Lire en VO ? You can indeed!

Coup de pouce pour vous aider à bien comprendre le début de l'histoire...

Agatha, qui a brillamment résolu le mystère de la quiche empoisonnée*, a décidé de s'installer pour de bon dans son petit coin d'Angleterre pittoresque. Mais elle doit reconnaître que les vacances qu'elle s'est accordées dans la foulée n'ont pas été une réussite... Le beau colonel en retraite James Lacey n'était pas au rendez-vous.

* *1er volume de la série, en VO et en Yes You Can.*

Chapter One

Agatha Raisin arrived at Heathrow Airport with a tan[1] outside and a blush of shame[2] inside. She felt an utter fool[3] as she pushed her load[4] of luggage towards the exit.

She had just spent[5] two weeks in the Bahamas in pursuit of her handsome neighbour, James Lacey, who had let fall that he was going to holiday there at the Nassau Beach Hotel. Agatha in pursuit of a man was as ruthless[6] as she had been in business. She had spent a great deal of money on a fascinating wardrobe[7], had slimmed[8] furiously so as to be able to sport[9] her rejuvenated[10] middle-aged figure[11] in a bikini, but there had been no sign of James Lacey. She had hired a car and toured[12] the other hotels on the island to no avail[13]. She had even called at the British High Commission in the hope they had heard of him. A few days before she was due to return[14], she had put a long-distance call through to Carsely, the village in the Cotswolds in which she lived, to the vicar's[15] wife, Mrs Bloxby, and had finally got around to[16] asking for the whereabouts of[17] James Lacey.

She still remembered Mrs Bloxby's voice, strengthening and fading on a bad line, as if borne towards Agatha on the tide[18]. 'Mr Lacey changed his plans at the very last[19] minute. He decided to spend his holiday with a friend in

1. bronzée
2. rouge de honte
3. une parfaite idiote
4. cargaison
5. venait de passer
6. impitoyable
7. garde-robe
8. maigri
9. de montrer à son avantage
10. rajeunie
11. silhouette
12. fait le tour
13. sans succès
14. la date prévue pour son retour
15. du pasteur
16. s'était résolue à
17. où se trouvait
18. comme portée vers Agatha par la marée
19. toute dernière

ro. He did say he was going to the Bahamas, remember, and Mrs Mason said, "What a surrise! That's where our Mrs Raisin is going." And the next thing we knew[1] this friend in Egypt had invited him over.'

How Agatha had squirmed[2] and was still squirming. It was plain to her[3] that he had changed his plans simply so as not to meet her. In retrospect, her pursuit of him had been rather blatant[4].

And there was another reason she had not enjoyed her holiday. She had put her cat, Hodge, a present from Detective Sergeant Bill Wong, into a cattery[5] and somehow[6] Agatha found she was worrying that the cat might have died.

At the Long-Stay Car-Park, she loaded in her luggage and then set out to drive to Carsely, wondering again why she had ever retired[7] so young – well, these days early fifties[8] *was* young – and sold her business to bury herself in a country village.

The cattery was outside Cirencester. She went up to the house and was greeted ungraciously by the thin rangy[9] woman who owned the place. 'Really, Mrs Raisin,' she said, 'I am just going out. It would have been more considerate[10] of you to phone.'

'Get my animal ... *now*,' said Agatha, glaring balefully[11], 'and be quick about it.'

The woman stalked off[12], affront in every line of her body[13]. Soon she came back with Hodge mewling[14] in his carrying basket. Totally deaf to further[15] recriminations, Agatha paid the fee[16].

Being reunited with her cat, she decided, was a very comforting thing, and then wondered if she was reduced to the status of village lady, drooling over[17] an animal.

2. Aga s'était sentie horriblement embarrassée

3. lui parut évident

4. flagrante

5. pension pour chats

6. curieusement,

7. pourquoi diable elle avait pris sa retraite

8. le début de la cinquantaine

9. longiligne

10. courtois

11. jetant un regard mauvais

12. s'éloigna d'un pas raide

13. avec la posture de celle que l'on a froissée

14. qui geignait

15. Sourde à toute autre

16. la note

17. à s'extasier devant

Her cottage, crouched under its heavy weight of thatch[1], was like an old dog, waiting to welcome her. When the fire had been lit, the cat fed, and with a stiff[2] whisky inside her, Agatha felt she would survive. Bugger[3] James Lacey and all men!

She went to the local store, Harvey's, in the morning to get some groceries and to show off her tan[4]. She ran into[5] Mrs Bloxby. Agatha felt uncomfortable about that phone call but Mrs Bloxby, ever tactful, did not remind her of it, merely[6] saying that there was a meeting of the Carsely Ladies' Society at the vicarage[7] that evening. Agatha said she would attend[8], although thinking there must be more to social life than[9] tea at the vicarage.

She had half a mind[10] not to go. Instead she could go to the Red Lion, the local pub, for dinner. But on the other hand, she had promised Mrs Bloxby that she would go, and somehow one did not break promises to Mrs Bloxby.

When she made her way out that evening, a thick fog had settled down on the village, thick, freezing fog, turning bushes into crouching assailants[11] and muffling[12] sound.

The ladies were all there among the pleasant clutter[13] of the vicarage sitting-room. Nothing had changed. Mrs Mason was still the chairwoman – chairpersons did not exist in Carsely[14] because, as Mrs Bloxby pointed out, once you started that sort of thing you didn't know where to stop[15], and things like manholes would become personholes[16] – and Miss Simms, in Minnie Mouse white shoes and skimpy[17] skirt, still the secretary. Agatha was pressed for details about her holiday and so she bragged[18] about the sun and the sand until she began to feel she had actually[19] had a good time.

1. tassé sous son lourd toit de chaume
2. bien raide
3. Au diable
4. montrer comme elle était bronzée
5. tomba sur
6. seulement
7. presbytère
8. y serait
9. qu'il il devait y avoir mieux à faire dans la vie qu'aller prendre
10. bien envie de
11. qui transformait les buissons en agresseurs prêts à bondir
12. étouffant
13. désordre
14. la présidente – à Carsely on ne se lançait pas dans les « un(e) président(e) »,
15. après on ne sait pas où s'arrêter
16. on se retrouve à mettre « un(e) individu(e) »
17. minimale
18. en fit des tonnes
19. vraiment

The minutes[1] were read, raising money[2] for Save the Children was discussed, an outing for the old folks, and then more tea and cake.

That was when Agatha heard about the new vet. The village of Carsely had a veterinary surgery[3] at last. An extension had been built onto the library building. A vet, Paul Bladen, from Mircester, held a surgery[4] there twice a week on Tuesday and Wednesday afternoons.

'We weren't going to bother at first,' said Miss Simms, 'because we usually go to the vet at Moreton, but Mr Bladen's ever[5] so good.'

'And ever so good-looking,' put in Mrs Bloxby.

'Young?' asked Agatha with a flicker[6] of interest.

'Oh, about forty, I think,' said Miss Simms. 'Not married. Divorced. He's got these searching eyes[7], and such beautiful hands.'

Agatha was not particularly interested in the vet, for her thoughts were still on James Lacey. She wished he would return so that she could show him she did not care for him at all. So, as the ladies gushed their praise for[8] the new vet, she sat writing scripts in her head about what he would say and what she would say, and imagining how surprised he would be to find out that ordinary neighbourly friendliness[9] on her part had been mistaken on his for pursuit[10].

But as the fates would have it[11], Agatha was destined to meet Paul Bladen the very next day[12].

She decided to go to the butcher's and get herself a steak and buy some chicken livers[13] for Hodge. 'Marnin'[14], Mr Bladen,' said the butcher, and Agatha turned round.

Paul Bladen was a good-looking man in his early forties with thick wavy fair hair dusted with[15] grey, light-brown eyes which crinkled up[16]

1. comptes rendus
2. une collecte de fonds
3. cabinet vétérinaire
4. des consultations
5. vraiment
6. pointe
7. ce regard perçant
8. se répandaient en louanges sur
9. une simple attitude de bon voisinage
10. du harcèlement
11. ironie du sort
12. lendemain même
13. des foies de volaille
14. B'jour
15. saupoudrés de
16. se plissaient

as though against the desert sun[1], a firm, rather sweet mouth, and a square chin. He was slim, of medium height, and wore a tweed jacket with patches[2] and flannels[3] and, for[4] it was a freezing day, an old London University scarf about his neck. He reminded Agatha of the old days when university students dressed like university students, before the days of T-shirts and frayed[5] jeans.

For his part, Paul Bladen saw a stocky[6] middle-aged woman with shiny brown hair and small, bearlike eyes in a tanned face. Her clothes, he noticed, were very expensive.

Agatha thrust out her hand and introduced herself, welcoming him to the village in her best lady-of-the-manor voice[7]. He smiled into her eyes[8], holding on to her hand, and murmuring something about the dreadful weather. Agatha forgot all about James Lacey. Or nearly. Let him rot[9] in Egypt. She hoped he'd got gippy tummy[10], she hoped a camel bit him.

'As a matter of fact,' cooed[11] Agatha, 'I was coming to see you. With my cat.'

Did a frost settle momentarily on those crinkled eyes? But he said, 'There is a surgery this afternoon. Why don't you bring the animal along? Say, two o'clock?'

'How lovely to have our own vet at last,' enthused[12] Agatha.

He gave her that intimate smile of his again and Agatha went out treading on air[13]. Fog was still holding the countryside in its grip[14] although, far, far above, a little red disc of a sun struggled to get through, casting a faint pink light on the frost-covered landscape, which reminded Agatha of the Christmas calendars of her youth where the winter scenes were decorated with glitter[15].

1. comme pour se protéger du soleil du désert
2. des coudières
3. un pantalon de flanelle
4. car
5. râpés
6. trapue
7. de son ton le plus aristocratique
8. en la regardant droit dans les yeux
9. Qu'il aille moisir
10. la turista
11. roucoula
12. s'enthousiasma
13. aux anges
14. Le brouillard enserrait toujours la campagne
15. des paillettes

She hurried past James Lacey's cottage without a glance, thinking what to wear. What a pity all those new clothes had been meant for[1] hot weather.

While the tabby[2], Hodge, watched curiously, she studied her face in the dressing-table mirror. A tan was all very well, but there was a lot to be said for thick make-up on a middle-aged face. There was a pouchy softness[3] under her chin which she did not like and the lines down the side of her mouth[4] appeared more pronounced since before she had gone away, reminding her of all the dire warnings[5] about what sun-bathing did to the skin[6].

She slapped on[7] skin-food[8] and then rummaged through her wardrobe[9], settling at last on[10] a cherry-red dress and black tailored coat with a velvet collar. Her hair was shiny and healthy, so she decided not to wear a hat. It was a bitterly cold day and she should wear her boots, but she had a new pair of Italian high heels and she knew her legs were good[11].

It was only after two hours of diligent preparation that she realized she had first to catch her cat, eventually running the animal to earth[12] in a corner of the kitchen and shoving him ruthlessly[13] in the wicker[14] carrying basket. Hodge's wails[15] rent the air. But deaf for once to her pet, Agatha tripped along[16] to the surgery in her high heels. By the time she reached the surgery, her feet were so cold she felt she was walking on two lumps of pain[17].

She pushed open the surgery door and went into the waiting-room. It seemed to be full of people: Doris Simpson, her cleaning woman[18], with her cat; Miss Simms with her Tommy; Mrs Josephs, the librarian, with a larger mangy[19] cat called Tewks;

1. prévus pour
2. chat tigré
3. zone toute bouffie
4. rides aux commissures des lèvres
5. terribles mises en garde
6. la nocivité du bronzage pour la peau
7. appliqua rapidement
8. une crème nutritive
9. fouilla dans sa garde-robe
10. se décidant finalement pour
11. qu'elle avait de belles jambes
12. et parvint enfin à le débusquer
13. sans ménagement
14. en osier
15. Les miaulements désespérés
16. partit gaiement
17. blocs douloureux
18. femme de ménage
19. galeux

and two farmers, Jack Page, whom she knew, and a squat burly[1] man she only knew by sight, Henry Grange. There was also a newcomer.

'Her be[2] Mrs Huntingdon,' whispered Doris. 'Bought old Droon's cottage up back. Widow.'

Agatha eyed the newcomer jealously. Despite the efforts of Animal Liberation to stop women from wearing furs, Mrs Huntingdon sported[3] a ranch mink[4] coat with a smart[5] mink hat. A delicate French perfume floated from her. She had a small pretty face like that of an enamelled[6] doll, large hazel[7] eyes with (false?) eyelashes, and a pink-painted mouth. Her pet was a small Jack Russell which barked furiously, swinging on the end of its lead[8] as it tried to get at the cats. Mrs Huntingdon seemed unaware[9] of the noise or of the baleful looks cast at her by[10] the cat owners. She was also sitting blocking the only heater.

There were 'No Smoking' signs all over the walls, but Mrs Huntingdon lit up a cigarette and blew smoke up into the air. In a doctor's waiting-room, where patients had only themselves to worry about, there would have been protests. But a vet's waiting-room is a singularly unmanning or unwomanning place[11], people made timid by worry about their pets[12].

Along one side of the waiting-room was a desk with a nurse-cum-receptionist[13] behind it. She was a plain girl with lank[14] brown hair and the adenoidal[15] accents of Birmingham. Her name was Miss Mabbs.

Doris Simpson was the first to go in and was only out of sight for five minutes. Agatha surreptitiously[16] rubbed her cold feet and ankles. This would not take long.

1. costaud
2. Elle, c'est
3. arborait
4. de vison [d'élevage]
5. élégant
6. émaillée
7. noisette
8. sa laisse
9. ne pas s'apercevoir
10. regards menaçants que lui lançaient
11. un lieu où curieusement hommes et femmes se résignent
12. animaux de compagnie
13. infirmière-réceptionniste
14. ternes et mous
15. nasillards
16. furtivement

But Miss Simms was next and she was in there for half an hour, emerging at last with her eyes shining and her cheeks pink. Mrs Josephs had her turn. After a very long time she came out, murmuring, 'Such a firm hand Mr Bladen does have,' while her ancient cat lay supine[1] in its basket as one dead.

Agatha went to the counter after Mrs Huntingdon was ushered in[2] and said to Miss Mabbs, 'Mr Bladen told me to call[3] at two. I have been waiting a considerable time.'

'Surgery starts at two. That's probably what he meant,' said Miss Mabbs. 'You'll need to wait your turn.'

Determined not to have got all dressed up[4] for nothing, Agatha sulkily[5] picked up a copy[6] of *Vogue*, June 1997, and retreated to her hard plastic chair.

She waited and waited for the merry widow plus dog to reappear, but the minutes ticked past and Agatha could hear a ripple of laughter[7] from the surgery and wondered what was going on in there.

Three quarters of an hour went by while Agatha finished the copy of *Vogue* and a well-preserved 1990 copy of *Good Housekeeping* and was absorbed in a story in an old *Scotch Home* annual about the handsome laird[8] of the Scottish highlands who forsook his 'ain true love'[9] Morag of the glens for Cynthia, some painted harlot[10] from London. At last Mrs Huntingdon came out, holding her dog. She smiled vaguely all around before leaving and Agatha glowered back[11].

There were only the two farmers and Agatha left. 'Reckon I won't be coming here again[12],' said Jack Page. 'Waste a whole day, this would.'

1. gisant
2. qu'on eut fait entrer Mrs Huntingdon
3. me présenter
4. à ne pas s'être bien habillée
5. la mine renfrognée
6. numéro
7. des rires en cascade
8. lord [écossais]
9. avait délaissé sa « douce amie »
10. une cocotte peinturlurée
11. lança un regard noir en retour
12. M'est avis que je suis pas prêt de revenir

But he was dealt with[1] very quickly, having come to collect a prescription[2] for antibiotics, which he handed over to Miss Mabbs. The other farmer also wanted drugs[3] and Agatha brightened as he reappeared after only a few moments. She had meant to berate the[4] vet for having kept her waiting so long but there was that sweet smile again, that firm clasp of the hand, those searching, intimate eyes.

Feeling quite fluttery[5] and at the same time guilty[6], for there was nothing up with Hodge[7], Agatha smiled back in a dazed way.

'Ah, Mrs Raisin,' said the vet, 'let's have the cat out. What's his name?'

'Hodge.'

'Same as Dr Johnson's cat.'

'Who's he? Your partner at Mircester?'

'Dr *Samuel* Johnson[8], Mrs Raisin.'

'Well, how was I to know?' demanded Agatha crossly[9], her private opinion being that Dr Johnson was one of those old farts[10] like Sir Thomas Beecham that people always seemed to be quoting[11] loftily[12] at dinner parties. James Lacey had suggested the name.

To hide her irritation, she raised Hodge's basket on to the examining table and undid the latch[13] and opened the front. 'Come on now, out you come,' cooed Agatha to a baleful Hodge who crouched at the back of the basket.

'Let me[14],' said the vet, edging Agatha aside[15]. He thrust a hand in and brutally dragged Hodge out into the light and then held the squirming, yowling animal by the scruff[16] up in the air.

'Oh, don't do that! You're scaring him,' protested Agatha. 'Let me hold him.'

1. son affaire fut réglée
2. prendre une ordonnance
3. des médicaments
4. se plaindre auprès du
5. émoustillée
6. coupable
7. Hodge n'avait rien du tout
8. [écrivain et lexicographe anglais du XVIIIe s.]
9. avec humeur
10. schnoques
11. citer
12. avec hauteur
13. défit le loquet
14. Laissez-moi faire
15. en poussant Agatha sur le côté
16. attrapa par la peau du cou l'animal qui se tortillait et miaulait de toutes ses forces

'Very well. He looks remarkably healthy. What's up with him[1]?'

Hodge buried his head in the opening of Agatha's coat. 'Er, he's off his food[2],' said Agatha.

'Any sickness, diarrhoea?'

'No.'

'Well, we'd best take his temperature. Miss Mabbs!'

Miss Mabbs came in and stood with head lowered. 'Hold the cat,' ordered the vet.

Miss Mabbs detached the cat from Agatha and pinned him down[3] with one strong hand on the examining table.

The vet advanced on Hodge with a rectal thermometer. Could it be, wondered Agatha, that the thermometer was thrust up poor Hodge's backside[4] with unnecessary force? The cat yowled[5], struggled free[6], sprang from the table and crouched in a corner of the room.

'I've made a mistake,' said Agatha, now desperate to get her pet away. 'Perhaps if he shows any severe signs I'll bring him back.'

Miss Mabbs was dismissed. Agatha tenderly put Hodge back in the basket.

'Mrs Raisin.'

'Yes?' Agatha surveyed him with bearlike eyes[7] from which the love-light had totally fled[8].

'There is quite a good Chinese restaurant in Evesham. I've had a hard day and feel like treating myself[9]. Would you care to join me for dinner?'

Agatha felt gratified warmth[10] coursing through[11] her middle-aged body. Bugger[12] all cats in general and Hodge in particular. 'I'd love to,' she breathed.

'Then I'll meet you there at eight o'clock,' he said, smiling into her eyes. 'It's called the Evesham

1. Qu'est-ce qui ne va pas
2. ne mange plus
3. l'immobilisa
4. dans le derrière du pauvre Hodge
5. hurla
6. se dégagea
7. le toisa d'un œil torve
8. qui n'avait plus rien de langoureux
9. j'ai bien envie de m'offrir ça
10. une douce vague de chaleur
11. parcourir
12. Au diable

Diner. It's in an old house in the High Street, seventeenth century, can't miss it.'

Agatha emerged grinning smugly into[1] the now empty waiting-room. She wished she had been the first 'patient' so she could have told all those other women she had a date[2].

But she stopped at the store on the road home and bought Hodge a tin of the best salmon to ease her[3] conscience.

By the time she had reached home and cosseted[4] Hodge and settled him in front of a roaring fire, she had persuaded herself that the vet had been firm and efficient with the cat, not deliberately cruel.

The desire to brag about[5] her date was strong, so she phoned the vicar's wife, Mrs Bloxby.

'Guess what?' said Agatha.

'Another murder?' suggested the vicar's wife.

'Better than that. Our new vet is taking me out for dinner this evening.'

There was a long silence.

'Are you there?' demanded Agatha sharply.

'Yes, I'm here. I was just thinking …'

'What?'

'Why is he taking you out[6]?'

'I should have thought that was obvious,' snarled[7] Agatha. 'He fancies me[8].'

'Forgive me. Of *course* he does. It's just that I feel there is something cold and calculating about him. Do be careful.'

'I am not sweet sixteen[9],' said Agatha huffily[10].

'Exactly.'

That 'exactly' seemed to Agatha to be saying, 'You are a middle-aged woman easily flattered by the attentions of a younger man.'

1. souriant avec suffisance à

2. rendez-vous [galant]

3. pour se donner bonne

4. dorloté

5. se vanter

6. vous invite-t-il à dîner

7. grinça

8. Je lui plais

9. une ado

10. avec humeur

'In any case,' Mrs Bloxby went on, 'do go very carefully on the roads. It's starting to snow.'

Agatha rang off, feeling flat[1], and then she began to smile. Of course! Mrs Bloxby was jealous. All the women in the village were smitten by[2] the vet. But what was that she had said about snow? Agatha twitched back[3] the curtain and looked out. Wet snow was falling, but it was not lying on the ground.

At seven thirty she drove off in all the discomfort of a tight body stocking[4] under a gold silk Armani dress embellished with a rope of pearls. Her heels were very high, so she kicked them off and drove up the hill from the village in her stockinged feet[5].

The snow was getting thicker and suddenly, near the top of the hill, she crossed over a sort of snow-line and found herself driving over thick snow. But ahead lay the tempting vision of dinner with the vet.

She pressed her foot on the brake to slow down as she neared the A44 and quite suddenly the car went into a skid[6]. It was all so quick, so breathlessly fast[7]. Her headlights[8] whirled crazily round[9] the winter landscape, and then there was a sickening crunch[10] as she hit a stone wall on her left. She switched off the lights[11] and the engine with a trembling hand and sat still.

A car going the other way, towards the village, stopped. A door opened and closed. Then a dark figure loomed up[12] on Agatha's side of the car. She opened the window. 'Are you all right, Mrs Raisin?' came James Lacey's voice.

Before the vet, before the fiasco of the Bahamas, Agatha had often fantasized about James

1. déprimée
2. en pinçaient pour
3. écarta
4. body très ajusté
5. en collants
6. partit en dérapage
7. d'une soudaineté à couper le souffle
8. phares
9. balayèrent follement
10. horrible craquement
11. phares
12. surgit

Lacey rescuing her from some accident. But all she could think about now was that precious date.

'I think nothing's broken,' said Agatha and then struck the wheel[1] in frustration. 'Bloody, bloody snow. I say[2], can you run me[3] into Evesham?'

'You must be joking. It's to get worse[4], or so the weather forecast said[5]. Fish Hill will be closed.'

'Oh, no,' wailed[6] Agatha. 'Maybe we could go another way. Maybe through Chipping Campden.'

'Don't be silly. Does your engine still work?'

Agatha switched it on and it sprang into life[7].

'What about the lights?'

Agatha switched them on, glaring out at a snow-covered wilderness.

James Lacey inspected the damage to the front of the car. 'The glass in your headlamps is all shattered and you'll need a new bumper[8], radiator, and number-plate[9]. You'd best back out[10] and follow me down to the village.'

'If you won't run me, then I'll get a cab[11].'

'You can try.' He walked off to[12] his own car and Agatha heard him starting up. She reversed[13] and followed him. He parked outside his own house, waved to her, and strode indoors.

Agatha leaped out[14] of her own car, forgetting she was in her stockinged feet, and ran into the house. She seized the phone and, looking at a list of taxi-cab companies pinned to the wall, she began to phone them one after the other, but no taxi driver was prepared to go to Evesham or anywhere else on such a night.

Dammit, thought Agatha furiously, my car still works. I'm going.

She pulled on a pair of boots over her wet feet and went out again. But she was half-way up the

1. le volant
2. Dites-moi
3. m'emmener
4. Il est prévu que ça s'aggrave
5. selon la météo
6. gémit
7. redémarra immédiatement
8. pare-chocs
9. plaque d'immatriculation
10. feriez mieux de faire marche arrière
11. taxi
12. regagna
13. fit marche arrière
14. bondit hors

hill again when both her headlamps blew[1], leaving her crawling along[2] in snowy darkness.

Wearily[3], she turned the car and headed back down to the village again. Back indoors, she phoned the Chinese restaurant. No, came a voice at the other end, Mr Bladen had not turned up[4]. Yes, he had booked[5] a table. No, he had definitely[6] not arrived.

Feeling very flat, Agatha phoned Directory Enquiries[7] and got a Mircester number for the vet. A woman answered the phone. 'I am afraid Mr Bladen is busy at the moment.' The voice was cool and amused.

'This is Agatha Raisin,' snapped[8] Agatha. 'He was to meet me in a restaurant in Evesham tonight.'

'You could hardly have expected him to drive in such weather.'

'Who is speaking, please?' demanded Agatha.

'This is his wife.'

'Oh!' Agatha dropped the receiver like a hot coal[9].

So he was still married after all! What was it all about? But if he were married, then he should not have asked her out[10]. Agatha had very firm views about dating married men.

She felt somehow as if he had set out to deliberately[11] make a fool of her. Men! And James Lacey! He had simply gone indoors without calling to see if she were indeed unharmed[12] after her accident.

Agatha felt silly and now she had only a ruined[13] car to show for[14] her dreams of a date with a handsome man. She passed the rest of the evening filling in[15] an accident claim form[16], the purring[17] Hodge on her lap.

* * *

1. s'éteignirent
2. avancer au pas
3. Avec lassitude
4. n'était pas arrivé
5. réservé
6. assurément
7. le service des renseignements
8. dit sèchement
9. tison brûlant
10. n'aurait pas dû l'inviter à dîner
11. avait fait exprès
12. elle était indemme
13. fichu
14. en témoignage de
15. à remplir
16. formulaire de déclaration d'accident
17. ronronnant

The next day dawned foggy as well as snowy[1]. Once more Agatha felt that old trapped feeling. She waited and waited for the phone to ring, sure that Paul Bladen would call her to say *something*. But it sat there, squat in its silence[2].

At last she decided to pay a visit to her neighbour, James Lacey, if only to explain to him, subtly, that she had not been pursuing him. But although a thin column of smoke rose from his chimney, although his snow-covered car was parked outside, he did not answer the door[3].

Agatha felt well and truly[4] snubbed[5]. She was sure he was in there.

Hodge, in the selfish way of cats, played happily in the snow in the garden, stalking[6] imaginary prey.

In the afternoon, the doorbell went[7]. Agatha peered at herself[8] in the hall mirror, grabbed a lipstick she always kept ready on the hall table and painted her mouth. Then, smoothing down[9] her dress, she opened the door.

'Oh, it's you,' she said, looking down into the round oriental features of Detective Sergeant Bill Wong.

'That's not much of a greeting[10],' he said. 'Any chance of a cup of coffee?'

'Come in,' said Agatha, leaning over his shoulder and peering hopefully up and down the lane.

'Who were you expecting?' he asked, when they were seated in the kitchen.

'I was expecting an apology[11]. Our new vet, Paul Bladen, invited me out for dinner in Evesham last night, but I had a skid at the top of the road and couldn't make it[12]. But as it turned out[13], he didn't even get to the restaurant. I phoned his

1. apporta autant de brouillard que de neige
2. buté dans son silence
3. ne vint pas ouvrir
4. bel et bien
5. snobée
6. traquant
7. retentit
8. se regarda
9. lissant
10. Comme accueil on fait mieux
11. des excuses
12. je n'ai pas pu m'y rendre
13. finalement

home and a woman answered it. She said she was his wife.'

'Couldn't be,' said Bill. 'He was separated from his wife for about five years and the divorce came through[1] last year.'

'What's he playing at?' cried Agatha, exasperated.

'You mean, who's he playing with. Snowy night, no way of getting to Evesham, had a bit of fun at home instead.'

'Well, he should have phoned anyway,' said Agatha.

'Talking about your love life, how did you get on in the Bahamas?'

'Nice,' said Agatha. 'Got some sun.'

'See anything of Mr Lacey?'

'Didn't expect to. He'd gone to Cairo.'

'And you knew that before you left?'

'What is this?' exclaimed Agatha. 'A police interrogation?'

'Just friendly questions. Glad to see Hodge is happy. Looking very fit[2].'

'Oh, Hodge is in the best of health.'

The almond-shaped eyes studying her so intently glittered slightly in the white light from the snow coming in the kitchen window.

'Then why did poor Hodge have to go to this vet?'

'Have you been spying on me?'

'No, I just happened to be passing[3] yesterday and I saw you carrying Hodge in a basket to the surgery. You should wear more sensible footwear[4] in[5] this weather.'

'I just wanted to check the cat had all his shots[6],' said Agatha, 'and what I choose to wear on my feet is my business.'

1. a été prononcé
2. Il a l'air en pleine forme
3. il se trouve que je passais par là
4. vous chausser mieux que ça
5. par
6. vaccins

He raised his hands and let them fall. 'Sorry. Funny thing about Bladen, though.'

'What?'

'He went into partnership with Peter Rice, the vet in Mircester, some time ago. What a queue of women there were during the first weeks! Right out[1] in the street. But then they stopped coming. Seems Bladen is no good with pets. He's a whiz[2] with farm animals and horses, but he loathes[3] cats and small dogs.'

'I don't want to talk about the man,' said Agatha hotly[4]. 'Haven't you got anything else to talk about?'

So Bill told her all about the trouble with the increase in car theft in the area and how a lot of the crime was being increasingly committed by juveniles[5], while Agatha listened with half an ear and hoped the phone would ring to salve her pride[6]. But by the time Bill left, the wretched machine[7] was still silent.

She phoned the local garage and told them to come and tow her broken car away[8] and give her an estimate[9], and then, after she had seen her vehicle carried off down the street on the back of a truck, she decided to go down to the Red Lion. There was no reason to dress up[10] any more. For months now she had worn only her best and smartest clothes when passing James Lacey's door. She put on a thick sweater, a tweed skirt and boots. But just as she was shrugging herself into[11] a sheep-skin[12] coat, the telephone suddenly shrilled[13], making her jump[14].

She picked it up, sure it would be Paul Bladen at last, but a voice she did not recognize said tentatively[15], 'Agatha?'

1. Jusque
2. un as
3. déteste
4. avec véhémence
5. des mineurs
6. préserver son amour-propre
7. ce fichu téléphone
8. venir prendre avec leur dépanneuse sa voiture cassée
9. de lui faire un devis
10. bien s'habiller
11. endossait
12. en peau de mouton
13. retentit, strident
14. sursauter
15. avec hésitation

'Yes, who is it?' said Agatha, made cross by disappointment[1].

'It's Jack Pomfret. Remember me?'

Agatha brightened. Jack Pomfret had run[2] a rival public relations company to her own, but they had always been on amicable terms.

'Of course. How's things?'

'I sold out[3] about the same time as you,' he said. 'Decided to take a leaf out of your book[4], have early retirement[5], have a bit of fun. But it get's boring, know what I mean?'

'Oh, yes,' said Agatha with feeling[6].

'I'm thinking of starting up again and wondered if you would like to be my partner[7].'

'Bad time,' said Agatha cautiously. 'Middle of a recession.'

'Big companies need PR[8] and I've got two lined up[9], Jobson's Electronics and Whiter Washing Powder.'

Agatha was impressed. 'Are you anywhere near here?' she asked. 'We need to sit down together and discuss this properly[10].'

'What I thought,' he said eagerly[11], 'was if you could take a trip up to London, we could get down to business[12].'

The thought of fleeing the village, of getting away from lost romantic hopes, made Agatha say, 'I'll do that. I'll book a place in town. What's your number? I'll call you back.'

She wrote down his phone number and then, about to[13] phone her favourite hotel, paused. Damn Hodge. She couldn't really dump that poor animal back[14] in the cattery. Then she remembered a block of expensive service flats[15] into which she had once booked visiting foreign clients and phoned them and managed to get

1. la déception l'ayant mise de mauvaise humeur
2. dirigé
3. J'ai liquidé ma boîte
4. de prendre exemple sur vous
5. de prendre une retraite anticipée
6. chaleur
7. associée
8. [public relations]
9. en vue
10. sérieusement
11. avec empressement
12. entrer dans le vif du sujet
13. sur le point de
14. relarguer ce pauvre minet
15. résidence haut de gamme [avec meublés et service de ménage et restauration]

a flat for two weeks. She was sure they did not allow pets but she wasn't even going to ask them. Hodge could survive indoors for two weeks. The weather was lousy[1] anyway.

1. pourri

Chapter Two

Agatha could not immediately plunge into business affairs, for[1] Hodge, who had kept all his destruction to the outdoors in Carsely, had started to scratch the furniture[2] in the service flat in Kensington, and so Agatha had to buy a scratching post[3] and spend some time crouched on the floor in front of it[4], raking it with her fingernails[5], to show the cat what to do.

Having seen her pet settled at last, she phoned Jack Pomfret, who said he would meet her at the Savoy Grill for lunch.

Carsely was whirling away to a small speck[6] in Agatha's mind. She was back in London, part of it again, not visiting, back in business.

Jack Pomfret, a slim Oxbridge[7] type, fighting the age battle[8] in denim[9] and hair-weave[10], enthused over Agatha's appearance[11]. Agatha curiously asked him why he had really decided to sell up.

'Just like you,' he said with a boyish grin. 'Thought retirement would suit me. Actually[12] we, that's my wife, Marcia, and I, moved to Spain for a bit, but the climate didn't suit us. Down in the south. Too hot. But tell me all about yourself and what you've been doing.'

Agatha settled back[13] and bragged about her part in a murder investigation, highly embroidered.

1. car
2. à faire ses griffes sur le mobilier
3. arbre à gratter
4. accroupie devant
5. en le griffant elle-même
6. n'était plus qu'un petit point tourbillonnant au loin
7. [contraction d'Oxford et Cambridge]
8. qui essayait de faire jeune
9. en jean
10. avec un postiche
11. complimenta Agatha pour son look
12. En fait
13. se mit à l'aise

'But village life must be absolutely stultifying[1] for you, darling,' he said, smiling into her eyes in a way that reminded Agatha of the vet. 'All those dead brains[2] and clodhoppers[3].'

'I must admit I get bored,' said Agatha, and then felt a pang of guilt[4] as the faces of the village women rose before her eyes. 'Actually, everyone's very nice, very kind. It's not them. It's me. I'm just not used to country life.'

They talked on until the coffee arrived and then got down to business. Jack said that there was an office up at Marble Arch they could rent. All they really needed to kick off[5] were three rooms. Agatha studied the figures[6]. He seemed to have gone into[7] everything very carefully.

'This rent is very high,' said Agatha. 'We would be better to get the end of a lease[8] somewhere. Then, before we even start thinking about it, we should be sure we had enough clients.'

'Would those two biggies[9] I mentioned to you, Jobson's Electronics and Whiter Washing Powder, convince you?'

'Of course.'

'The managing directors of both companies happen to be in London for a business conference. Tell you what.[10] Lay on[11] some drinks and fiddly bits[12] and I'll bring them round to your flat. I'll phone you later today and give you a time.'

'I must say, if you have contacts like this, we'll shoot[13] to the top of the league in a few weeks,' said Agatha.

He did phone later, the managing directors came round to Agatha's the following day and it was a jolly[14] meeting, particularly for Agatha, as both men flirted with her.

1. abêtissante
2. débiles
3. bouseux
4. pointe de culpabilité
5. pour démarrer
6. les chiffres
7. étudié
8. une fin de bail
9. grosses boîtes
10. Tu sais quoi ?
11. Prépare
12. des petits-fours
13. allons nous propulser
14. jovial

As Jack got up to leave, having stayed on for an extra drink[1] after the businessmen had left, he kissed Agatha on the cheek and said, 'I'll give you a round figure[2] for your share of the concern[3], you give me a cheque and leave all the nitty-gritty business side[4] to me. You're the whiz[5] with the clients, Agatha. Always were. Look at the way you had those two eating out of your hand!'

'How much?' demanded Agatha.

He named a figure[6] which made her blink[7]. He sat down again and took out sheaves[8] of facts and figures. Agatha thought hard. The sum he had named would take away all her savings[9]. She still had the cottage in Carsely, but she wouldn't need that any more now she was back in business.

'Let me sleep on it[10],' she said. 'Leave the papers with me.'

After he had gone, she wished she had not drunk so much. She stared down at the figures. They needed all the basic things like computers and fax machines, desks and chairs. Party to launch it. Paper and paper-clips[11]. 'I'm not sure,' she said slowly. 'What do you think, Hodge? Hodge?'

But there was no sign of the cat. She searched the small flat, under the bed, in the cupboards[12] and closets[13], but no Hodge.

The cat must have slipped out when her guests were leaving.

She threw on her coat and went down by the stairs, not the lift[14], calling 'Hodge! Hodge!' A woman opened a door and said in glacial tones, 'Do you mind keeping that noise down[15]?'

'Get stuffed[16],' snarled Agatha, sick with worry. If this were Carsely, said a voice in her head, the whole village would turn out to help you[17]. She opened the street door. Outside lay anonymous,

1. dernier verre
2. chiffre global
3. participation à l'affaire
4. détails pratiques
5. d'enfer
6. donna un chiffre
7. la fit tiquer
8. tout un assortiment
9. lui prendrait toutes ses économies
10. y réfléchir jusqu'à demain
11. des trombones
12. placards
13. les penderies
14. ascenseur
15. Ça vous ennuierait de baisser le ton
16. Allez vous faire voir !
17. serait venu à l'aide

uncaring[1] London. She trekked round and round[2] the squares and gardens of Kensington while the traffic often drowned the sound of her frantically calling voice[3].

'If I was you, dear,' said a woman's voice at her elbow, 'I'd wait till after the traffic dies down[4]. Cat, is it? Well, the traffic scares them.'

But Agatha ploughed on[5], her feet cold and aching.

She asked in all the shops up the Gloucester Road, but she was just another woman looking for a lost pet and no one had seen the cat, nor did they look at all interested or concerned.

She wandered dismally back into[6] Cornwall Gardens. Someone was stumbling through[7] a Chopin sonata in an amateurish way. Someone else was having a party, a press of people standing shoulder to shoulder in a front room.

And then Agatha saw a cat walking slowly towards her, a tabby[8] cat. She advanced slowly, praying under her breath[9]. Hodge was a tabby, a striped grey and black, hardly an original-looking animal.

'Hodge,' said Agatha gently.

The cat stopped and looked up at her. 'Oh, it *is* you,' said Agatha gratefully and scooped[10] the cat up into her arms.

'I'm glad someone's picked up that poor stray[11],' said a man who was walking[12] his dog. 'I was going to phone the RSPCA[13]. Been living in these gardens for about two weeks. In this cold, too. Still, cats are great survivors.'

'It's *my* cat,' said Agatha, and clutching[14] the animal as fiercely[15] as a mother does her hurt child, she stalked off to[16] her flat.

1. indifférent
2. sillonna en tous sens
3. appels frénétiques
4. l'arrêt de la circulation
5. s'obstina
6. s'en revint, lugubre, jusqu'aux
7. était aux prises avec
8. tigré
9. tout bas
10. souleva
11. chat errant
12. promenait
13. SPA
14. en agrippant
15. farouchement
16. repartit avec raideur vers

She opened the door and closed it firmly behind her, put the cat on the floor and said, 'Hot milk is what you need.'

Agatha went into the minuscule kitchen. Hodge rose from a kitchen chair and stretched and yawned[1].

'How did you get there?' demanded Agatha, bewildered[2]. She swung round. The tabby she had picked up in Cornwall Gardens came into the kitchen, mewing softly. In the full glare of the fluorescent light, Agatha saw that it was a skinny thing[3], not at all like Hodge.

'Two of them,' groaned Agatha. She couldn't keep two. One was worry enough. Where had Hodge been? thought Agatha, who was not yet well enough versed in the ways of[4] cats and did not know they could appear to vanish into thin air[5]. She thought of putting the new cat back out in the gardens. But that would be cruel. She could take it to the RSPCA but they would probably gas it, for[6] who would want a plain tabby cat?

She warmed milk and put down two bowls of it and then two bowls of cat food. Hodge seemed to have placidly accepted the newcomer. Agatha changed the litter in the tray[7], hoping the new animal was house-trained[8].

When she went to bed, the cats settled down on either side of her[9]. It was comforting. What would they say in Carsely when she returned with two? But then, she would only be returning to Carsely to pack up[10].

But the village was still fresh in her mind when she awoke the next morning. She decided to phone Bill Wong and tell him her news.

1. puis s'étira et bailla
2. abasourdie
3. tout maigrichon
4. ne s'y connaissait pas encore assez en
5. sembler se volatiliser
6. car
7. plateau de la litière
8. propre
9. de chaque côté d'elle
10. faire ses bagages

At police headquarters in Mircester, they said it was his day off[1] and so Agatha phoned his home.

Bill listened carefully while she outlined[2] all her plans and told him of the visit of the two managing directors.

There was a silence. Then he said in his soft Gloucester accent, 'That's odd.'

'What is?' demanded Agatha.

'I mean, *two* managing directors of big companies turning up just like that[3] . I don't know much about business …'

'No, you don't,' put in[4] Agatha.

'But I would have thought a meeting would have been set up for you, liaison[5] with the advertising department, the firms' public relations officers, that sort of thing.'

'Oh, they both happened to be in town for some business meeting.'

'And what do you really know about this Jack Pomfret? You're not just going to hand over[6] any money or anything like that?'

'I'm not stupid,' said Agatha, angry now, for she was beginning to think she was.

'A good way to find out about people,' said Bill, 'is to call at their home. You can usually get an idea of how flush they are[7] from where they live and what the wife is like.'

'So you think I should spy on him? And you're always telling me I don't know how to mind my own business[8].'

'I think you're a Nosy Parker[9] when you don't have to be and touchingly naïve when you do have to be,' said Bill.

'Look, copper[10], I ran a successful business for years.'

1. de congé
2. exposait
3. tombant du ciel
4. coupa
5. en collaboration
6. [leur] remettre
7. de leur situation financière
8. que je ferais mieux de m'occuper de mes oignons
9. fouineuse
10. poulet

'Maybe Carsely's made you forget what an evil place[1] the world can be.'

'What? After all that murder and mayhem[2]?'

'Different sort of thing.'

'Well, I've finished with Carsely.'

There was an amused chuckle[3] from the other end of the phone. 'That's what you think.'

Agatha settled down with a coffee and cigarette to go through the papers Jack had given her again. Did he really expect her just to hand over a cheque without seeing his equal contribution? The new cat and Hodge were chasing each other over the furniture, the stray[4] seeming to have recovered amazingly.

Agatha opened her briefcase and found a clipboard and put the papers on it. She phoned Roy Silver, the young man who had once worked for her.

'Aggie, love,' his voice lilted down the line[5]. 'I was thinking of coming down to see you. What are you up to[6]?'

'I need some help. Do you remember Jack Pomfret?'

'Vaguely.'

'You wouldn't happen to have an address for him[7]?'

'As a matter of fact I have, sweetie. I pinched[8] your business address book when I left. Don't squawk[9]! You'd probably have forgotten about it. Let me see ... aha, 121, Kynance Mews, Kensington. Do you want the phone number?'

'I've got that, but it doesn't seem like a Kensington one. Never mind. I'll walk round. It's only round the corner.'

'How long are you in London? I gather[10] you are in London. Want to meet up?'

1. endroit malfaisant
2. pagaille
3. gloussement
4. chat errant
5. chanta sa voix au téléphone
6. Que fais-tu de beau
7. n'aurais pas son adresse, par hasard
8. t'ai piqué
9. Ne pousse pas des cris d'orfraie
10. J'en conclus

'Maybe later,' said Agatha. 'Did you get married?'

'No, why?'

'What about that girl, what's-her-name[1], you brought down to meet me?'

'Ran off and left me for a lager lout[2].'

'I'm sorry.'

'I'm not,' said Roy waspishly[3]. 'I can do better than that.'

'Look, I'll call you. I've got something to deal with first.' Agatha said goodbye and put the phone down. Why hadn't Jack said he was living just round the corner?

She walked along to the end of Kynance Mews to 121 and pressed the bell.

A thin, tweedy[4] woman answered the door, the kind Agatha didn't like, the kind who wore cultured[5] pearls and green wellies[6] in London.

'Mr Pomfret?' asked Agatha.

'Mr Pomfret no longer lives here,' said the woman acidly. 'I bought the house from him. But I am not his secretary and I refuse to send any more letters on to him. All he needs to do is to pay a small amount of money to the post office in order to get his mail redirected[7].'

'If you give me his address, I can take any letters to him,' said Agatha.

'Very well. Wait there and I'll write it down.'

Agatha stood in the freezing cold on the frost-covered cobbles[8] of the mews[9]. A skein of geese[10] flew overhead on their way from the Round Pond in Kensington Gardens to St James's Park. Her breath came out in a little cloud of steam in front of her face. Two dog lovers stood at the entrance to the mews and unleashed[11] their animals, which peed their way down from door to door[12] and then both squatted down[13] and defecated, before

1. Trucmuche
2. pignouf porté sur la bière
3. d'un ton mordant
4. en tenue chic et décontractée
5. de culture
6. bottes
7. faire réadresser son courrier
8. pavés couverts de givre
9. ruelle chic [a priori semi-piétonne, avec anciennes écuries]
10. vol d'oies
11. détachèrent
12. longèrent la ruelle en faisant pipi de porte en porte
13. s'accroupirent

the satisfied owners called them to heel[1]. There was no more selfish animal lover than a[2] Kensington animal lover, thought Agatha.

'Here you are,' said the woman, 'and here's the address.' She handed Agatha a slip[3] of paper and a pile of letters. Agatha thanked her and put the letters in her briefcase and then looked down in surprise at the address as the woman firmly closed the door: 8A Ramillies Crescent, Archway. Well, there were some mansions[4] in Archway and some rich people left in that declining suburb, but 8A suggested[5] a basement flat[6].

She headed off to the Gloucester Road tube[7], and not wanting to make a lot of changes took the District Line to Embankment and then the Northern Line to Archway. Once she was settled on the Northern Line, she took out the letters. They were mostly junk mail[8] but there was one from the income tax[9].

Agatha's heart sank down to her cold feet. Law-abiding, financially secure people were the ones that kept in touch with the Inland Revenue[10].

She then took out a pocket atlas of London and looked up Ramillies Crescent, which was in a network[11] of streets behind the hospital.

Everyone at the main road junction in Archway at the exit to the tube[12] looked depressed. You could, thought Agatha bleakly[13], take the lot and dump them[14] on the streets of Moscow and no one would notice they were foreigners. She ploughed up the steep hill[15] from the tube[16] and turned off towards Ramillies Crescent when she got to the hospital.

It turned out to be a run-down crescent[17] of Victorian houses. No one here was obviously feeling[18]

1. ne les rappellent
2. plus égoïste qu'un
3. bout
4. hôtels particuliers
5. indiquait plutôt
6. appartement en sous-sol
7. station de métro
8. de la pub
9. un courrier des impôts
10. Les gens honnêtes et solvables restent en contact avec le fisc
11. réseau
12. métro
13. abattue
14. les coller en bloc
15. monta difficilement la côte
16. depuis la station
17. rue décrépite [en arc de cercle]
18. ne souffrait visiblement

the recession[1], for no one had ever got to any point from which to recess *to*[2].

The gardens were untended[3] and most of them had been concreted over[4] to make space for some rusting car. Agatha arrived at Number 8. Sure enough[5], 8A was the basement flat. Edging her way around[6] a broken pram[7] which looked as if it had been thrown there rather than left to rot, she rang the doorbell. Marcia Pomfret, she vaguely remembered, was a statuesque[8] blonde.

At first she did not recognize Marcia in the woman who opened the door to her, a woman with a faded, lined[9] face and black roots[10], who looked at her without a spark of recognition[11].

'What are you selling?' asked Marcia in a weary[12], nasal voice.

Agatha made up her mind to lie. 'I'm not selling anything,' she said brightly[13]. 'Your name was given to me because I believe you and your husband lived in Spain. I am doing research for the Spanish government. They would like to know why various British families did not settle in Spain but returned.'

Agatha scooped[14] the clipboard and papers out of her briefcase and stood waiting.

'You may as well come in,' said Marcia. 'I usually stand talking to the walls here, and that's a fact[15].'

She led the way into a dark living-room. Agatha's sharp eyes[16] recognized what she called landlord's furniture[17] and she sat down on a worn[18] sofa in front of a low glass-and-chrome coffee-table.

'Now,' she said brightly, 'what took you to Spain?'

'It was my husband, Jack,' said Marcia. 'He'd always wanted to run a bar. Thought he could do

1. d'une baisse de la croissance

2. puisque nul n'avait connaissance d'une quelconque croissance

3. n'étaient pas entretenus

4. bétonnés

5. Et comme de juste

6. Après avoir contourné

7. poussette

8. sculpturale

9. ridée

10. racines [de cheveux]

11. avoir du tout l'air de la reconnaître

12. lasse

13. enjouée

14. sortit rapidement

15. vrai de vrai

16. L'œil averti

17. un mobilier de meublé

18. fatigué

it. So he sold the business and the house and we bought this little bar on the Costa Del Sol. He called it Home from Home[1]. Made it British-like[2]. San Miguel beer and steak-and-kidney pud[3]. We had a little flat above the bar. Slave labour, it was. While he was out chatting up[4] the birds[5] in the bar, I was in the kitchen, wasn't I, turning out those hot English meals when it was cooking-hot[6] outside.'

'And were you successful?' asked Agatha, pretending to take notes.

'Naw[7]. We was just another English bar among all them other English bars. Couldn't get help[8]. The Spanish'll only work for top wages[9]. Nearly died with the heat, I did. "Soon it'll be all right," Jack said. "Spend the days on the beach and let someone do the work for us." But the place never really got off the ground[10]. Once the tourist season was over, that was that[11]. I said to Jack he'd have been better to make it Spanish, get the locals and the better-class tourists who don't come all this way for English muck[12], but would he listen? So we sold up and came back to nothing.'

Agatha asked a few more questions about Spain and the Spanish to keep up the pretence[13]. Then she put the clipboard away and rose to go. 'I hope you will soon be on your feet again.'

Marcia shrugged wearily[14] and Agatha suddenly remembered what she had looked like ten years ago at a party, blonde and beautiful. Jack's latest bimbo[15], they had called her, but he had married her.

'Have you any children?' Agatha asked.

Marcia shook her head. 'Just as well,' she said sadly. 'Wouldn't want to bring them up[16] here.'

1. Un deuxième chez-soi
2. De style britannique
3. tourte à la viande
4. draguait
5. nénettes
6. alors qu'on crevait de chaud
7. Nan
8. embaucher du renfort
9. de gros salaires
10. n'a jamais décollé
11. fichu
12. de la bouffe british dégueulasse
13. garder les apparences
14. haussa les épaules avec lassitude
15. la dernière conquête pulpeuse
16. [avoir à] les élever

And just as well, indeed, thought Agatha miserably as she trailed off down[1] the street. For when he finds[2] I haven't been suckered[3], he'll search around for a new wife, and one with money this time. She remembered his letters and stopped beside a pillar-box[4], readdressed the lot and popped them in[5].

Jack Pomfret was standing on the up escalator at Archway tube when he saw the stocky figure[6] of Agatha Raisin on the down escalator and opened his copy of *The Independent* and hid behind it. He ran all the way home once he was out in the street.

'Was that Raisin woman here?' he demanded.

'What Raisin woman?' demanded Marcia. 'There was only some woman from the Spanish government asking questions about British who had left Spain.'

'What did she look like?'

'Straight brown hair, small brown eyes, bit of a tan[7].'

'You silly bitch[8], that was Agatha Raisin smelling out[9] God knows what kind of rats[10]. What did you tell her?'

'I told her how we couldn't make that bar work. How was I to know …'

Jack paced up and down. The money he'd spent feeding that old cow[11] at the Savoy! The money he'd paid to those two actor friends to impersonate[12] businessmen! Perhaps he could still save something.

Agatha packed up her stuff[13] and left the rented flat for a new one, sacrificing the money she'd paid in advance. She moved to another rented service flat in Knightsbridge, behind Harrods. She

1. en repartant d'un pas lent dans
2. découvrira
3. que je ne me suis pas fait pigeonner
4. boîte aux lettres
5. les glissa dans la boîte
6. silhouette trapue
7. légèrement bronzée
8. Imbécile heureuse
9. flairant
10. Dieu sait quelle embrouille
11. vieille dinde
12. afin qu'ils se fassent passer pour
13. remballa ses affaires

would see a few shows and eat a few good restaurant meals before returning to that grave[1] called Carsely.

She knew Jack would come looking for her and she did not relish the confrontation[2], for like all people who have been tricked[3], she felt ashamed of her own gullibility[4].

So when Jack Pomfret, sweating lightly despite the cold, called at her old flat, he did not find anyone there. The owners did not know she had left, for she had not returned[5] her keys, and assumed[6] she was out, and so Jack called and called desperately in the ensuing days[7] until even he had to admit to himself that there was little hope of getting any money out of Agatha Raisin.

Apart from going to shows and restaurants, Agatha took the new cat to the Emergency Veterinary Clinic in Victoria, learned it was female, got it its shots[8], named it Boswell[9] despite its gender, with some idea of keeping up the literary references[10], and decided that two cats were as easy to keep as one.

One evening, walking home from the theatre through Leicester Square, she was just priding herself[11] at how easily she fitted back[12] into city life when a youth[13] tried to seize her handbag. Agatha hung on like grim death[14], finally managing to land a hefty kick[15] on her assailant's shins[16]. He ran off. Passers-by stared at her curiously but no one asked her if she was all right. When one lived in town, thought Agatha, one became street-wise[17], developed an instinct for danger. But in sleepy Carsely, where she often did not bother to lock her car at night, such instincts had gone. She walked on purposefully[18], striding out with a confident step which declared,

1. bled mortel
2. appréhendait la rencontre
3. les gens qui se sont fait avoir
4. crédulité
5. rendu
6. supposèrent
7. les jours suivants,
8. le fit vacciner
9. [écrivain mort en 1795 ; biographe de Samuel Johnson]
10. allusions
11. se félicitait
12. de la facilité avec laquelle elle s'était réinsérée dans
13. jeune homme
14. avec acharnement
15. décocher un grand coup de pied
16. les tibias
17. on apprenait à se débrouiller dans la rue
18. résolument

don't mug me[1], I'm loaded for bear[2], the step of the street-wise.

At the end of a week, she headed back to Carsely, carrying two cat baskets this time.

For the first time, she had an odd feeling of coming home. It was a sunny day, with a faint hint[3] of warmth in the air. Snowdrops were fluttering shyly[4] at village doorsteps.

She thought of the vet, Paul Bladen, again. Now she had a new cat, she had every excuse[5] to take it to the vet for a check-up. On the other hand, if Bill Wong was to be believed, Paul Bladen did not like cats. She decided to go along and say she needed some eye ointment[6].

She had really only half believed Bill, however, and was surprised to find the waiting-room empty. Miss Mabbs looked up listlessly[7] from a torn magazine and said Mr Bladen was up at Lord Pendlebury's racing stable but would be back soon. Agatha waited and waited.

After an hour, Paul Bladen walked into the waiting-room, nodded curtly[8] to Agatha and disappeared into the surgery. Agatha had half a mind[9] to leave.

But after only a few moments, Miss Mabbs told her to go through[10].

He listened to Agatha's tale of the cat's eye infection and then scribbled out a prescription[11], saying they were out of the ointment[12], but that she could get it at the chemist's in Moreton-in-Marsh. He then obviously waited for Agatha to leave.

'Don't you think you owe me[13] an explanation?' demanded Agatha. 'I tried to go to that restaurant in Evesham but the snow was so bad, I crashed[14]. I tried to phone you but some woman answered

1. ne cherchez pas à m'agresser
2. ou vous me trouverez
3. léger soupçon
4. timidement
5. toutes les excuses du monde
6. une pommade ophtalmo
7. d'un air absent
8. sèchement
9. presque envie
10. d'entrer [dans le cabinet du docteur]
11. griffonna une ordonnance
12. que la pommade était en rupture de stock
13. que vous me devez
14. que j'ai eu un accident

the phone, saying she was your wife. I thought you might have had the decency to phone *me*.'

He was suddenly all charm. 'Mrs Raisin, I am very sorry. The weather was so dreadful, I was sure you would not even try to make it[1]. The woman on the phone was my sister, being silly. Do forgive me. Look, what about tonight? There's a new Greek restaurant in Mircester, just near the abbey. We could meet there at eight.' But when he smiled into her eyes, Agatha was reminded bitterly of Jack Pomfret.

She hesitated, looking out of the surgery window. It was then that she saw James Lacey, looking the same as ever. He was a very tall, well-built man with a handsome, tanned face and bright blue eyes. His thick black hair had only a trace of grey at the sides. He was strolling past with that easy, rangy stride of his[2], James Lacey without a care in the world[3].

'I'd love to go,' she said. 'See you then.'

When Agatha got home, the phone was ringing and she picked up the receiver. Jack Pomfret's voice sounded down the line. 'Agatha, Agatha, I can explain ...'

Agatha slammed the receiver back on its stand. The phone immediately began to ring again.

She snatched it up. 'Look[4], bugger off[5], you useless con[6],' she snarled[7]. 'If you think –'

'Mrs Raisin, it's me, Bill.'

'Oh! I told you to call me Agatha.'

'Sorry. Agatha. So business wasn't business?'

'No,' said Agatha curtly.

'Pity. What about dinner tonight?'

'What?'

'You, me, dinner.'

1. que n'alliez même pas essayer de venir au rendez-vous

2. de sa démarche ample, décontractée

3. exempt de tout souci

4. Écoute

5. va te faire voir

6. arnaqueur à la noix

7. dit-elle, hargneuse

Bill Wong was in his twenties, so any invitation to dinner was prompted by pure friendship[1]. Nonetheless she was flattered and almost tempted to dump the vet[2]. But the vet was nearer her age.

'I've got a date[3], Bill. What about next week?'

'Right. I'll probably see you before then. Who's your date with? Lacey?'

'No, the vet.'

'Out of the frying pan into the fire[4].'

'What the hell does that mean? You mean he's after my *money*? Well, let me tell you, Bill Wong, that a lot of men find me attractive.'

'Sure, sure. Talking off the top of my head[5]. See you soon. Only joking. He's probably loaded[6].'

1. n'était dictée que par l'amitié
2. lâcher le véto
3. rendez-vous
4. De Charybde en Scylla
5. Je parlais comme ça, sans réfléchir
6. plein aux as

Chapter Three

Agatha tried on one dress after the other, gave up and changed into an old skirt and blouse[1], was about to leave and hurried back indoors to put on the body stocking, the Armani dress, the pearls, and gummed on[2] a pair of false eyelashes she had bought in London.

James Lacey saw her drive off. He noticed that she no longer went slowly past his house, looking eagerly[3] out of the car window.

Agatha drove along the Fosse to Mircester, an old cobbled[4] town dominated by a great medieval abbey. She found the restaurant without difficulty. It was more like a dingy[5] shop with closed curtains rather than a restaurant, but she was sure all would be warmth and elegance inside.

The Stavros Restaurant came as a bit of a shock to her when she walked inside. There was cracked linoleum on the floor and checked[6] plastic tablecloths[7] covered the tables. A few rather dingy enlarged photographs of views of Greece, the Acropolis, Delphi, and so on[8] stared down from the walls.

Paul Bladen rose to meet Agatha. He was wearing his old tweeds and an open-necked shirt.

'You look very grand[9],' he said by way of[10] greeting.

1. chemisier
2. se colla sur les yeux
3. avidement
4. pavée
5. minable
6. à carreaux
7. nappes
8. ainsi de suite
9. êtes magnifique
10. en guise de

'I didn't know it would be such a … quaint[1] … restaurant,' said Agatha, sitting down.

'The food makes up for[2] the decor.' He poured her[3] a glass of retsina[4] from a carafe, and Agatha took a swig[5], mentally damning it as lighter fuel[6] but hoping the alcohol content was enough to give courage.

A skinny waitress with dead-white *Return of the Mutant Women* make-up[7] came up with a notebook.

'Watyerwant[8]?' she asked laconically.

Agatha, who would normally have told her to buzz off[9] and give her time to choose something had, that evening, decided to play the feminine and submissive[10] woman, so she batted her false eyelashes at Paul and said, 'You choose for me.'

The dish was supposed to be stuffed vine leaves. Agatha, poking at it[11] after it had arrived at their table with depressing speed, decided the vine leaves were cabbage[12] and the filling was watery[13] rice.

She found that by dint of breaking[14] the little packets open and spreading them about her plate she could actually make it look as if she[15] had at least eaten some of it.

Paul Bladen talked all the while about his hopes to supply Carsely with a really good veterinary service and ordered another large carafe of retsina, as Agatha was making up[16] in drink what she was not getting in the way of food.

'Now,' he said, smiling into her eyes, 'tell me all about yourself. How is it that such a sophisticated lady ends up in a Cotswold village?'

A sober Agatha might have remembered that the Cotswolds, being fashionable[17], abound in quite a lot of interesting people, but the tipsy[18]

1. pittoresque
2. rachète
3. lui versa
4. [vin grec résiné]
5. gorgée
6. un carburant un peu trop léger
7. maquillage d'un blanc cadavérique, façon *Le Retour des mutantes*,
8. Kèssvous-voulez
9. de repartir vite fait
10. soumise
11. les ayant tâtées du doigt
12. du chou
13. gorgé d'eau
14. en cassant
15. donner l'impression qu'elle
16. rattrapait
17. chic
18. éméchée

Agatha was flattered and told him all about her childhood dream of owning a cottage in the country, how she had built up a successful business, sold it and retired early. '*Very* early,' said Agatha.

He reached across the table and took her hand. 'You haven't mentioned your husband.'

Agatha shrugged. 'I left him years and years ago. I suppose he's dead.' Agatha had never even bothered[1] to get a divorce. Paul's hand was warm and dry and firm. She felt fluttery[2] and breathless, almost as if she were on a first date.

'I'm doing all the talking,' she said. 'What about you?'

'I am working on a dream,' he said. He released her hand as the waitress came up and put two Levantine sticky cakes[3], oozing watery honey[4], in front of them and two cups of black sludge[5] masquerading under the name of[6] Greek coffee[7].

'I plan to create a really good veterinary hospital,' he said, 'but that takes money.'

'You should ask the Carsely Ladies' Society,' said Agatha. 'They're terribly good at fund-raising.'

'Unlike you, I think they are all too provincial to grasp[8] such a grand[9] concept.'

'I wouldn't say that.' Agatha thought of Mrs Bloxby. 'They're really dedicated workers[10] ... I tell you what. I'll give you a contribution to start your fund off.'

Twenty pounds, thought Agatha charitably. After all, he is paying for this quite hideous dinner.

He seized her hand again. 'You don't seem to like your coffee.'

'I like filter coffee.'

'Then let's go to my place and have some.' He stroked his thumb over the palm of her hand.

1. ne s'était même jamais donné la peine
2. fébrile
3. gâteaux levantins très collants
4. dégoulinant de miel coupé d'eau
5. gadoue
6. se faisant passer pour du
7. café turc
8. saisir
9. splendide
10. dévouées

Well, this is it[1], thought Agatha, as she drove after his car through the dark winding streets[2] of the old town, this is what I got all dressed up for. But the euphoria induced[3] by all she had drunk was leaving her.

Paul, in the car in front, stopped outside a small Victorian villa on the outskirts of the town.

As Agatha followed him into a gloomy hall, she was suddenly seized with panic as he turned and smiled slowly and intimately at her. Sex! Here it was and here were all the fears. She hadn't shaved her armpits[4]. What if[5] she wasn't … er … gymnastic enough[6]? The house was cold. One of her false eyelashes was beginning to slip. She could feel it. What if she had to undress in front of him and he saw her trying to get out of that body stocking?

'I've got to go,' she said suddenly. 'I forgot to leave the cats any water.'

'Agatha, Agatha, they'll be all right. Come here.'

'And I'm expecting an important phone call from New York and … I mean, thanks for the dinner. My treat[7] next time. Honestly, got to rush.'

Agatha fled down the garden path, stumbling[8] on her high heels.

She unlocked her car and dived into the driving seat and then drove off, not feeling the panic ebb[9] until she was safely back out of the town and on her road home. Along the Fosse, a police car loomed up[10] in her rear-view mirror. She thought of all she had drunk and prayed they would not stop her and breathalyse her[11]. She dropped her speed to thirty and the police car moved out and passed her.

She felt bewildered[12] by her reactions to the handsome vet. She had not had an affair[13] with anyone in quite a long time. What a fool she had

1. nous y voilà
2. rues sombres et tortueuses
3. provoquée
4. aisselles
5. Et si
6. suffisamment acrobate
7. C'est moi qui régale
8. trébuchant
9. l'angoisse s'atténuer
10. surgit
11. pour la soumettre à un Alcootest
12. était effarée
13. de liaison

been. Not once did she allow the thought to form in her head that the idea of love-making without love had become repugnant to her. That was too old-fashioned an idea to admit to, and Agatha Raisin was determinedly modern.

The next day Paul Bladen went back to Lord Pendlebury's racing stables. He was to perform[1] Hobday's operation[2] on a racehorse to stop its roaring[3]. This involved cutting the vocal cords. He filled a syringe with a drug called Immobilon to anaesthetize the animal. Beside him on a small rickety[4] table which he had carried into the stable for the purpose[5], he placed a glass bottle of Revivon to inject the horse when the operation was over[6], and also a glass bottle of Narcon, a powerful antidote in case he got any of the Immobilon into his bloodstream[7] by mistake.

'There now, boy, easy[8],' he said, patting the horse on the nose as it shuffled[9] and whinnied[10]. He felt irritated that Lord Pendlebury had not even bothered to supply him with a stable-boy to help. The sun was shining in through the open stable door, casting a huge gold rectangle on the cobbles at his feet. He raised the syringe to inject the horse in the jugular vein. The gold at his feet darkened as if a cloud had passed over the face of the sun. Then something struck him savagely on the back of the head and he fell sprawling[11]. Winded[12] but not unconscious, he twisted round on the cobbles. 'What the hell are you …?' he began.

A hand twisted the syringe out of his grasp and the next thing he knew[13], the syringe had been plunged into his chest. He scrabbled[14] desperately at[15] the table where the antidote lay. Even

1. procéder à
2. une intervention chirurgicale de Hobday
3. mettre fin au cornage [sifflement dû à une paralysie du larynx]
4. bancale
5. dans ce but
6. serait finie
7. système sanguin
8. tout doux
9. s'agitait
10. hennissait
11. s'affala de tout son long
12. Le souffle coupé
13. l'instant d'après
14. Il tâtonna
15. pour tenter d'attraper

Revivon, the drug to revive the horse, would work if he couldn't reach the Narcon, but the table was kicked over[1] and he died a few seconds later.

Agatha heard about his death the following day from Bill Wong, and her first feeling was one of selfish relief[2] that the vet was no longer around to gossip about the way[3] she had fled from his house.

Agatha had replaced the electric cooker in her kitchen with an Aga stove[4]. The door of the stove was open and a wood fire was burning briskly[5]. A jug of early daffodils[6] from the Channel Islands[7] stood on the window-ledge[8]. The square plastic table was gone and now there was a solid wooden one with a scrubbed top[9].

'It was a tragic accident,' said Bill. 'Some vets won't work with Immobilon. It's deadly[10]. There was a case not long ago where the vet put the syringe full of the stuff in his breast pocket and approached the horse. The horse nudged him[11] on the chest, the syringe pricked the vet and that was enough. He died almost instantly.'

'You'd think[12] they'd have some sort of antidote,' said Agatha.

'Oh, they do, but there's not often time to reach it. In Paul Bladen's case, it was on a little table, but either he kicked it over in his death agonies[13], or the horse kicked it over.'

'You mean it's like cyanide? You writhe about[14]?'

'Come to think of it, you don't[15],' said Bill. 'Good way to commit suicide … quick and painless. There was one curious thing.'

'Yes?' Agatha's eyes brightened.

'No, not that[16] curious. Not murder. There was a lump[17] on the back of his head, but of course it

1. quelqu'un renversa la table d'un coup de pied

2. le soulagement égoïste

3. raconter comment

4. un gros poêle en fonte

5. bien vif

6. jonquilles précoces

7. îles Anglo-Normandes

8. rebord de la fenêtre

9. au plateau récuré

10. mortel

11. lui a donné un petit coup de museau

12. On pourrait espérer

13. en agonisant

14. On se tort de douleur

15. Maintenant que j'y pense, non

16. si

17. une bosse

was assumed[1] he got that striking his head when he fell, although he was found lying on his side[2]. His fingerprints were on the edge[3] of the table, as if he'd made an attempt to get to[4] the antidote.'

'And he was all alone?'

'Yes. The reason for that, reading between the lines of old Lord Pendlebury's statement, is that he high-handedly demanded[5] help. Lord Pendlebury said his stable staff[6] were all too busy and then made sure they were. It was an operation to stop the horse roaring. A lot of racehorses make a roaring sound on the course.'

'Seems brutal.'

'Everything to do with animals is brutal.'

James Lacey hovered[7] outside Agatha's door. She had baked him a pie two months ago and he knew he should have returned[8] the pie dish. He had been putting it off[9]. But the fact that Agatha had apparently ceased to pursue him had given him courage. He rang the bell, thinking that with any luck she might be out around the village, and then he could safely leave the pie dish on the doorstep.

But Agatha answered the door[10]. 'Come in and have coffee,' she said, taking the pie dish. 'We're in the kitchen.'

That 'we' encouraged James Lacey to step inside. He was writing a military history, and like most writers spent his days looking for excuses not to work.

He knew Bill Wong and nodded a greeting[11]. James settled down over a cup of coffee, relieved that Agatha was not staring at him in the intense way she usually did.

1. on a supposé
2. sur le côté
3. le bord
4. se saisir de
5. avait exigé, avec arrogance
6. ses palefreniers
7. hésitait
8. lui rendre
9. repoussait sans cesse
10. lui ouvrit
11. le salua de la tête

'We've just been talking about Paul Bladen's death,' said Agatha. She described what had happened.

The retired colonel despised what he called 'women's gossip[1]' and would have been amazed had anyone pointed out to him[2] that he was just like the rest of the human race, a gossip himself[3].

'I'm not surprised,' he said cheerfully, 'that a man so generally loathed[4] should be bumped off[5].'

'But he wasn't bumped off,' protested Agatha.

The people who claim[6] not to be gossips are usually the worst kind, and James Lacey weighed in[7]. 'How can you be sure?' he demanded. 'For a start, did you hear about poor Mrs Josephs? You know she was devoted to that old cat of hers, Tewks. Well, she kept going to Bladen with one excuse or another. One day he asked her to leave the cat with him for a full examination. When she went back to collect[8] her beloved pet, he had put it to death. He said the cat was too old and needed to be put out of its misery[9]. Mrs Josephs was distraught[10].

'Then there was Miss Simms. She kept going along on one pretext or another. The last time she went, she said, and I believe her, it was because the cat had a genuine complaint[11]. It was scratching and scratching. Bladen told her coldly the cat had fleas[12], and not to waste his time and be more thorough with her housekeeping[13]. She took her cat back to her former[14] vet, who told her the animal had an allergy. Miss Simms returned to Bladen and ripped him up and down[15]. You could hear it all over the village. But then Bladen had told Jack Page, the farmer, that he was sick of those women and their dreary[16] pets. He only had time for working animals.'

1. des commérages
2. si on lui avait fait remarquer
3. une commère lui aussi
4. détesté
5. supprimé
6. prétendent
7. insista
8. rechercher
9. qu'il fallait abréger ses souffrances
10. désespérée
11. était vraiment malade
12. des puces
13. de faire son ménage plus à fond
14. ancien
15. l'a engueulé
16. assommants

'This must have all happened when I was in London,' said Agatha. 'I mean, they all went to him when he first came[1].'

'They were all in love with him,' said James. 'Then for some reason[2] he started to get nasty[3] to a few of them. There are still some who think he's the best vet ever ... or was.'

'Who are they?' asked Bill.

'Mrs Huntingdon, the pretty newcomer with the Jack Russell; Mrs Mason, the chairwoman of the Carsely Ladies' Society; Mrs Harriet Parr from the lower village; and Miss Josephine Webster, who runs that shop which seems to sell nothing other than dried flowers.'

'How did you learn all this?' exclaimed Agatha, and then turned pink, for she realized in that moment that he was every bit as much[4] pursued by the village women as Paul Bladen had been.

'Oh, people talk to me,' he said vaguely.

'You had a dinner date with Bladen,' said Bill Wong, looking at Agatha. 'The night before his death, in fact, for[5] I asked you out for dinner and you told me you couldn't go because you had a date with him.'

'So what[6]?' demanded Agatha.

James Lacey looked at her curiously. She was quite attractive, he supposed, in a pugnacious sort of way. In fact, now that she was not oiling all over him[7], he could see that she did have certain good points. She had a trim, if rather stocky figure, excellent legs[8], rather small, intelligent brown eyes, and shiny healthy brown hair, worn straight but cut by some no doubt expensive hair-dressing master.

'So I'm interested,' Bill was saying. 'Where did you go for dinner?'

1. à son arrivée
2. bizarrement
3. à être désagréable
4. tout autant
5. car
6. Et alors
7. n'était plus mielleuse avec lui
8. Plutôt mince bien que trapue, elle avait des jambes parfaites

'That new Greek place in Mircester.'

'Horrible dump[1],' said James. 'Took someone there for dinner myself. Never again.'

Agatha wondered immediately whom he had taken for dinner, but she said, 'I didn't find out all that much about him[2]. Oh, he said his dream was to open a veterinary hospital.'

'Aha[3],' said Bill maliciously. 'Tried to get money out of you, did he?'

'No, he did not!' yelled Agatha, and added in a quieter voice. 'It may come as a surprise to you, but he fancied me.'

'I'm glad about that. I mean, you'd suffered enough already with that chap[4] in London trying to cheat you[5],' said Bill.

'More coffee?' said Agatha, glaring at him[6].

'Yes, please,' said James Lacey.

'Not for me,' said Bill. 'Back to work.' And he left the kitchen too quickly for James to change his mind and escape.

Determined to be as remote and cool[7] as possible, Agatha served James with another cup of coffee and then sat at the far end of the table from him. More for something to say than because she was interested, she said, 'So you think someone might have murdered Paul Bladen?'

'It did cross my mind,' he said. 'I mean, it would be so easy to do. Creep up on him[8] when he had a syringe full, knock him on the head … No, that won't do. He hadn't been knocked on the head.'

'But he might have been,' said Agatha. 'I mean, he had a lump on his head. They decided he might have got it falling on the floor, but he was lying on his side.'

'I suppose the police know what they are doing,' said James. 'I mean, if anyone else had

1. Un endroit pourri

2. Je n'en ai pas appris tellement sur lui

3. Tiens, tiens

4. ce type

5. de vous arnaquer

6. lui jetant un regard mauvais

7. détachée

8. S'approcher de lui tout doucement

been around Lord Pendlebury's racing stables, he or she would have been seen. This is the country. You can't sneak around places quietly[1] like you can in the city.'

'I wonder,' said Agatha. 'I would like to see those racing stables. Do you know Lord Pendlebury?'

'No. But all you have to do is go up there and ask him to contribute to one of those charities[2] you're always raising money for. Then, when you leave the house, all you have to do is go to the stables and take a look around.'

'I wish you would come with me,' said Agatha. He looked at her nervously, but she had not said it in any flirtatious way.

He thought of the work he had to do, he thought of the joys of writing and found himself saying, 'I don't see why not[3]. We could go up this afternoon, say, about two[4].'

'That is very kind of you,' said Agatha calmly.

She saw him[5] to the door, ushered him out[6], and then performed a war dance[7] in her little hall. The impossible was about to happen. She was going to spend an afternoon with James Lacey.

By two o'clock, Agatha, weary of trying on clothes, had settled[8] for a cherry-red sweater, a neat tweed skirt, brogues[9], and a sheepskin[10] coat.

She stood by the window of the dining-room, which faced the front of the house, so that she could watch him arriving. And there he came with his long rangy stride[11]. Although in his fifties, he was a handsome man, over six feet tall[12], with crisp dark hair with only a trace of grey, humorous eyes and a powerful[13] nose. He was wearing a moth-eaten[14] old shooting sweater with worn suede patches[15] on the shoulders over a checked shirt[16]

1. Impossible de se faufiler n'importe où tranquillement
2. œuvres de bienfaisance
3. Je n'y vois pas d'inconvénient
4. vers deux heures
5. le raccompagna
6. le fit sortir
7. exécuta un pas de danse victorieux
8. s'était décidée
9. de bonnes chaussures basses
10. en peau de mouton
11. ample démarche
12. faisait plus de 1,80 m
13. imposant
14. mité
15. de vieux renforts en daim
16. par-dessus une chemise à carreaux

and olive-green cords[1]. Agatha had a good stare at him to compensate for the fact that she intended to remain cool and detached when she actually met him again[2].

Lord Pendlebury's home, Eastwold Park, lay at the end of a long drive[3] which led off[4] the road from the village. Agatha felt quite elated[5]. The only time she had been inside the doors of a grand house[6] before was as a tourist. She wondered if she should curtsy[7] – no, that was for royalty – and should she call him 'my lord'? Best to watch how James Lacey went on and copy him.

They drove up and parked outside the front of one of those rambling[8] Cotswold mansions which cover quite a bit of ground without appearing to do so. The door was answered not by a butler[9], but by one of the village women, Mrs Arthur, wearing an overall[10] and brushing wisps[11] of grey hair from her eyes. Mrs Arthur was a member of the Carsely Ladies' Society, but Agatha had not known she worked for Lord Pendlebury.

'I wanted to ask Lord Pendlebury if he would contribute to our fund-raising for Save the Children,' said Agatha.

'You can *ask*,' said Mrs Arthur. 'No harm in *asking*, I always say.' She stayed put[12].

'Why don't you ask Lord Pendlebury then if we may see him?' demanded James Lacey.

'On your own heads be it[13],' said Mrs Arthur. 'He's in the study, over there.' She jerked a thumb towards[14] a door at the end of the hall.

It was all very disappointing, thought Agatha, as she followed James Lacey across the hall. There should have been a butler to take a visiting card on a silver tray[15]. But James was already holding open the study door for her.

1. pantalon en velours côtelé
2. le reverrait
3. allée
4. débouchait sur
5. était sur un petit nuage
6. dans une maison de maître
7. faire une révérence
8. délabrée
9. majordome
10. blouse
11. des mèches
12. ne bougeait pas d'un pouce
13. À vos risques et périls
14. D'un coup de pouce elle désigna
15. plateau d'argent

Lord Pendlebury was seated in a battered[1] leather armchair before a dying wood fire. He was fast asleep[2].

'Well, that's that[3],' whispered Agatha.

James crossed to the window. 'The stable block[4] is out the back[5],' he said, not bothering to lower his voice. 'You can see it from here.'

'Shhh[6],' urged[7] Agatha. The room was so silent, book-lined[8], dim[9], with two walls of calf-bound[10] books, a large desk, bowls of spring flowers on odd little tables, and the solemn tick of clocks intensifying the silence.

'Who are you?' Lord Pendlebury was awake now and staring straight at her.

Agatha jumped and said, 'I am Agatha Raisin from Carsely. The gentleman there is Mr Lacey.' She longed to[11] call him Colonel but was sure James would object. 'I am collecting money on behalf of[12] the Carsely Ladies' Society for Save the Children.'

Like an American swearing the oath of allegiance[13], Lord Pendlebury put an arm across his chest, no doubt to protect his wallet.

'I have already given money to Cancer Research,' he said.

'But this is Save the Children.'

'I don't *like* children,' said Lord Pendlebury petulantly[14]. 'Too many of them. Go away.'

Agatha opened her mouth to blast him[15], but James Lacey said quickly, 'Fine-looking stables you have, sir. Mind if we walk over and take a look?'

'Doesn't matter if I mind, does it?[16]' said Lord Pendlebury. 'A landowner[17] no longer has any privacy. If it's not busybodies[18] like you, it's those damn environmentalists, walking over my land

1. défraîchi
2. dormait à poings fermés
3. point final, quoi
4. Les écuries
5. sont à l'arrière
6. Chut
7. le pressa
8. garnie de livres
9. sombre
10. à reliure de vélin
11. avait très envie de
12. pour le compte de
13. prêtant le serment à la patrie
14. avec humeur
15. l'invectiver
16. Que ça me dérange ou non, c'est pareil, non ?
17. propriétaire [foncier]
18. des petits curieux

with their rucksacks[1], eating health-food nut bars[2] and farting[3]. Do you know what causes the damage to the ozone layer? It's health fanatics, eating ghastly[4] bran[5] and nut bars and farting about the landscape[6]. Sending out poisonous gases and wind[7]. Ought to be put down[8].'

'Quite,' said James indifferently while Agatha glared at Lord Pendlebury.

'You don't seem a bad sort of chap,' said Lord Pendlebury, peering at James in the gloom of the study. 'But that woman looks like one of those hunt saboteurs[9], slavering on about[10] the darling foxes.'

'Listen, you,' said Agatha, advancing on him.

James took her firmly by the arm and guided her towards the door. 'Thank you for your kind invitation, Lord Pendlebury,' he said over his shoulder. 'We shall enjoy seeing your stables.'

'Rude old bugger[11],' raged Agatha when they were out in the hall.

James shrugged. 'He's old. Leave him be. We get to see the racing stables and that's why we came.'

But Agatha was still smarting[12]. She felt she had been grossly insulted. Worse than that, she thought Lord Pendlebury had been able to see right through[13] her expensive sheepskin and sweater, right down into her working-class soul[14].

'I'm going to have a firm talk with Mrs Arthur,' said Agatha as they walked together towards the stable block. 'She could probably earn more[15] working in a factory or a supermarket.'

'She and her husband work for Lord Pendlebury,' pointed out James Lacey. 'They get a rent-free[16] cottage on the estate[17] and all the free vegetables they want from the market garden[18]. Anyway, you

1. sacs à dos
2. barres diététiques
3. pétant
4. d'horribles
5. au son
6. dans le paysage
7. gaz et haleines empoisonnés
8. On devrait les faire piquer
9. activistes anti-chasse
10. toujours à gâtifier sur
11. Sale type malpoli
12. était toujours piquée au vif
13. n'avait pas été dupe de
14. et vu clairement son âme de prolétaire
15. gagner plus
16. sans payer de loyer
17. à l'intérieur de la propriété
18. ferme maraîchère

want to persuade Mrs Arthur to leave to get your revenge on the old man because he thought you were a flatulent fox preserver[1].'

This was the truth, and so Agatha decided James was really quite an uninteresting and charmless man after all.

The other thing that was irritating was that although James Lacey had spent less time in and around the village compared to herself, he seemed to know a remarkable number of people. He hailed[2] Lord Pendlebury's trainer[3], Sam Stodder, and introduced him to Agatha.

'Lord Pendlebury said we could take a look around the stables, Mr Stodder,' said James. 'Sad thing about that vet's death, wasn't it?'

'Sad, for sure. Happened right over there. He were[4] doing that operation to stop Sparky roaring.'

'And no one else was about[5] at the time?'

'No. Lord Pendlebury had a new filly[6] out in the paddock and took us all off to have a look[7]. We was[8] all talking and smoking and admiring the filly, 'cos[9] it's not often the old man lets us slack[10]. Devil for work, he is. Then Bob Arthur, him what does for[11] my lord, he strolls off[12] and says he's going for to see[13] how the vet is getting on and the next thing[14] he comes out, yelling and crying that Bladen is dead. "Looks like someone's done fer him[15]," he says, so his lordship[16] says for to[17] call the police.'

'And it was in here?' asked Agatha, approaching the right wing of the stable block.

Both men followed her in. There was nothing to be seen. The row of loose boxes[18] stretched off into the gloom[19], the horses' heads poking out[20]. 'Oldest bit of the stables,' said Sam. 'In the rest of

1. flatulente militante en faveur des renards
2. interpella
3. l'entraîneur
4. [was]
5. n'était là
6. pouliche
7. nous a tous emmenés la voir
8. [were]
9. [because]
10. nous laisse un peu de mou
11. l'homme à tout faire de
12. s'en va peinard
13. qu'y va voir
14. deux secondes après,
15. On dirait qu'y s'est fait buter
16. monsieur le comte
17. y veut qu'on
18. rangée de box ouverts
19. s'enfonçait dans le noir
20. on ne voyait que les têtes des chevaux qui dépassaient

it, the loose boxes open right out on to the courtyard[1], not inside like here.'

Agatha stared at the floor, but there was nothing to be seen, not even a sliver of glass[2].

'Why did Mr Arthur say that it looked like someone had done for him?' she asked.

'Reckon[3] he waren't none[4] too popular, like[5]. Wizard with[6] horses, mind[7]. Lord Pendlebury thought him a cheeky sort[8] and wanted Mr Rice, Bladen's partner from Mircester, but Mr Rice don't like Lord Pendlebury and that's a fact[9], and so he do make excuses not to come.'

'I don't suppose anyone likes Lord Pendlebury, horrible old man that he is,' said Agatha.

'You're entitled to[10] your opinion, I'm sure,' said Sam, 'but don't expect none of us here to say a word against the old man. Course you haven't been as long in these parts as Mr Lacey here, or you'd know that criticism of his lordship is not welcome; no, that it's not.'

'I've been here a considerable time longer than Mr Lacey,' said Agatha huffily.

'Well, there's folks that fit in[11] and folks that don't,' said Sam. 'Afternoon.' He touched his cap and strolled off[12].

'What a feudal peasant[13],' said Agatha.

'Sam's a good man, and we're the peasants in this case.'

'What?'

'Vulgarly poking our noses in[14] where they don't belong[15]. What on earth are we doing here, Mrs Raisin?'

'Agatha.'

'Agatha. The man died because of an unfortunate accident.'

1. direct dans la cour
2. bout de verre
3. J'pense
4. [wasn't]
5. quoi
6. Un vrai magicien avec
7. remarquez
8. du genre impertinent
9. ça c'est sûr
10. avez le droit d'avoir
11. y a des gens qui s'intègrent
12. repartit d'un pas tranquille
13. paysan arriéré
14. Nous fourrons le nez avec grossièreté
15. dans des affaires qui ne nous regardent pas

'I'm not so sure,' said Agatha, more out of a desire to be contrary[1] than because she believed it.

They strolled round to the front of the house where Agatha's car was parked. It looked new and shiny after all the expensive repairs. Lord Pendlebury came towards them.

His tall, thin, heron-like figure loped up to them[2]. 'What do you think you're doing?' he said angrily. 'There's an open day once a year, on June the first; otherwise keep off private property.'

'It's us,' said James Lacey patiently. 'You gave us permission to go and look at your stables.'

His pale watery eyes blinked at them[3] and then focused on Agatha. 'Oh, the hunt saboteur,' he said. 'The people one has to put up with[4] these days.'

He headed off towards the stables, leaving James amused and Agatha fuming[5].

'You're hardly the flavour of the month[6],' said James.

'The man's senile,' snapped Agatha. She had often lingered longingly[7] while on the tour[8] of some stately[9] home outside the roped-off[10] private part hoping a member of the family would recognize her as one of their own kind[11] and ask her to tea. That fantasy[12] seemed totally ridiculous now.

She drove James back to the village, feeling hurt and gauche[13] and inadequate[14]. He glanced at her sideways and something prompted him to[15] say, 'I haven't been to the Red Lion for ages[16]. Fancy[17] a drink there this evening?'

Agatha's spirits[18] rocketed[19] like the pheasant which rose up before the wheels of her car and over the hedge[20] beside the road. But she kept her voice light and casual[21]. 'That would be nice. What time?'

1. par esprit de contradiction
2. vint jusqu'à eux à grands pas souples
3. Il cilla de ses yeux pâles et larmoyants
4. qu'on doit supporter
5. furieuse
6. n'êtes guère en odeur de sainteté
7. s'était souvent attardée avec envie
8. pendant une visite
9. majestueuse
10. interdite d'accès
11. une des leurs
12. rêve
13. maladroite
14. pas à la hauteur
15. le poussa à
16. depuis des lustres
17. Ça vous dirait
18. Le moral
19. monta en flèche
20. la haie
21. détachée

'Oh, about eight. I have to go to Moreton for something, so I'll see you there.'

He was already regretting his invitation, and yet there was no sign of any return of that predatory look he had noticed before in Agatha's eyes.

Agatha, guessing that he would not bother to change, restrained herself from changing her own clothes. She fed the cats and played with them and tried not to watch the clock. Excitement built up in her as eight o'clock approached. Although she had, with the help of Mrs Bloxby, been training herself to cook, she put a frozen lasagne in the microwave for her dinner so as not to waste more time on elaborate preparations. It tasted foul[1]. How could she ever have eaten such stuff[2]?

As she walked to the Red Lion, a full moon was shining down, washing[3] everything with silver[4], outlining[5] the skeletal arms of trees against the starry[6] sky. White and pink verbena flowers[7] scented the air, reminding Agatha unromantically of expensive bath soap. At exactly three minutes past eight, she pushed open the door of the Red Lion.

James Lacey was there in the low-raftered[8] pub, standing at the bar, talking to the landlord. 'What'll you have?' he asked by way of greeting.

'Gin and tonic,' said Agatha, settling herself happily on a bar stool.

'I was wondering,' he began as he paid for her drink. But Agatha was never to know[9] what he was wondering, for the pub door opened and the yapping[10] of a Jack Russell and the heavy smell of French perfume heralded[11] the arrival of Mrs Huntingdon, Carsely's newest incomer.

1. Elles avaient un goût infect
2. des trucs pareils
3. baignant
4. d'une lumière argentée
5. soulignant
6. étoilé
7. des verveines
8. bas de plafond et à poutres apparentes
9. ne saurait jamais
10. jappement
11. annoncèrent

To Agatha's dismay[1], James said, 'Evening, Freda. What'll you have? Do you know Agatha Raisin? Agatha, this is Freda Huntingdon.'

So it was Freda, was it? thought Agatha gloomily. The widow was wearing a cherry-red sleeveless jacket over a black cashmere sweater and short black wool skirt. Her legs in fine black stockings were very good.

'Let's sit at that table over there,' said James after he had bought Freda a whisky and water.

'Perhaps Freda is meeting someone,' suggested Agatha hopefully.

'No,' she said in a husky[2] voice, 'all on my lonesome[3]. Thought I might find you here, James. How's the writing going?'

James! Freda! Rats[4]! Agatha plumped herself down[5] at the table by the log fire[6] and tried not to let her bitter disappointment[7] show on her face.

'The writing's not going at all well,' said James. 'I look for every excuse not to get started. This morning I defrosted the fridge, and this afternoon Mrs Raisin –'

'Agatha, please.'

'Sorry, Agatha and I went to see Lord Pendlebury.'

'Isn't he an old duck[8]?' murmured Freda. 'Quite one of the old school.'

'How do you know him?' asked Agatha.

'I talked to him outside the church last Sunday,' said Freda. 'I found him quite charming.'

'I don't think Agatha found him at all charming,' said James. 'He mistook her for[9] a hunt saboteur.'

Freda Huntingdon laughed merrily. Her dog peed[10] against the leg of the table and she said 'Tut-tut[11]' and picked up the revolting yapping creature and cuddled it[12] on her lap.

1. la consternation
2. rauque
3. toute seulette
4. Les salauds
5. se laissa tomber
6. près de l'âtre
7. amère déception
8. un chou
9. l'a prise pour
10. pissa
11. Tss-tss
12. la serra

'Have you seen the latest Russell Crowe movie, James?' asked Freda. She lit a cigarette and blew a cloud of smoke in Agatha's direction.

'I haven't seen any Russell Crowe movie, let alone[1] the latest,' replied James.

'But you should! They're tremendous fun. The new one's on[2] at Mircester. Tell you what, come with me tomorrow.'

At that moment, Agatha saw Jack Page, the farmer, come in. She felt she could not bear any more of Freda and James. She rose and picked up her unfinished drink.

'Just going to have a drink with Jack.'

Jack Page hailed her. 'Nights are drawing out[3], Agatha,' he said. 'Be spring before you know it[4]. Sorry to hear about that crash you had.'

He was a cheerful man with an easy manner[5]. Agatha told him at length[6] about her crash. He bought her another drink. Agatha sat down on a bar stool next to him and tried to forget about the pair in the corner.

'Bad thing about that vet,' said Jack.

'You went to him[7], didn't you?' said Agatha. 'I saw you there the first time I took my cat along. What did you make of him[8]?'

'The surgery was handy[9] to nip down to[10] and get antibiotics and things,' said Jack. 'Never thought about him much one way or t'other. Then I heard what he done[11] to poor Mrs Josephs's cat, so I stopped going. That was right[12] cruel.'

'You don't think someone bumped him off, do you?'

'Ah, you're looking for another murder to solve,' he teased[13]. 'Sad accident, it were[14]. Funeral's next Monday in Mircester, at St Peter's.'

'I might go,' said Agatha.

1. encore moins
2. se joue
3. Les jours rallongent
4. Le printemps sera là, on ne l'aura pas vu venir
5. cordial
6. en détail
7. le voir
8. Qu'en avez-vous pensé
9. commode
10. y faire un saut
11. [had done]
12. carrément
13. dit-il pour la taquiner
14. [was]

'Was you friendly with him then?'

'Had dinner with him one night,' replied Agatha, 'but not really friendly.'

He drained[1] his tankard[2] and set the empty glass down on the bar. 'I'd best be getting back[3]. I told the wife I'd only stop for the one[4]. Why not come back and say hello?'

Agatha had a sudden longing[5] to turn round. But Mrs Huntingdon let out a trill[6] of laughter and her dog gave a volley of barks[7].

'I'd like that,' said Agatha, picking up her handbag.

She turned at last and gave a casual wave[8] to James before leaving with the farmer.

James Lacey watched her go with some surprise. And he had thought she was pursuing him!

1. vida
2. sa chope
3. ferais mieux de rentrer
4. un petit verre
5. envie
6. laissa échapper des trilles
7. jappa plusieurs fois
8. un coucou

Chapter Four

Snow was falling as Agatha entered the church of St Peter in Mircester the following Monday. She was already wishing she had not come. A doggedness[1] to find out something about the vet's death had prompted[2] this visit. So long as she was worrying about the vet's death, Agatha did not need to worry about James Lacey.

The church was very old, with fine stained-glass windows[3] and a dreadful seventeenth-century altar[4] of some dark wood. Agatha took a pew[5] at the back, unhitched the hassock from its hook[6], knelt in pretended prayer and then studied the congregation[7]. But all she saw was backs of heads. There seemed to be quite a number of women present. One turned her head. Mrs Huntingdon! And then Agatha recognized the solid bulk[8] of Mrs Mason, the chairwoman[9] of the Carsely Ladies' Society, two pews in front of her. She changed her seat and went to sit next to her.

Mrs Mason was clutching[10] a damp handkerchief in her hand. 'So sad,' she whispered to Agatha. 'Such a fine young man.'

'Hardly[11] young,' said Agatha and received a look of reproach.

The coffin was carried in and placed in the aisle[12] in front of the altar. 'That's Mr Rice, Mr Bladen's partner[13],' said Mrs Mason. 'The one on the left at

1. entêtement
2. occasionné
3. vitraux
4. autel
5. prit place sur un banc
6. détacha le coussin de son crochet
7. assemblée des fidèles
8. silhouette massive
9. présidente
10. serrait
11. Pas vraiment
12. allée
13. l'associé

the front.' Among the men who had carried in the coffin, Agatha saw a burly[1] middle-aged man with curly ginger hair[2].

'Who is here from the village, apart from us and that Mrs Huntingdon?' asked Agatha.

'Over there to the right, Mrs Parr and Miss Webster.'

Agatha leaned forward. Both women were crying. Mrs Parr was small and quite pretty and Miss Webster of an indeterminate age, possibly late thirties[3]. She recognized Miss Webster as the woman who ran[4] the dried flower shop.

'I'm surprised you are all so upset[5],' whispered Agatha, 'after what he did to Mrs Josephs' cat.'

'What he did was *right*,' muttered[6] Mrs Mason fiercely. 'That cat was too old for this world.'

'I hope no one thinks that about me,' said Agatha.

'Shhh!' said a man in front waspishly[7].

The service began.

Mr Peter Rice paid a tribute to[8] his dead partner, the vicar quoted[9] St Francis of Assisi, hymns were sung, then the coffin was raised up again and the congregation filed out after it to the graveyard.

It was strange, thought Agatha, but one never thought of people being buried in old church graveyards any more. A short service in a crematorium was more what was expected. She had always wondered about those churchyard graveside scenes in television dramas and had assumed[10] that the television company had paid a nice sum to the church to dig up an appropriate hole for the show. One always assumed that the old churchyards of England had been full to bursting point[11] since the end of the nineteenth century.

1. costaud
2. des cheveux roux bouclés
3. vers la fin de la trentaine
4. tenait
5. que vous soyez tous si affectés
6. marmonna
7. d'un ton acerbe
8. rendit hommage à
9. cita
10. supposé
11. étaient pleins à craquer

Snow fluttered down among the leaning gravestones[1] and a magpie[2] swung on the branch of a cedar and cocked a curious eye[3] at the proceedings[4].

'That's his ex-wife,' said Mrs Mason. A thin, grey-haired woman with a weak face was looking bleakly[5] straight in front of her. She was wearing a fox coat over a red suit. No mourning weeds[6] for her.

But the graveside service was so moving[7] and so dignified that Agatha thought there was a lot to be said for[8] staking your claim to your six-by-four in a country churchyard[9]. When the service was over[10], she muttered a goodbye to Mrs Mason and set out in pursuit of the vet's ex-wife, catching up with her at the lych gate[11].

'My name is Agatha Raisin,' she said. 'I gather you are poor Mr Bladen's wife.'

'I was,' said Mrs Bladen a trifle[12] impatiently. 'It is really very cold, Mrs Raisin, and I am anxious[13] to get home.'

'My car is just outside. Can I drop you[14] somewhere?'

'No, I have my own car.'

'I wonder if we could have a talk?' said Agatha eagerly.

A look of dislike came into Mrs Bladen's eyes. 'My life seems to have been plagued by[15] women wanting to talk to me after my husband had dumped them[16]. It is just as well he is dead.'

She stalked off[17].

I seem to be getting snubbed all round[18], thought Agatha. But there's one thing for sure: our vet was a philanderer[19]. If only I could prove it wasn't an accident, that it was murder, then they'd all sit up and take notice[20]!

* * *

1. pierres tombales inclinées
2. pie
3. pencha la tête avec curiosité
4. sur le déroulement des évènements
5. d'un air sombre
6. de vêtements de deuil
7. émouvant
8. qu'il y avait bien des avantages à
9. revendiquer sa parcelle dans un cimetière de campagne
10. terminé
11. au porche du cimetière
12. un rien
13. impatiente
14. vous déposer
15. Toute ma vie j'ai été tourmentée par
16. avoir été plaquées par mon mari
17. partit d'un pas raide
18. partout
19. coureur de jupons
20. feraient tous attention à moi

Carsely had frequent power cuts[1], some lasting days, some only a few seconds.

James Lacey pressed Agatha's doorbell the following day. He did not know there was one of the brief power cuts because one could not usually hear the bell ringing from outside.

He glanced down at the front lawn. There was a lot of moss[2] on it. He wondered if Agatha knew how to treat it. He bent down for a closer look[3]. Agatha, who thought she had heard someone outside, put her eye to the spy-hole[4], but not seeing anyone, retreated to the kitchen. James Lacey straightened up and pressed the bell again. By this time the power had come back on but Agatha had found crumbs[5] on the carpet and had plugged in the vacuum cleaner[6] in the kitchen at the back.

James retreated, feeling baffled[7]. He remembered all the times he had pretended to be out[8] when Agatha had called[9].

He went into his own cottage, made himself a cup of coffee and sat down at his desk. He switched on his new computer and then stared bleakly at the screen waiting for it to boot up[10], before finding the right file[11] and flicking his written words up on to[12] the green screen. There it was. 'Chapter Two'. If only he had written just one sentence[13]. Why had he decided to write military history anyway? Just because he was a retired[14] soldier did not necessarily mean he was confined to[15] military subjects. Besides, why had he chosen the Peninsular Wars[16]? Was there anything to add more than what had been already written? Oh, dear, how long the day seemed. It had been fun going to see Pendlebury. Of course it had been an accident. And yet there was that bump[17] on the back of the head.

1. coupures de courant
2. mousse
3. regarder de plus près
4. au judas
5. des miettes
6. branché l'aspirateur
7. perplexe
8. fait semblant d'être sorti
9. était passée
10. qu'il démarre
11. bon répertoire
12. faire apparaître sa prose sur
13. ne serait-ce qu'une phrase
14. à la retraite
15. qu'il devait se limiter à
16. guerre d'Indépendance espagnole [1807-1813]
17. cette bosse

It might be more fun to write mystery stories. Say, for example, the vet had been murdered, how would one go about[1] finding out what had really happened? Well, the first step would be to find out *why* he was murdered, for the why would surely lead to the *who*.

1. comment s'y prendre pour

If Agatha had answered her door to him and not looked as if she were avoiding him, he might have dropped the subject[2]. Had he[3] really wanted to write military history, he still might have dropped it. He gave an exclamation of disgust, switched off the machine and went out again. There would be no harm in trying Agatha's door again. He had obviously been mistaken when he had thought she was pursuing him. And he had invited *her* for a drink, not Freda Huntingdon. It was not his fault that Agatha had suddenly decided to leave with that farmer.

2. aurait peut-être laissé tomber le sujet

3. S'il avait

It was a fine spring day, light and airy[4], smelling of growing things. This time, Agatha's front door was open. He went in, calling, 'Agatha,' and nearly fell over her. She was sitting cross-legged[5] on the floor of the hall, playing with her cats.

4. une brise légère soufflait

5. assise en tailleur

'Am I seeing things, or have you two of them?' he asked.

'The new one's a stray[6] I picked up in London,' said Agatha, scrabbling to her feet[7]. 'Like a coffee?'

6. chat errant

7. en se mettant péniblement debout

'Not coffee. I seem to have been drinking it all morning. Tea would be nice.'

'Tea it is[8].' Agatha led the way into the kitchen.

'About the other night,' he said, hovering[9] in the kitchen doorway, 'we didn't have much of a chance to talk.'

8. Allons-y pour du thé

9. planté

'Well, that's pubs for you[10],' said Agatha with seeming indifference. 'You never end up talking to the person you go in with. Milk or lemon?'

10. c'est toujours comme ça dans les pubs

'Lemon, please. I've been thinking, this business about the vet. Did you go to the funeral?'

'Yes. Lot of women there. Seems to have been popular with[1] quite a lot of women, so he can't have gone around[2] putting down *their* cats unasked[3].'

'Who was there from this village?'

'Apart from me, his four remaining fans: your friend, Freda Huntingdon; Mrs Mason; Mrs Harriet Parr; and Miss Josephine Webster. Oh, and his ex-wife. Hey, that's odd.'

'What is?'

'When I was supposed to be having dinner in Evesham that night I crashed[4] and I phoned Paul's house and this woman answered the phone saying she was his wife ...' Agatha broke off[5].

'Well?'

'Well, Paul Bladen told me afterwards that the woman who answered the phone was his sister, being silly or something. But no one else has mentioned his sister. I forgot to ask for her at the funeral.'

'We could drive into Mircester and find out,' he volunteered.

Agatha turned away quickly and fiddled with[6] the kettle[7] to hide the sudden look of rapture[8] in her eyes. 'Do you think it's murder then?' she asked.

He sighed. 'No, I don't. But it might be fun to go through the motions[9]. I mean, ask people, just as if it were[10].'

'I'll get my coat.' Agatha nipped smartly upstairs[11], gazing in the glass at her outfit of sweater and skirt. But there was no time to change, for[12] if she did not hurry up, he might decide to call the whole thing off[13].

1. avoir eu du succès auprès de
2. n'a pas pu passer son temps à
3. piquer leurs chats sans leur demander leur avis
4. le soir de mon accident
5. s'interrompit
6. tripota
7. bouilloire
8. éclair de ravissement
9. de se dire qu'on cherche, juste comme ça
10. comme s'il s'agissait bien d'un meurtre
11. fila à l'étage
12. car
13. de tout annuler

'Just going to get some money,' he called up the stairs.

Agatha cursed[1] under her breath[2]. What if he were way-laid[3] in the short distance between her house and his? She went down the stairs and out of the door.

Freda Huntingdon was talking to him, laughing and holding that wretched yapping dog[4] under her arm. Agatha clenched her hands into fists[5] as they both disappeared into James's cottage. She stood there in her own front garden, irresolute[6]. What if he[7] forgot about her? But he emerged with Freda after only a few moments. Freda was tucking[8] a paperback[9] into her pocket.

She waved goodbye to him and he walked towards Agatha. 'Shall we take my car?' he asked. 'No need to take two.'

'Mine will be fine,' said Agatha. He climbed into the passenger seat. As Agatha drove past Freda, she turned and stared at them in surprise. Agatha gave a cheerful fanfare on the horn[10] and drove fast round the corner out of the lane.

'What did the merry widow[11] want?' she asked.

'Freda? She had lent me a paperback and had come to collect it[12].'

Agatha would have chatted on merrily all the way to Mircester and probably would have driven James away again[13] , but just at that moment she sensed there was a pimple[14] growing on the end of her nose. She squinted down[15] and the car veered wildly[16] to the side of the road before she corrected the steering[17].

'Are you all right?' asked James. 'Do you want me to drive?'

'I'm fine.' But Agatha sank into a worried silence. She could feel that pimple growing and

1. jura
2. entre ses dents
3. détourné
4. maudit cabot jappeur
5. serra les poings
6. indécise
7. Et s'il
8. glissait
9. livre de poche
10. klaxonna gaiement
11. veuve joyeuse
12. le récupérer
13. aurait à nouveau fait fuir James
14. bouton
15. loucha vers le bas
16. dévia violemment
17. redresse la trajectoire

growing, an itchy soreness[1] on the end of her nose. Why should such a thing happen to her on this day of all days[2]? This was what came of eating 'healthy' food, as recommended by Mrs Bloxby. Years of fast food had not produced one blemish[3]. The only[4] solution, Agatha decided, was when they reached Mircester, she would say she needed to buy something from the chemist's – no gentleman would ask what – and then say she was dying for a drink.

She parked in the last space in the town's main square. A woman who had been in the act of carefully reversing into it[5] before Agatha beat her to it by driving straight in nose first[6], stared in hurt anger. When they got out of the car, Agatha, keeping her face averted[7], said, 'Got to go to the chemist's over there. Meet you in that pub, the George, in a few moments.' And then, like jesting Pilate[8], did not stay for an answer[9], but scuttled across the square[10].

In the chemist's, she bought a stick of Blemish Remover[11], astringent lotion, and, for good measure, a new lipstick, Hot Pink.

James looked up and waved as Agatha came into the pub, but she scuttled past him to the Ladies'[12], her face still averted.

Agatha cleaned her face, applied the astringent lotion and then wiped it off with a tissue[13]. She peered at her nose. There was a bright little red spot at the end of it. She carefully applied the stick of Blemish Remover, which resulted in a beige blotch[14] on the end of her nose. She covered it with powder. The light in the Ladies' was not working, so she could only guess at the effect. She stared upwards. There was a light socket[15] up on the ceiling, but she noticed the light bulb[16] was

1. démangeaison douloureuse
2. justement aujourd'hui
3. un seul bourgeonnement
4. seule
5. s'apprêtait à l'occuper moyennant une prudente marche arrière
6. ne la devance en s'y introduisant en marche avant
7. sans la regarder
8. tel le Ponce Pilate railleur [chez Francis Bacon]
9. partit sans écouter la réponse
10. et traversa la place sans demander son reste
11. stick anti-bouton
12. le dépassa pour filer aux toilettes [pour femmes]
13. mouchoir en papier
14. tache
15. douille
16. ampoule

missing and what light there was[1] in the room filtered through the grimy panes[2] of a window high up over the hand basin[3]. Then she remembered she had bought a packet of 100-watt light bulbs the day before and had left them in her car. She scuttled out again. Again James waved and again she ran past him, her face averted, and out the door. He drank his beer thoughtfully[4]. He had once thought Agatha Raisin deranged. Perhaps he had been right. There she came again, running sideways[5], and back into the Ladies'.

Agatha looked up at the ceiling. In order to reach the light socket, she would need to stand on the hand basin. She hitched up[6] her skirt and climbed into the large Victorian hand basin and gingerly stood up[7]. She reached up to the light socket.

With a great rending sound[8], the hand basin came away from the wall. Agatha swayed wildly[9] and then grabbed hold of[10] a dusty windowsill[11] as the hand basin slowly continued to detach itself and fell with an almighty crash[12] on the floor, taking the brass taps[13] with it. A ferocious jet of cold water from a now broken and exposed pipe[14] shot straight up Agatha's skirt.

With a whimper[15] she let go of[16] the windowsill, jumped to the flooding floor and skirting[17] the debris shot back[18] into the pub after firmly closing the door behind her.

'Let's go,' she said to James.

He stared at her in surprise. 'I've just bought you a gin and tonic.'

'Oh, thanks,' said Agatha desperately. 'Cheers!' She threw the drink down her throat in one gulp[19]. 'Come on!' Out of the corner of her eye, she could

1. le peu de lumière
2. filtrait au travers des vitres crasseuses
3. lavabo
4. pensivement
5. de profil
6. remonta
7. se releva avec précaution
8. grand bruit de cassure
9. vacilla désespérément
10. saisit
11. rebord de fenêtre
12. énorme fracas
13. robinets en laiton
14. tuyau
15. gémissement,
16. lâcha
17. contournant
18. retourna précipitamment
19. d'un trait

see a flood of water[1] appearing from under the door of the Ladies'.

James followed her out. He noticed to his dismay[2] that the back of her skirt had a dark stain[3] on it and he wondered whether to tell her. She was not *that* old[4], but perhaps she had bladder trouble[5].

'Now, *this* pub looks much nicer,' said Agatha, pushing open the door of the Potters Arms and diving in. Once more, she went to the Ladies'. To her relief[6] it was a modern place with a hot-air hand dryer. She took off her skirt and held it under the dryer until the water stain began to fade[7]. Then she lay down on the floor and held her wet feet up under it. Time passed. When she emerged, a worried James was on his second pint of beer. 'I was just about to[8] send someone to look for you[9],' he said. 'Are you all right?'

'Yes,' said Agatha, radiant again, for she had discovered that the new make-up[10] had done the job effectively[11] and she was once more warm and dry.

'I bought you another gin,' he said, indicating the glass on the table.

Agatha smiled at him. 'Here's to detection[12],' she said, raising her glass. And then she slowly lowered it, a look of ludicrous dismay on her face[13]. For into the pub had just marched Bill Wong and a tall policewoman. 'Dropped my handbag,' said Agatha and dived[14] under the table.

It was to no avail[15]. 'Come out, Agatha,' said Bill.

Agatha miserably[16] crawled out from[17] under the table, her face red with shame[18].

'Now, Agatha,' said Bill, 'what have you been up to? PC[19] Wood here called me into the George. A

1. nappe d'eau
2. consterné,
3. tache
4. vieille à ce point
5. des problèmes de vessie
6. soulagement,
7. à s'estomper
8. J'allais
9. à votre recherche
10. maquillage
11. efficacement
12. Buvons à la recherche des coupables
13. un air de consternation ridicule sur le visage
14. elle plongea
15. en pure perte
16. piteusement
17. s'extirpa de
18. de honte
19. l'agent de police [police constable]

woman answering your description went in and vandalized the ladies' room, tearing a hand basin out of the wall and flooding the place. People in the square saw you running in here. What have you to say for yourself[1]?'

'I had a spot[2] on my nose,' mumbled[3] Agatha.

'Speak up[4]. I can't hear you.'

'*I had a spot on my nose*,' roared[5] Agatha. Everyone looked at her and James Lacey desperately wished himself elsewhere.

'And how did that make you tear the hand basin out of the wall[6]?' asked Bill.

'I bought make-up at the chemist's.' Agatha's voice was now reduced to a flat even tone[7]. 'I wanted to cover up the spot, but the light in the Ladies' wasn't working and I thought it probably needed a new bulb. I remembered I had a packet of light bulbs in the car and went to get one. But the only way I could get to the light was by standing on the basin. It came away from the wall. I was so shocked I decided to say nothing about it.'

'I am afraid you are going to have to come with me,' said Bill severely.

The fact that James Lacey did not offer to accompany her, that he muttered something awkwardly[8] about staying put[9] and reading the newspapers, plunged him low in Agatha's estimation[10] despite her distress. So much for the knight errant[11] of her dreams. He was going to sit safely while she dealt with a no doubt enraged landlord[12].

James went out a few moments after they had left. He bought two newspapers and then returned to the pub. But he could not concentrate on the stories. Damn Agatha. What a woman. What a stupid thing to do! And then the ridiculous side of it all struck him and he began to laugh and, once

1. pour votre défense

2. bouton

3. marmonna

4. plus fort

5. rugit

6. détacher le lavabo du mur

7. à un ton monocorde

8. d'un ton embarrassé

9. sur le fait de rester là

10. l'estime

11. Adieu au chevalier errant

12. faisait face à un patron [de pub] sans doute furieux

started, couldn't seem to stop, although people edged away from[1] his table nervously. He finally mopped his eyes[2] and, tucking the unread papers under his arm, strode over to the George.

Agatha was holding out a cheque which the landlord of the George was refusing. 'Ho, no, you don't get off that easily[3],' he said. He was an unpleasant-looking man with a face like a slab of Cheddar cheese[4], the skin yellow and slightly sweating with rage. 'You charge[5] this woman, officer,' he said to Bill, 'and I'll see her in court. You charge her with wilful[6] vandalism.'

James twitched the cheque out of[7] Agatha's fingers and blinked slightly[8] at the large sum. 'You can't afford this,' he said to Agatha. 'A lady like yourself, existing on a widow's pension, cannot afford a sum like this. Declare yourself bankrupt[9] and then, even if he takes you to court, he won't get a penny. I know a good solicitor[10] just around the corner.'

'Good idea,' said Bill. 'You need a solicitor anyway. He'll want to know why there was no light bulb in the Ladies' in the first place[11], why the basin fell away from the wall so easily. The wiring[12] in this pub had better be checked, too.'

'I'll take the cheque,' growled[13] the landlord desperately.

'You'll take another cheque,' said James firmly. 'Agatha, get your cheque-book[14] and write out one for half this sum.'

The Cheddar cheese looked ready to explode again, but a steely look[15] from James silenced him.

Agatha wrote out the new cheque while James tore up the old one.

When they were all outside in the square, Bill said, 'If that had been a nice, respectable land-

1. s'écartaient de
2. s'essuya les yeux
3. n'allez pas vous en tirer aussi facilement
4. tranche de cheddar
5. inculpez
6. délibéré
7. prit le chèque des
8. tiqua légèrement
9. insolvable
10. avocat
11. déjà d'une part
12. L'installation électrique
13. grogna
14. chéquier
15. coup d'œil glacé

lord, I might have charged you, Agatha. Anyway, thanks to Mr Lacey, it's all sorted out[1]. What about dinner tonight?'

Agatha hesitated. She had originally thought her day with James might end in an intimate dinner. On the other hand, better to continue to play it cool. 'Yes, that would be nice. Where do you live? I know your phone number but not your address.'

'It's number 24, The Beeches. You go out of town on the Fosse and take the first left[2] along Camden Way until you come to a set of traffic lights[3], turn right, then take the first left, and that's The Beeches. It's a cul-de-sac.'

Agatha scribbled[4] the information down on the back[5] of a gas bill[6]. 'What time?'

'Six o'clock. We eat early.'

'We?'

'My parents. You forget, I live at home. You come too, Mr Lacey.'

Please, please, *please*, God, prayed Agatha.

James looked surprised but then said, 'I'd like that. I'd more or less decided to have the day off. Is it all right if I come dressed like this?'

Bill looked amused. 'We're not formal[7],' he said. 'See you then.'

He moved off, with the tall and still silent police-woman walking beside him.

'I think we need something to eat now,' said James. 'What about a beer and a sandwich, and then we'll decide who we ask about the sister. We should have asked Bill Wong. Still, we can always do that this evening.'

He did not mention the ruined toilet and Agatha was grateful for that. But she felt obliged to say gruffly[8], 'I'm hardly penniless[9].'

1. tout est arrangé
2. la première à gauche
3. des feux de signalisation
4. griffonna
5. au dos
6. facture
7. Nous ne faisons pas de cérémonies
8. d'un ton bourru
9. je ne suis pas sans le sou

'I know,' he said amiably, 'but the minute that[1] landlord thought you were broke[2], then he was glad to take any money.'

Once they had eaten, he drew out a notebook and pen and said, 'Why don't we pretend[3] it's murder and start by writing down all the names of the people we should speak to.'

'I think the ex-wife would be a good idea, said Agatha, 'although she wasn't very friendly[4]. I know, we can call at the vet's here, his partner, Peter Rice. He'll know whether Bladen had a sister, and that would be a start.'

Mr Peter Rice was a pugnacious man with a large bulbous nose, small eyes and a small mouth. The ugly nose, which dominated his face, was disconcerting, rather like a face pressed too close to a camera lens. His thatch[5] of thick red curly hair looked as if someone had dropped a small wig[6] casually[7] on the top of his rather pointed head. His neck was thick and strong, as were his shoulders. In fact, his body seemed too strong and broad for his small head, as if he had thrust his head through a Strong Man cardboard cutout on a fairground[8].

He was not pleased to learn that they had queued up in his surgery, not to consult him about some animal, but to ask him questions about his dead partner.

'Sister?' he said in answer to their questions. 'No, he didn't have a sister. Got a brother somewhere in London. Fell out a time ago[9]. Brother didn't bother turning up for the funeral.' His hands covered in thick red hair like fur[10] moved restlessly[11] over a shelf of small bottles, as if looking for a label that said 'Vanish'[12]. 'Now if that's all …'

'Was he a wealthy[13] man?' asked James.

1. dès que
2. fauchée
3. ne pas supposer
4. aimable
5. tignasse
6. perruque
7. au petit bonheur
8. comme s'il avait mis sa tête dans la découpe en carton d'un Hercule de foire
9. Plus de contact depuis quelque temps
10. de la fourrure
11. fébrilement
12. une étiquette avec l'inscription 'Disparaissez'
13. riche

'No.'

'Oh. How do you know?'

'I know because he left everything to me.'

'How much was that?' asked Agatha eagerly.

'Not enough,' he said. 'Get out of here and leave me to deal with my customers.'

'So he inherits[1] and not the brother. Now there's a motive,' crowed[2] Agatha when they were outside. 'Who would know how much money was involved?'

'The lawyer. But I doubt if he would tell us. Let's try the local newspaper editor,' said James. 'They pick up all sorts of gossip[3].'

The offices of the *Mircester Journal* came as a disappointment to[4] Agatha, even though the newspaper consisted of little more than three pages. She had naïvely expected something like the newspaper offices she had occasionally seen on news programmes, great enormous rooms with lines of computers and busy reporters. Time and printing changes had passed the *Mircester Journal* by[5]. The offices consisted of several dark rooms at the top of a rickety staircase[6]. A pale young woman with straight lank hair[7] was pounding[8] an old-fashioned typewriter and a young man with his hands in his pockets was standing by a window, whistling tunelessly[9] and looking down into the street.

'May we see the editor[10]?' asked James.

The pale girl stopped typing. 'If it's births, deaths, or marriages, I do that,' she said.

'None of those.'

'Complaints[11]? Wrong name under the photo?'

'No complaint.'

1. Donc c'est lui qui hérite
2. fanfaronna
3. potins
4. déçurent
5. n'avaient pas touché le *Mircester Journal*
6. escalier branlant
7. aux cheveux raides et ternes
8. martelait
9. sifflant faux
10. rédacteur en chef
11. Une réclamation

'That makes a change[1].' She got to her feet. She was wearing a long patchwork skirt and baseball boots[2] and a T-shirt which said 'Naff Off[3]'. 'Names?'

'Mrs Raisin and Mr Lacey.'

'Right.'

She pushed open a scarred door[4] and vanished inside. There was a murmur of voices and then she popped out again. 'You're to go in. Mr Heyford will see you now.'

Mr Heyford rose to meet them. After the vision in the T-shirt and baseball boots he came as a conservative surprise[5], being a small, neat man with a smooth olive face[6], black eyes and thin strips of oiled black hair combed straight back from his forehead. He was dressed in a dark suit, collar and tie.

'Sit down,' he said. 'What can I do for you? I recognize your name, Mrs Raisin. That was quite a lot of money you raised for charity last year.' Agatha preened[7].

'We both knew the vet, Paul Bladen,' said James. 'We're having a sort of a bet[8]. Mrs Raisin here said he was worth a lot of money[9], but I got the impression he didn't have that much[10]. Do you know how much he left?'

'I can't tell you exactly how much because I can't quite remember,' said Mr Heyford. 'About eighty-five thousand, I think. Would have been a fortune once, but that sort of money won't even buy you a decent house now. He left a house, of course, but he had taken a double mortgage[11] out on that, and with house prices being what they are, Mr Rice, who inherited, will barely get enough to[12] cover the mortgages. I never thought the day would come in this country when we would consider

1. Ça nous change
2. des baskets
3. Tire-toi
4. porte éraflée
5. faisait étonnamment classique
6. au teint lisse et basané
7. se rengorgea
8. pari
9. très riche
10. tant que ça
11. double hypothèque
12. aura à peine de quoi

eighty-five thousand not very much money, so it looks as if you've won the bet, Mr Lacey.'

'So he couldn't have been killed for his money,' said Agatha mournfully[1] when they had said goodbye to the editor. 'And yet ...'

'And yet what?'

'If he did have eighty-five thousand pounds, why the two mortgages? I mean, the interest must have been crippling[2]. Why not pay off some of the money owing[3]?'

'The trouble,' said James, 'is that we are making ourselves believe an accident to be murder.'

Agatha thought quickly. If he gave up the idea of investigating anything at all, then she would have little excuse to spend any time in his company. 'We could try the wife,' she suggested. 'I mean, as we're here and we've still got time to kill before we go to Bill's.'

'Oh, very well. Where do we find her?'

'We'll try the phone book[4] and hope she is still using her married name,' said Agatha.

They found a name, G. Bladen, listed. The address was given as Rose Cottage, Little Blomham. 'Where's Little Blomham?' asked Agatha.

'I saw a sign[5] to it once. It's off[6] the Stroud road.'

A pale mist[7] was shrouding[8] the landscape, turning the countryside into a Chinese painting, as they drove down into Little Blomham. It was more of a hamlet[9] than a village, a few ancient houses of golden Cotswold stone hunched[10] beside a stream.

No one moved about, no smoke rose from the chimneys, no dog barked.

Agatha switched off the engine and both listened as the eerie[11] silence settled about them.

1. tristement

2. les intérêts devaient être accablants

3. ne pas rembourser une partie de la somme due

4. annuaire

5. panneau

6. donne sur

7. brume

8. voilait

9. plutôt un hameau

10. blotties

11. étrange

1. étrier
2. reprenait doucement sa place
3. le martèlement des sabots eut cessé [d'un poème de Walter de la Mare, où personne ne répond aux paroles et au bruits du voyageur solitaire]
4. avec humeur
5. inculte
6. incompétent
7. pour frimer
8. claqua la portière
9. masures pittoresques
10. jardin enchevêtré et mal entretenu
11. avec un toit de chaume
12. d'une profusion de plantes grimpantes
13. terrier

James suddenly quoted:

'Ay, they heard his foot upon the stirrup[1],
And the sound of iron on stone,
And how the silence surged softly backward[2],
When the plunging hoofs were gone[3].'

Agatha looked at him crossly[4]. She did not like people who suddenly quoted things at you, leaving you feeling unread[5] and inadequate[6]. In fact, she thought they only did it to show off[7].

She got out of the car and slammed the door shut[8] with unnecessary force.

James got out of the passenger seat and wandered to a stone wall and looked down at the slowly moving stream. He seemed to have gone into some sort of dream, to have forgotten Agatha's presence. 'So very quiet,' he said, half to himself. 'So very English, the England they fought for in the First World War. So little of it left.'

'Would you like to stand here and meditate while I find out which one of these picturesque hovels[9] is Rose Cottage?' asked Agatha.

He gave her a sudden smile. 'No, I'll come with you.' They walked together down the road by the stream. 'Let me see, this one has no name and the next one is called End Cottage, although it's not at the end. Perhaps one of the ones further on.'

They nearly missed Rose Cottage. It was set well back from the road at the end of a thin, narrow, tangled and unkempt garden[10]. It was small and thatched[11], with the walls covered in thick creeper[12]. 'Looks more like an animal's burrow[13] than a house,' commented James. 'Well, here we go. We can't say we think he was murdered. We'll offer our sympathy and see where that gets us.'

He knocked on the door. And waited. They stood wrapped in[1] the silence of the dream countryside. Then, as if a spell[2] had been broken, a bird suddenly flew up from a bush near the door, a dog barked somewhere, high and shrill in the road outside, and Mrs Bladen opened the door.

Why[3], I believe she's older than I, thought Agatha, looking again at that grey hair and at the tell-tale lines[4] on the thin neck.

Mrs Bladen looked past James to Agatha and her face settled in lines of dislike. 'Oh, it's you again.'

'Mr Lacey wished to offer you his sympathy[5],' said Agatha quickly.

'Why?' she demanded harshly. 'Why should someone come all this way to offer sympathy for the death of a man I've been divorced from?'

'We're very neighbourly people[6] in Carsely,' said James, 'and wondered if we could do anything to help.'

'You can help by going away.'

James looked helplessly[7] at Agatha. Agatha decided to take the bull by the horns. 'Are you sure your husband died a natural death?' she asked.

Mrs Bladen looked amused. 'Meaning someone killed him? It's more than likely. He was a thoroughly nasty man[8] and I'm glad he's dead. I hope that satisfies you.'

She slammed the door in their faces.

'That's that[9],' said James, as they walked down the weedy[10] path.

'We got something,' said Agatha eagerly[11]. 'She didn't laugh in our faces[12] when I suggested murder to her. Now did she[13]?'

'You know what I think?' he said, holding the gate open for her. 'I think we're two retired people with not enough to do with our time.'

1. enveloppés par
2. sortilège
3. Eh bien
4. rides révélatrices
5. vous présenter ses condoléances
6. bons voisins
7. jeta un regard d'impuissance
8. homme vraiment méchant
9. Ben voilà
10. envahi d'herbes
11. avec enthousiasme
12. ne nous a pas ri au nez
13. N'est-ce pas

'Just because you can't get started writing,' said Agatha shrewdly[1], 'don't take it out on me[2].'

'This is a lovely little place,' he said to change the subject. 'So quiet and peaceful. I wonder if there's anything for sale here.'

'Oh, you wouldn't want to live here,' said Agatha, alarmed. 'I mean, Carsely's bad enough, but there's *nothing* here, not even a shop or a pub.'

'What's wrong with that, in this age of the motor car? Oh, look. That sign[3] there. The Manor House. I didn't notice it before. Let's go and have a look.'

Agatha followed him silently up a winding drive[4]. She did not want to look at any manor house because manor houses belonged to James Lacey's world and not to hers. The drive, edged with[5] rhododendron bushes, opened up and there stood the manor house. The mist had thinned and pale sunlight washed[6] the golden walls. It was low and rambling[7] and settled[8] and charming, exuding centuries of peace[9]. Even Agatha sensed that wars and conflicts, plague[10] and pestilence[11] had passed this old building by[12].

A small square woman in a twin set[13] and tweed skirt came out with a black retriever[14] at her heels. 'Can I help you?' she called.

'Just admiring your beautiful home,' said James, approaching her.

'Yes, it is beautiful,' she said. 'Come inside and have some tea. I don't often get visitors until the summer, when all my relatives[15] decide they would like a free holiday[16].'

James introduced them[17]. The woman said she was Bunty Vere-Dedsworth. She led the way into a dark hall and then through into a large old kitchen gleaming with copper pans[18] and white-and-

1. finement
2. ne vous défoulez pas sur moi
3. panneau
4. allée sinueuse
5. bordée de
6. baignait
7. plein de coins et de recoins
8. stable
9. exhalant des siècles de tranquillité
10. épidémies
11. fléaux
12. n'avaient pas touché cette vieille bâtisse
13. tailleur
14. chien de chasse
15. les membres de ma famille
16. des vacances gratuites
17. fit les présentations
18. vaisselle de cuivre

blue china[1] on an old dresser which ran the length of one wall.

'Lacey,' she said, as she plugged in an electric kettle. 'I used to know some Laceys down in Sussex.'

'That's where my family comes from,' said James.

'Really!' She had cornflower-blue eyes[2] in a reddish face. 'Old Harry Lacey?'

'My father.'

'Gosh[3], small world. Do you ever see the ...'

Agatha, excluded from that intimidating conversation of the upper classes which consisted of names and exclamations of recognition thrown back and forth[4], moodily[5] sipped[6] her tea and felt James moving out of her sphere. She could picture him[7] living in a place like this with an elegant wife, not with some retired public relations woman such as herself who would only be able to swap[8] names with someone from the rather nasty Birmingham slum[9] in which she had grown up.

'What brings you here?' said Bunty at last.

James said, 'Our vet in Carsely died and we went to offer Mrs Bladen our sympathies, but she doesn't seem in need of any.'

'No, she wouldn't,' said Bunty. 'She had a very unhappy marriage.'

'Other women?' suggested Agatha.

'I think it was more a question of money, or the lack[10] of it. Greta Bladen was a wealthy woman when she married Paul, and he seemed to spend a great deal of her money. When she left him, that dingy[11] little cottage was all she could afford[12]. She really hated him. I heard how Bladen died. Now if he had been found dead because someone had biffed him with the frying-pan[13], that some-

1. porcelaine
2. des yeux couleur de bleuet
3. Seigneur !
4. en un ping-pong de gens qu'on connaît en commun
5. d'un air boudeur
6. sirotait
7. le voyait très bien
8. ne pourrait échanger
9. quartier pauvre
10. manque
11. minable
12. s'offrir
13. lui avait flanqué un coup de poêle à frire

one being Greta, I wouldn't have been at all surprised. But you'd really need to know about veterinary things to shove a syringe full of deadly stuff in him. I mean, think of it. How many of the population would know that stuff was deadly? Maybe his partner wanted the business for himself,' And Bunty laughed.

James looked at his watch. 'We really must go.'

'Must you?' Bunty smiled at Agatha. 'Then do come back and see me. I'd like that.'

Agatha smiled back, feeling all her social inadequacies fade away[1], feeling welcome.

'She had a point[2],' said Agatha as she drove out of the village. 'I mean about Rice. Surely it would need to be someone with a knowledge[3] of veterinary medicine.'

'Not necessarily,' he remarked. 'That story about the vet who died last year when the horse nudged[4] his breast pocket with the syringe in it and caused his death was in all the local papers[5]. I read it. Anyone could have read it and got the idea.'

'But it would need to be someone who knew where he was going and what he was doing on that day.'

'Any of his lady friends might know. "What are you doing tomorrow, Paul?" "Oh, I'm cutting the vocal cords of one of Pendlebury's horses." That sort of thing.'

'Yes, but say he had said that to me. I wouldn't immediately think of Immobilon.'

'No, but a vet might talk about it, saying how deadly it was and talking about the accident of the previous year. I've got a feeling a woman did it.'

Agatha was about to exclaim, 'So you *do* think it was murder,' but decided to remain silent in the hope of more days of investigation together.

1. perdant d'un coup son sentiment d'infériorité sociale
2. n'avait pas tort
3. certaine connaissance
4. a donné un coup de museau sur
5. journaux

Bill's home came as a surprise to Agatha. She had naïvely expected something, well, more oriental and exotic. The Beeches was one of those closes[1] designed by builders[2], each house different, with trim suburban lawns[3], oozing[4] respectability and dullness[5]. Agatha knew that Bill's father was Hong Kong Chinese and his mother from Gloucestershire, but she had not expected him to live somewhere so ordinary. Bill's house was called Clarendon, the name being poker-worked[6] on a wooden sign hung on a post at the gate. They went up a trim path between regimented flower-beds and rang the bell, which played a chorus[7] of 'Rule, Britannia[8]'.

Bill himself answered the door. 'Come in. Come in,' he cried. 'I'll just put you in the lounge and go and get the drinks. Ma's in the kitchen getting dinner ready.'

Agatha and James sat in the lounge, not looking at each other. There was a three-piece suite[9], shell-backed[10], in a nasty sort of grey wool material[11]. There were venetian blinds[12] drawn down over the 'picture' windows[13] and ruched curtains[14]. The fitted carpet[15] was in a noisy[16] geometric design of red and black. The wallpaper was white and gold Regency stripe. There were little occasional pie-crust tables[17] on spindly legs[18]. A display cabinet[19] full of Spanish dolls and little bits of china stood against one wall. A gas fire with fake[20] coals and logs burned cheerfully but threw out very little heat.

Agatha longed for a cigarette but could not see an ashtray.

Bill came in with a small tray on which were three tiny glasses of sweet sherry.

1. quartiers résidentiels

2. entrepreneurs

3. pelouses soignées de banlieue

4. suintant

5. l'ennui

6. inscrit au tisonnier

7. carillon

8. [chant patriotique britannique]

9. canapé et deux fauteuils

10. à dossier en coquillage

11. tissu [d'ameublement]

12. des stores

13. des baies vitrées

14. des rideaux à ruches

15. moquette

16. tapageur

17. guéridons

18. à pieds filiformes

19. vitrine

20. faux

'You're honoured,' said Bill. 'We don't use this room much. Keep it for best[1].'

'Very nice,' said Agatha, feeling strange and awkward[2] at seeing her Bill, chubby[3] and oriental as usual, in these cold English suburban surroundings.

'May I use your toilet?' she asked.

'Top of the stairs. But don't go standing on the hand basin.'

Agatha climbed up thickly carpeted stairs and pushed open the door of a bathroom which contained a suite in Nile green[4]. The toilet had a chenille cover[5]. A flowery notice[6] on the back of the bathroom door stated, 'When you have had a tinkle, please wipe the seat[7].'

She tugged at[8] the toilet roll to get a piece of tissue to blot[9] her lipstick and started in alarm[10] as the toilet-roll holder[11] chimed out[12] 'The Bluebells of Scotland'.

'Dinner's ready,' said Bill when she arrived downstairs again.

He led them across the hall and into another small room, the dining-room, where at the head of the table sat his father, a small morose Chinese gentleman with a droopy[13] moustache, a grey baggy[14] cardigan and large checked[15] carpet slippers.

Bill performed the introductions. Mr Wong grunted by way of reply, picked up his knife and fork and stared at the polished surface of the laminated top of the table. Agatha looked down at a place-mat[16] depicting Tewkesbury Abbey and wished she had not come.

A hatch[17] from the kitchen shot up[18] and a Gloucester accent said shrilly, 'Bill! Soup!'

1. Elle est réservée pour les grandes occasions
2. étrangement mal à l'aise
3. potelé
4. ensemble vert-bleu pâle
5. Le couvercle des toilettes était recouvert de tissu chenille [à fines bandes de velours]
6. inscription fleurie
7. En cas de goutte, prière d'essuyer la lunette
8. tira sur
9. tamponner
10. sursauta
11. porte-rouleau de papier toilette
12. chantonna
13. tombante
14. ample
15. à carreaux
16. set de table
17. La trappe d'un passe-plat
18. fut brusquement soulevée

Bill collected plates of soup and passed them round. 'Have you got that bottle of Liebfraumilch, Ma?' he called.

'In 'er[1] fridge.'

'I'll get it.'

Mrs Wong appeared. She was a massive woman with a discontented, suspicious face and appeared to resent[2] having guests. Bill poured wine.

The soup was canned oxtail[3]. Little triangles of bread were passed around. Even James Lacey seemed stricken into silence[4].

'Roast beef next,' said Bill. 'Nobody does roast beef quite like Ma.'

'That's for sure[5],' said Mr Wong suddenly, making Agatha jump.

The roast beef was incredibly tough and the table knives were blunt[6]. It took all their concentration to hack pieces off[7]. The cauliflower was covered in a coat of thick white sauce, the carrots were overcooked[8] and oversalted, the Yorkshire pudding was like salted rubber[9] and the peas were those nasty processed kind out of a can[10] which manage to turn everything on the plate green.

'Days are drawing out[11],' said Mrs Wong.

'That's for sure,' said Mr Wong.

'Soon be summer,' pursued Mrs Wong, glaring fiercely[12] at Agatha, as if blaming her for the seasons.

'I hope we get another nice summer,' said James.

Mrs Wong rounded on him[13]. 'You call last summer nice? Did you hear that, Father? He called last summer nice?'

'Some people[14],' muttered Mr Wong, taking more cauliflower.

'So hot, it nearly brought on one of my turns[15],' said Mrs Wong. 'Didn't it nearly, Father?'

1. [= in the]
2. ne pas apprécier d'
3. C'était de la soupe de queue de bœuf en boîte
4. frappé de mutisme
5. Y a pas de doute
6. émoussés
7. se couper des morceaux
8. trop cuites
9. du caoutchouc
10. du genre atroce industriel en boîte
11. rallongent
12. jetant un regard furieux à
13. s'en prit à lui
14. Y a des gens
15. j'ai failli en faire une de mes crises

'That's for sure.'

Silence.

'I'll get the pudding,' said Bill.

'Sit down,' said his mother. 'These are your guests. I told you I wanted to watch that quiz on the telly, but you would have them[1].'

Soon bowls of stewed apples[2] and custard[3] were banged[4] in front of them. I want to go home, thought Agatha ... Oh, please God, let this evening be over[5] quickly.

'Take them through to the lounge,' said Mrs Wong when the dreadful meal was over. 'I'll bring the coffee.'

'You really must show me your garden,' said James. 'I'm very interested in gardens.'

'We're not going out in the evening air to catch our deaths,' said Mrs Wong, looking outraged[6]. 'Are we, Father?'

'Funny thing to suggest,' said Mr Wong.

To Agatha's and James's relief, they had only Bill for company over coffee. 'I'm so glad you could come,' said Bill. 'I'm really proud of my home. Ma's made quite a little palace out of it.'

'Really cosy,' lied Agatha. 'Bill, are you sure there is nothing odd about Bladen's death?'

'Nothing that anyone could find,' he said. He looked amused. 'You two have been sleuthing[7].'

'Just asking around,' said Agatha. 'Bill, do you mind if I have a cigarette?'

'I don't, but Ma would kill you. Come out into the back garden and have one there.'

They followed him out into the garden. James let out a gasp[8]. It was beautifully laid out[9]. A cluster of cherry trees[10] at the bottom raised white-and-pink branches to the evening sky. A wisteria[11] just beginning to show its first leaves coiled over[12]

1. as voulu les inviter
2. compote de pommes
3. avec de la crème anglaise
4. déposés brutalement
5. que cette soirée finisse
6. l'air indigné
7. avez joué aux détectives
8. laissa échapper un cri de surprise
9. composé de façon ravissante
10. massif de cerisiers
11. glycine
12. montait en torsade au-dessus

the kitchen door. 'This is my patch[1],' said Bill. 'Makes a change from policing[2].'

James marvelled that Bill, who obviously had such an eye for[3] beauty, could see nothing wrong with his parents' home. Agatha wondered how Bill could have such admiration and affection for such a dreary[4] couple and then decided she admired him for it.

James was becoming happy and animated as he discussed plants and Agatha thought again of her own neglected garden and decided that if this investigation fell through[5], then gardening[6] might be a subject they would have in common. By the time they returned to the dreadful lounge for more horrible coffee served in doll's cups which Mrs Wong called her best 'demytess'[7], the three were at ease with each other.

'I like to return hospitality,' said Bill to James. 'I'm always dropping in to Agatha's[8] for a coffee, but she's never been here. Now you know the road, you're welcome to come any time.'

'Have you moved[9] here recently?' asked James.

'Last year,' said Bill proudly. 'Dad's got this dry-cleaning[10] business in Mircester and he's really built it up[11]. Yes, we're moving up in the world[12].' His good nature seemed to transform his home into the palace he thought it to be and Agatha and James thanked Mrs Wong very warmly for her hospitality before they finally left.

'It will be a cold day in hell[13] before I go back there again,' said Agatha, as they drove off.

'Yes, I'm still hungry. I cut up that beef and pushed it under the vegetables to make it look as if[14] I'd eaten it,' said James. 'We'll stop somewhere for a drink and a sandwich.' He said this almost absent-mindedly[15], as if to an old friend, taking

1. domaine
2. Ça me change du maintien de l'ordre
3. un tel sens de
4. assommant
5. tombait à l'eau
6. le jardinage
7. ses plus jolies demi-tasses
8. Je n'arrête pas de passer chez Agatha
9. emménagé
10. de teinturerie
11. l'a vraiment développé
12. nous montons dans la hiérarchie sociale
13. Il neigera en enfer
14. pour faire croire que
15. distraitement

her acceptance[1] for granted[2], and Agatha felt so ridiculously happy, she thought she might cry.

Over beer and sandwiches, they decided to continue their investigations the next day. 'What about Miss Mabbs?' asked Agatha suddenly. 'Look, we know Bladen was a womanizer[3]. Miss Mabbs was that pallid[4] female who worked as receptionist. What of her?[5] She must have known all about the operation on that horse. I wonder where she is now?'

'We'll find her tomorrow. You can smoke if you like.'

'I feel like an endangered species[6],' said Agatha, lighting up[7]. 'People are becoming so militant about smokers.'

'They're puritans,' said James. 'Who was it said that the reason the puritans were against bear-baiting[8] was not because it gave pain to the bear but because it gave pleasure to the crowd[9]?'

'I don't know. But I should give it up.'

'Bill said an odd thing when we were leaving,' said James. 'He said, "Don't go about stirring up muck[10] or you may promote a real murder[11]." '

'Oh, he was joking. He's a great one for jokes.'

1. accord
2. comme allant de soi
3. coureur de jupons
4. blafarde
5. Que penser d'elle ?
6. espèce menacée
7. allumant une cigarette
8. les combats d'ours
9. la foule
10. Ne vous amusez pas à remuer la boue
11. risquez d'encourager un vrai meurtre

Chapter Five

Agatha would have been most surprised if anyone had called her a romantic. She considered herself hard-headed[1] and practical[2]. So she did not realize the folly of wild dreams and fantasies[3].

In her mind, since she had said goodbye to him the evening before, she was married to James Lacey, and most of her dreams had been of a passionate honeymoon, and the lovely thing about dreams is that one can write the script, and James said beautiful and loverlike things.

So Agatha, next morning, forgot all her plans of being cool and detached. James had said he would call for her around noon and that they might have a bite to eat[4] in the pub before trying to find out what had become of Miss Mabbs.

Agatha decided to make a romantic lunch. So when James turned up on her doorstep, he shied[5] nervously before an Agatha in a low-cut[6] blouse[7], tight skirt and very high heels, who was glowing at him. He fidgeted[8] nervously in the hall as she waved a hand in the direction of the dining-room and said she'd thought they may as well have lunch at her place[9].

Through the open door of the dining-room, James saw the table set with fine china and crystal and candles burning in tall holders[10] – candles in the middle of the day!

1. se croyait du genre qui a la tête sur les épaules

2. pragmatique

3. des fantasmes

4. aller manger un morceau

5. recula

6. très décolleté

7. chemisier

8. resta à s'agiter

9. chez elle

10. chandeliers

Panic set in. He backed out of the door[1]. 'Actually[2], I came to apologize,' he said. 'Something's come up[3]. Can't make it[4].' And he turned and fled.

Agatha could practically hear the ruins of her dreams tumbling[5] about her ears, brick by brick. Red with shame, she blew out the candles, put the china away, went upstairs, scrubbed off[6] her thick make-up and put on a comfortable old dress like a sack, thrust her feet into slippers and shuffled back down[7] to stare at the soaps on television and try not to brood on[8] her gaffe.

She had had a nearly sleepless night and so she dozed off[9] in front of the television set with the cats on her lap, waking an hour later at the sound of the doorbell.

She hoped he had come back – if only he would come back! – but it was Mrs Bloxby, the vicar's wife, who stood there.

'I was just passing,' said Mrs Bloxby, 'and wondered whether you remembered that the Carsely Ladies are having a meeting tonight.' For a moment, something unlovely darted through[10] Agatha's eyes. She was thinking, Screw the[11] Carsely Ladies.

'I do hope you will come,' said Mrs Bloxby. 'Our new-comer, Mrs Huntingdon, is going to be there, and Miss Webster, who has the shop. We expect quite a crowd. And Miss Simms is bringing along some of her home-made cider, so I thought we would have cheese and biscuits with that.'

Agatha realized Mrs Bloxby was still standing on the doorstep and said, 'Do come in[12].'

'No, I'd better get home. My husband is wrestling with a tricky sermon[13].'

So this is what life has come down to[14], thought Agatha gloomily; another evening with the ladies.

1. passa la porte à reculons
2. En fait
3. Un imprévu
4. Je ne vais pas pouvoir, pour le déjeuner
5. s'effondrant
6. ôta
7. redescendit en traînant les pieds
8. ruminer
9. s'assoupit
10. quelque chose de déplaisant fusa dans
11. Rien à foutre des
12. Entrez donc
13. se débat avec un sermon un peu délicat
14. à quoi ma vie se limite

Even the knowledge[1] that Mrs Huntingdon was going to be there could not give Agatha enough energy to change out of her old dress.

But on her way to the vicarage, she remembered that Josephine Webster, she[2] of the dried-flower shop, she who had admired the vet, was to be there. There was no James Lacey, but there was still the interest of amateur detection.

The vicarage sitting-room was full of chattering[3] women. Mrs Bloxby handed Agatha a tankard[4] of cider. 'Where is Miss Webster?' asked Agatha.

'Over there, by the piano.'

'Of course.' Agatha studied her with interest. She was a neat[5] woman of indeterminate age, neat fair hair crisply permed[6], neat little features, neat little figure[7]. Talking to her was Freda Huntingdon, who had not bothered to dress up either[8], Agatha noticed. Agatha did not want to interrupt their conversation. She took another pull at her tankard and blinked[9]. The cider was very strong indeed. She found Miss Simms next to her. 'How did you get such powerful stuff?' she asked.

Miss Simms giggled[10] and whispered in Agatha's ear. 'Let you into[11] a secret. I thought I would spice it up a bit[12].' She waved her own tankard towards a firkin[13] on a table. 'So I poured a bottle of vodka into it.'

'You'll get us all drunk,' said Agatha.

'Well, some of us need cheering up. Look at Mrs Josephs. She's looking better already. I thought she was going to go into mourning for[14] that cat of hers forever.'

Agatha sat down beside Mrs Josephs. 'Glad to see you looking better,' said Agatha politely.

'Oh, much better,' said the librarian in a tipsy voice[15]. 'Revenge is mine.'

1. Même le fait de savoir
2. celle
3. occupées à bavarder
4. chope
5. soignée
6. parfaitement permanentés
7. personne
8. n'avait pas non plus fait d'effort pour sa tenue
9. tiqua
10. gloussa
11. Je vais vous révéler
12. le relever un peu
13. petit fût
14. porter le deuil de
15. éméchée

'Really?'

'I am to get what is rightfully mine[1].'

Agatha looked at her impatiently. 'What do you mean?'

'Silence, ladies,' called Mrs Mason. 'Our meeting is about to begin.'

'Call on me[2] at ten tomorrow,' said Mrs Josephs loudly, 'and I'll tell you all about Paul Bladen.'

'Shhh!' admonished[3] Mrs Bloxby.

Agatha waited restlessly[4] while the proceedings dragged on[5]. But before they were finished, Mrs Josephs suddenly got up and left. Agatha shrugged and approached Miss Webster. 'I saw you at Paul Bladen's funeral,' she said.

'I didn't know you were a friend of his,' said Miss Webster.

'Not exactly a friend,' said Agatha, 'but I felt I should pay my respects[6]. You must have been very sorry to lose him.'

'On the contrary,' said Miss Webster, 'I went to make sure he was really dead. Now, if you will excuse me, Miss ...?'

'Mrs Raisin.'

'Mrs Raisin. I find all these chattering women give me a headache[7].'

She got up abruptly and left the room. Curiouser and curiouser[8], thought Agatha. Damn James. All this was interesting stuff, hints here, hints there[9]. She would call on him before she went to see Mrs Josephs.

James heard his doorbell at quarter to ten the following morning. Feeling like an old spinster[10], he twitched[11] the front-room curtain and looked out. There was Agatha Raisin. That old feeling of being hunted came back again. He went through

1. Je vais récupérer ce qui me revient de plein droit
2. Passez me voir
3. gronda
4. avec impatience
5. la réunion traînait en longueur
6. lui rendre hommage
7. me donnent mal à la tête
8. De plus en plus bizarre [d'après Lewis Carroll]
9. des allusions par-ci, des allusions par-là
10. vieille fille
11. écarta

to his kitchen and sat there. The bell went on and on and then there was blessed silence[1].

Agatha stumped grumpily through the village[2]. A car slid to a stop[3] beside her and Bill Wong's cheerful face looked out. 'What's the matter, Agatha? Where's James?'

'Nothing's the matter, and where James Lacey is I neither know nor care.'

'Which means you've scared him off again[4],' commented Bill cheerfully.

'I have done nothing of the kind, and for your information I am on my way to see Mrs Josephs, the librarian. She has something important to tell me about Paul Bladen's death.'

Bill gave a little sigh. 'Agatha, when there actually has been a murder[5], a lot of distasteful scandal[6] usually comes to light[7] which has nothing to do with the case. A lot of people get hurt. Now if you're going to dig around an English village trying to make an accident look like murder it will have the same effect, and without any justification. Drop it. Do good works[8]. Go abroad[9] again. Let Paul Bladen rest in peace.'

He drove off. Well, I may as well go, thought Agatha stubbornly[10]. She'll be expecting me.

Mrs Josephs lived at the end of a terrace[11] of what were once workers' cottages. Hers was neat and trim, with a pocket-sized garden where forsythia spilled over[12] the hedge[13] into the road in a burst of golden glory[14]. A blackbird[15] sang on the roof. From a field above the village came the sound of a hunting horn[16], and as Agatha turned and looked up the hill, she saw the hunt streaming across a meadow[17], looking oddly out of perspective[18] from her angle of vision.

1. enfin le silence
2. traversa le village à pas lourds et en rogne
3. s'arrêta doucement
4. à nouveau fait fuir
5. un meurtre a vraiment eu lieu
6. ragots déplaisants
7. éclatent au grand jour
8. Occupez-vous de bonnes œuvres
9. à l'étranger
10. avec obstination
11. rangée de maisons
12. débordaient par-dessus
13. la haie
14. explosion de splendeur dorée
15. merle
16. cor de chasse
17. la file des chasseurs traverser une prairie
18. et ils semblaient curieusement hors de proportion

If Lord Pendlebury was part of the hunt, she hoped he broke his neck. And with that pious thought[1], she pushed open the small wrought-iron[2] gate and walked up to the door and rang the bell. There was no reply. The sound of the hunt disappeared into the distance. A jet screamed above, tearing the pale spring sky apart with sound.

Agatha tried again, feeling almost weepy[3], wondering dismally[4] if all the inhabitants of Carsely were going to hide behind their sofas when they saw her on the doorstep[5].

But Mrs Josephs had asked her to call. Mrs Josephs had no right to snub her[6]. Agatha turned the handle of the front door. It opened easily. A small hall with a narrow stair leading straight up from it.

'Mrs Josephs!' called Agatha.

The little house had thick walls, and silence pressed in on[7] Agatha. She looked in the downstairs rooms, small parlour, small dining-room, and tiny cubicle of a kitchen[8] at the back.

Agatha stood at the bottom of the stairs and shifted from foot to foot[9].

How sinister that dim staircase looked. Perhaps Mrs Josephs was ill. Emboldened by that thought[10], Agatha climbed the stairs. Bedroom on the right at the top, bed made, everything tidy. Box-room[11] full of pathetic[12] pieces of broken china and old furniture and dusty suitcases. No drama here.

May as well use the bathroom while I'm here, thought Agatha. Oh, I know! She probably meant me to go to the library[13]. What a fool I am! But how crazy to go out and leave the house unlocked. This must be the bathroom. She pushed open a door which had a pane of frosted glass[14].

1. pieuse pensée
2. en fer forgé
3. presque au bord des larmes
4. lugubrement
5. pas de leur porte
6. n'avait pas le droit de l'ignorer
7. s'abattit sur
8. un minuscule espace cuisine
9. se balança d'un pied sur l'autre
10. Enhardie à cette pensée
11. Un débarras
12. dérisoires
13. voulait probablement que j'aille à la bibliothèque
14. dont un panneau était en verre dépoli

Mrs Josephs was lying[1] on the bathroom floor, her eyes staring sightlessly up at the ceiling[2]. Agatha let out a whimper[3]. She forced herself to bend down, pick up an arm and feel the pulse[4]. Nothing.

She turned and ran down the stairs, looking for the phone. She found one in the parlour[5] and dialled[6] police and ambulance.

The first to arrive was PC[7] Fred Griggs, the village policeman. He looked like a village policeman in a children's story, large and red-faced.

'She's dead,' said Agatha. 'Upstairs. Bathroom.'

She followed the bulk of the policeman[8] up the stairs. Fred looked sadly down at the body. 'You're right,' he said. 'Can tell by just looking at her. Mrs Josephs was a diabetic.'

'So it wasn't murder,' said Agatha.

'Now what put such an idea into your head?' His small eyes were shrewd[9].

'She said last night in front of everyone at the Carsely Ladies' Society that she had something to tell me about Paul Bladen.'

'The vet what died[10]! What's that got to do with the poor woman's death?'

'Nothing,' muttered Agatha. 'I think I'll wait outside.'

As she went out into the garden again, she could hear the wail[11] of sirens; and then an ambulance, followed by two police cars, came racing up. She recognized Detective Chief Inspector Wilkes and Bill Wong. There were two other detectives she did not know and a policewoman.

Bill said, 'Did you find her?' Agatha nodded dumbly[12]. 'What time?'

'Ten o'clock,' said Agatha. 'I told you I was going to see her.'

1. gisait
2. fixant le plafond sans le voir
3. gémissement
4. son pouls
5. petit salon
6. appela
7. l'agent
8. massif agent de police
9. Il avait de petits yeux malins
10. [= that died]
11. hurlement
12. fit silencieusement oui de la tête

'Go home,' said Bill. 'We'll be around to take a statement[1].'

James Lacey stood on his doorstep, peering down the lane[2]. He had heard the sirens. Ever since he had failed to[3] answer the door to Agatha's ring, he had been staring at that heading[4] 'Chapter Two' on his computer screen. Then he saw Agatha trailing along the lane[5]. Her face was very white.

'What's happened?' he called, but she flapped a hand at him[6] and said, 'Later.'

He felt frustrated. He felt that Agatha held the key to some excuse to take him away from writing for the day. He should not have run away from her lunch like a schoolboy.

He returned to his machine and glared at it. Then he heard the sound of a car turning into the lane and dashed outside again. It was a police car. He watched eagerly as it drove up to Agatha's cottage and stopped. He recognized Bill Wong with another detective and a policewoman. They went inside.

He had brought it on himself[7], he thought gloomily. The wretched[8] Raisin woman was on to something[9] and he was excluded.

Inside her home, Agatha answered all questions put to her. How long had she been in Mrs Josephs's cottage? Just a few minutes? Had anyone seen her just before she arrived? Detective Wong. The Chief Inspector nodded, as though Bill had already confirmed that.

'What did she die of?' asked Agatha.

'We'll need to wait for the pathologist's report[10],' said Wilkes. 'Now, I gather[11] this arrangement to

1. Nous passerons prendre votre déposition
2. scrutant la ruelle
3. s'était abstenu de
4. titre
5. qui remontait lentement la ruelle
6. balaya la question d'un geste
7. l'avait bien cherché
8. Cette satanée
9. tenait quelque chose
10. rapport du médecin légiste
11. Bon, si j'ai bien compris

see her was made at the vicarage last night. What exactly did she say?'

Agatha replied promptly, 'She said, "Call on me at ten tomorrow and I'll tell you all about Paul Bladen." '

'Anything else?'

'Let me see. I think I remarked she was looking better and she said an odd thing, she said, "Revenge is mine." '

'You're sure of that?'

'Absolutely. She added …' Agatha screwed up her eyes[1] in an effort of memory. 'She added, "I am to get what is rightfully mine." '

'Indeed,' commented Wilkes. 'Very cryptic[2]. Quite like a novel.'

'I am not making it up[3],' snapped Agatha[4]. 'I have a very good memory.'

'Now, Mrs Josephs said, "Call me at ten," yet[5] you went to her house. Wouldn't you think she meant you to phone her?'

'No,' said Agatha, 'we don't use the phone much in this village to talk to each other. We call in person[6].'

'Mrs Josephs was due on duty[7] at the library. Why didn't you go there?'

'Because I didn't *think*!' howled[8] Agatha, exasperated. 'What the f –, what the devil is all this about? She just died of natural causes, didn't she?'

'Odd you should think that, when I gather from[9] Detective Sergeant Wong here that you are very ready to believe the death of Paul Bladen was murder.'

Agatha threw Bill Wong a reproachful look. 'I was interested in Paul Bladen's death and I was just asking a few questions,' she said defensively.

1. plissa les yeux
2. énigmatique
3. Je ne l'invente pas
4. lança Agatha d'un ton sec
5. et pourtant
6. On se voit en direct
7. aurait dû être de service
8. gueula
9. alors que d'après

1. Qui étaient toutes les personnes présentes au thé hier soir au presbytère
2. toute personne présente à
3. que cela nous suffit

'Who all was at the vicarage tea-party last night[1]?'

'It wasn't a tea-party. Cider and cheese. I can give you most of the names, but if you ask Miss Simms, the secretary, she makes a note of everyone who attends[2] each meeting.'

Wilkes stood up. 'I think that will do[3] for now, Mrs Raisin. We'll probably be talking to you again. Not thinking of travelling anywhere, are you?'

'What?' Agatha stared at him. 'Me? Not travel – You think it's murder.'

4. Allons, allons

'Now, now[4], Mrs Raisin, at the moment we are simply investigating the death of a diabetic. Good day to you.'

5. fit un clin d'œil à Agatha
6. articula

Bill gave Agatha a wink[5] behind his superior's back and mouthed[6] silently, 'This evening.'

7. ne vint pas ouvrir
8. fut peu réconfortée par

After they had left, Agatha decided to try James again. Forget about romance. This was too exciting to keep to herself. But he did not answer his door[7] and she took small comfort in[8] the fact that this time his car was gone.

9. Pour se réconcilier
10. envisagé
11. trouvé

James had driven into Mircester. To heal the breach[9] with Agatha, he had considered[10] an offer of flowers or chocolates and then had hit upon[11] a better idea. If he found out Miss Mabbs's address, that would be a better excuse than anything to call on her.

12. avec ardeur
13. gens du village
14. pompette

Agatha went along to the Red Lion and eagerly[12] discussed the death of Mrs Josephs with the locals[13] but without really learning anything that she did not know already. She returned home rather tipsy[14] and fell asleep, and did not wake up until five o'clock to hear her door-bell ringing.

15. Les yeux brouillés
16. avec la gueule de bois

Feeling bleary-eyed[15] and hung-over[16], she went to answer it. Bill Wong stood there.

'Come in! Come in!' cried Agatha. 'Tell me all about it, but let me get a cup of strong coffee first. I had too much to drink in the pub.'

'How did you scare Lacey off[1]?' asked Bill, ambling into the kitchen after her[2].

'I didn't ... Oh, well, I did invite him for lunch yesterday, light the candles on the dining-table and flash the old cleavage[3]. You couldn't see him for dust[4].'

The doorbell rang. 'I'll get it,' said Bill.

He came back a few moments later followed by James.

'Don't raise your voice,' said Bill. 'Our Agatha's got a hangover. She's been drowning her sorrows[5] in the pub. She got all dolled up like a dog's dinner[6] expecting an old flame[7] from London for lunch yesterday and he didn't show[8] and she'd forgotten about you calling but you scuttled off[9] anyway.'

'Oh,' said James. 'It's a good thing I'm not a vain man[10] or I might have thought it was all for me.'

Bill smiled happily. 'Our Agatha's usually got bigger fish to fry[11], haven't you, Agatha? Why didn't your flame turn up, anyway?'

I can lie[12] as easily as you, thought Agatha. 'Threatened with a merger[13],' she said. 'But he's going to take me to the Savoy[14] for dinner to make up for[15] his absence.'

James felt silly. I really must stop imagining this woman's pursuing me, he thought.

'So,' said Agatha, putting down cups of coffee in front of them, 'tell us all, Bill. Why have I not to leave the country?'

'What *is* all this?' cried James, exasperated. 'It's about that librarian's death, isn't it? It's all the talk[16] at Harvey's.'

1. avez-vous fait fuir Lacey
2. en la suivant tranquillement dans la cuisine
3. fait entrevoir mon petit décolleté
4. Il est parti à toute allure
5. noyer son chagrin
6. Elle s'est pomponnée à outrance
7. un ex
8. n'est pas venu
9. vous vous êtes débiné
10. que je ne sois pas prétentieux
11. des problèmes plus importants à traiter
12. mentir
13. Menacé par une fusion
14. [hôtel cinq étoiles à Londres]
15. pour se faire pardonner
16. On ne parle que de ça

Agatha told him about the arranged call on[1] Mrs Josephs and of finding Mrs Josephs dead. 'You, now, Bill,' she said. 'Is it murder?'

'We're waiting for the pathologist's report,' said Bill. 'I'll tell you this off the record[2]. There's something funny.'

'Like what?' asked Agatha.

'Forensic[3] found scuff marks[4] on the stairs, all the way up from the parlour to the bathroom. Mrs Josephs was wearing brown leather walking shoes. The stairs aren't carpeted. There were scuff marks which could have come from her shoes, and she was wearing those thick stockings and there are a couple of stocking threads caught in a crack on the stairs.'

Agatha's eyes gleamed. 'You mean someone could have killed her in her parlour and then dragged her[5] upstairs and dumped her in her bathroom?'

'I don't understand that,' said James. 'If someone's going to kill her, why bother dragging the body up to[6] the bathroom?'

'I'm speculating[7],' said Bill. 'I'm going out on a limb[8] and neither of you must breathe a word of this[9] to anyone,'

They both nodded like mandarin dolls[10].

'Everyone seems to have known she was a diabetic and injected herself with insulin. What if someone gave her a jab of something lethal[11] and then dragged her up to the bathroom where she kept her syringes and left her there hoping we would think she had died as she was giving herself one of her usual injections?'

James shook his head, to Agatha's irritation. 'I still don't like it,' he said. 'Everyone knows about the wonders of forensic science these days.'

1. visite convenue chez
2. entre nous
3. La police scientifique
4. des éraflures
5. traînée
6. se coltiner le corps jusqu'en haut dans
7. Je ne fais qu'une hypothèse
8. Je prends des risques
9. ne doit en piper mot
10. des petites poupées chinoises
11. Et si quelqu'un lui avait injecté un produit mortel

'Any murderer is usually desperate[1] or deranged[2],' said Bill. 'It would amaze you how little they think.'

'Did the neighbours see anyone calling at the house?' asked James.

'No, but there's a lane runs along the end of the back gardens. Mrs Dunstable at the other end of the terrace said she thought she heard a car stopping just at the end of the back lane – you can't get a car along there – about eight in the morning. But she's deaf[3]! She says she felt the *vibrations* of a car, can you believe it?'

'It would be odd if it turned out to[4] be murder,' said James slowly. 'After what she said to Agatha in front of all those women, it might cast doubts on[5] the death of Paul Bladen.'

'She might have committed suicide,' Bill pointed out. 'Everyone said she was very depressed since the death of her cat. The scuff marks could have been made when she dragged herself upstairs. That's the news so far[6]. I've got to get back to work. Thanks for the coffee, Agatha.'

When Bill had left, Agatha returned and sat down at the coffee-table and closed her eyes. 'Want me to go?' asked James.

'No, I'm thinking. If I had murdered Mrs Josephs and injected her with something, I wouldn't leave that lethal something among her bottles and pills in the bathroom. I'm not a very clever murderer. Think of the scuff marks. So I'm driving off with this bottle or ampoule I've used in my pocket. I'm sweating and panicky[7].' She opened her eyes. 'I'd chuck it out[8] the car window.'

'It's a thought,' said James. 'And the road from the end of the back lane goes up to Lord Pendlebury's. No harm in just having a look[9], I suppose.

1. prêt à tout
2. déséquilibré
3. sourde
4. ça se révélait
5. remettre en question
6. pour l'instant
7. affolé
8. Je le balancerais par
9. On peut toujours jeter un coup d'œil

We'll take rubbish sacks[1] so that people will think we're volunteers from the village keeping the countryside tidy. But if you find anything sinister[2], leave it there and call the police or they might think you planted it[3].'

They took Agatha's car. She drove to the back lane and sat there with the engine idling[4] imagining she had just committed murder. She then drove off up the hill and suddenly stopped.

'Why here?' asked James.

'Because here's where I would chuck it[5] if I were a murderer,' said Agatha.

They started searching up and down the road on the right-hand side where anything a driver might have thrown out would have landed. Fortunately people in the Cotswolds are very litter-minded[6] and so there was hardly anything after an hour's careful search to be found but an old broken fountain-pen[7] and one sandal.

'The light's fading and I'm hungry,' complained James.

'Let's try further up, nearer the estate[8],' pleaded Agatha. 'Just a bit more.'

'Damn, I promised Freda Huntingdon a few days ago that I would meet her for a drink at seven in the Red Lion. Besides, it's getting dark.'

'I've a torch in the car,' said Agatha, now determined to keep him out as long as possible.

'Oh, well, just a little longer.'

They drove farther up the road and got out again, Agatha taking the torch and James poking aimlessly now in the hedgerow[9].

When Agatha after half an hour of patient walking and searching suddenly cried, 'Eureka!' James said crossly, 'Look, is it another shoe or something? Freda will be –'

1. des sacs-poubelle
2. d'inquiétant
3. l'avez déposé là
4. tournant au ralenti
5. le jetterais
6. contre les détritus
7. stylo-plume
8. domaine
9. fourgonnant maintenant un peu au hasard dans la haie

'Come here! Look at this!'

He stumped over[1]. Agatha pointed the torch at some tangled shrubbery and nettles[2] in the ditch[3]. Down in the bottom of the ditch was a little brown pharmacist's bottle.

'Well, I'll be damned,' he said, giving her a hug[4].

Glad of the darkness, Agatha blushed with pleasure.

'You wait here and guard it,' she said excitedly. 'I'm off[5] to phone Bill Wong.'

James waited and waited. He glanced at his watch, noticing by the luminous dial that it was nearly eight. Then he thought, I don't really need to stand here. He took a stick which he had cut earlier from the hedgerow to help him in poking around, stabbed it down[6] into the ditch beside the bottle and tied his handkerchief like a flag to the top of it. Now he could go safely off to the pub and the police and Agatha would easily find his marker. He strode off down the road.

Agatha waited on her doorstep, biting her nails[7]. Bill had said, 'Wait right where you are,' and so she had done just that[8]. But James must be wondering what had happened.

With a sigh of relief, she saw the police car nosing round[9] into the lane and ran out to meet it. Bill and another detective were in the car. 'Hop in[10],' he said, 'and take us to this clue[11] of yours. We couldn't raise[12] Fred Griggs. It's his night off[13].'

Agatha could not believe it as they drove up the road and found no sign of James. Worse than that, she could not remember exactly where they had found the bottle and so they searched up and down the roadside for quite a long time before Bill finally found the stick with the handkerchief on top.

1. Il la rejoignit à pas pesants
2. un enchevêtrement d'arbustes et d'orties
3. dans le fossé
4. en la serrant contre lui
5. Je pars
6. le planta
7. en se rongeant les ongles
8. c'est ce qu'elle avait fait
9. l'avant de la voiture de police tourner
10. Montez
11. indice
12. joindre
13. soir de congé

'At least he's marked the spot,' said Bill, squatting down[1]. He shone[2] a powerful flashlight down beside the stick.

1. en s'accroupissant
2. dirigea

'There doesn't seem to be anything there, Agatha.'

Agatha peered over[3] his shoulder. 'But it *was* there,' she cried. 'Oh, where *is* James? If he just calmly went off to the pub to meet that tart[4], I'll kill him.'

3. regarda par-dessus
4. retrouver cette pétasse

Bill and the other detective searched slowly and carefully, but there was no sign of that bottle.

He finally straightened up with a sigh. 'Do you think Lacey's in the pub?'

'Oh, I'm quite sure he is,' said Agatha viciously.

It was a busy evening at the Red Lion. The whole village seemed to be crammed[5] into the pub. James was surprised when he received a tap on the shoulder and a voice murmured, 'Police. Would you step outside, Mr Lacey?'

5. entassé

He followed the man out and started guiltily[6] as he was confronted with an unusually serious Bill Wong and a baleful[7] Agatha.

6. eut un sursaut coupable
7. menaçante

'I shouldn't have left, I suppose,' he said in a rush[8], 'but didn't you find the stick with the handkerchief on it?'

8. hâtivement

'We found that all right, but no bottle,' said Bill. 'When did you get to the pub?'

'Just after eight. I was meeting Freda … Mrs Huntingdon.'

'Did you tell Mrs Huntingdon or anyone else in the pub what you had found?'

'Well …' James shifted awkwardly from foot to foot[9].

9. se balançait, gêné, d'un pied sur l'autre

The policeman who had summoned him from[10] the pub had gone back in and now emerged again in time to hear Bill's last question.

10. l'avait interpellé dans

'If I might have a word with you, sir.' He drew Bill aside. James Lacey stared at the ground.

Bill came back and looked up at James. 'So, I gather you said to Mrs Huntingdon that you and Mrs Raisin had found a clue to Mrs Josephs's death, that there was a pharmacist's bottle in the ditch and you had left your handkerchief as a flag to mark the spot. Mrs Huntingdon had said in a loud voice to a circle of locals, "We've got a sleuth in our midst[1]. Isn't James clever?" And she told about the bottle.'

'Look,' said James desperately, 'I'm not a policeman. I've looked on it all as a sort of game. But I may have put the stick in the wrong place. Let's go back and look again.'

'Come along, then,' said Bill. 'I'd already thought of that and sent for reinforcements.'

Agatha said not a word to James but climbed into the back of Bill's car. 'If you please, sir,' said a policeman and ushered James to[2] another police car.

There seemed to be policemen all over the place when they returned, searching and searching the hedgerows.

Then there was a shout of triumph. One policeman crouching down[3] a few yards from where James had marked the spot waved them excitedly over[4]. And there, as he pulled some long grass aside, lay a small pharmacist's bottle.

It was tenderly lifted up with tweezers[5] and placed on a clean cloth[6] and shown to Agatha.

'I am sure that's a different shape[7],' said Agatha. 'And it hasn't got any label. I'm sure the one I saw had a bit of a label on it.'

'You may as well go home, Mrs Raisin,' said Bill. 'We'll call on you when we need you.'

1. un détective parmi nous

2. fit monter James dans

3. accroupi

4. les appela à grands gestes, tout excité

5. soulevée délicatement avec des pincettes

6. tissu

7. forme

1. piteusement

2. que je suis vraiment un imbécile

3. le souvenir précis

4. l'avait aidée à se dépêtrer de

5. À côté d'elle, il régla son pas sur le sien

6. sort en vitesse

7. s'avérera avoir contenu

8. d'inoffensif

9. aurait commencé par ne pas la jeter là

10. absorbé dans ses pensées

11. chez lord Pendlebury

12. lui flanque un coup sur la tête

13. surprend

'I'm awfully sorry ...' began James miserably[1].

'You too, Mr Lacey. We'll be in touch with you.'

James faced Agatha. 'You must think I'm all sorts of a fool[2].'

Agatha opened her mouth to say that, yes, she did think him a fool, but a sharp memory[3] of how he had helped to extricate her over[4] her own foolishness with the hand basin came into her mind and she said instead, 'Let's walk back to my place for some coffee and think about this.'

He fell into step beside her[5]. 'I can't help thinking,' said Agatha, 'that the murderer might have been in the pub and heard Freda. So he or she nips out[6], up the road, and takes that bottle, hides nearby and sees the police arrive, waits till they've gone to the pub to question you and then puts another bottle there which will prove to have contained[7] something innocuous[8].'

'But a clever murderer would not have thrown the bottle there in the first place[9],' protested James.

They walked on in silence, each buried in thought[10].

Once in Agatha's kitchen and drinking coffee, Agatha, who had been silent for a very long time for her, suddenly burst out, 'I've been thinking.'

'What?'

'Surely clever murderers belong in fiction. To take a life you must be insane, or temporarily insane. What if some woman knew Paul was going to be up at Lord Pendlebury's[11] on that day? Mad with rage, she biffs him on the head[12], and then jabs the syringe into him without even knowing the contents of the syringe are lethal. He's dead. She runs off. Now she has committed murder, she really is deranged and terribly frightened. She overhears[13] Mrs Josephs talking to me at the vicarage and feels she's got to be silenced[1] and she knows she is a diabetic. She injects her with God knows what, panics again, thinks if the body is found in the bathroom, natural death will be assumed[2]. Again, she's in the pub, and hears Freda. More panic. Take the bottle away. More panic. Replace it with another.'

They talked for another hour, writing out lists of the women who were at the vicarage and all the women in the pub that James could remember. Then the phone rang. Agatha went to answer it and then came back and sat down wearily[3] at the table.

'That was Bill. Mrs Josephs was murdered. Someone shot a good dose of Adrenalin into her bloodstream.'

'But where would anyone get Adrenalin?'

'At first I thought of Peter Rice because vets have it, but he was nowhere near the village. Bill said farmers usually have a supply[4], although their drugs cabinets are checked[5] from time to time[6] to make sure they are safely locked.'

'Miss Mabbs!' said James suddenly.

'What about her?'

'That's why I called on you in the first place[7]. I found her address. She's living in Leamington Spa.'

'But wait a bit. She wasn't at the vicarage, nor was she in the pub this evening, surely.'

'No, but she might have been lurking around somewhere[8]. In any case, surely she would know more about Paul Bladen than most. She worked with him.'

Agatha made up her mind.

'We'll go tomorrow.'

1. qu'il faut la faire taire
2. présumée
3. avec lassitude
4. en ont habituellement en réserve
5. on contrôle leurs armoires à pharmacie
6. périodiquement
7. pour ça que je venais vous voir au départ
8. a pu rôder dans le coin

Chapter Six

Agatha and James were not able to set out for Royal Leamington Spa until late the next day, for another drama had hit Carsely. The veterinary surgery had been broken into[1] and the drugs cabinet smashed open. It had been neatly and efficiently done. A pane of glass on the back door had been broken, allowing the thief to reach in and unlock the door.

'So that's probably where the Adrenalin came from,' said a harassed-looking Bill Wong[2], 'except that PC Griggs says he kept checking the premises[3] on his rounds[4] and there was no sign of a break-in[5] before last night.'

'He probably didn't even notice the broken pane of glass,' commented James.

'Fred Griggs is a conscientious village bobby[6],' said Bill.

'Then do you think someone meant the police to think the Adrenalin came from there?' asked Agatha.

'That could be the case. But how unnecessarily complicated! And this throws suspicion[7] on the death of Paul Bladen. No one we can think of wanted Mrs Josephs dead.'

Then statements were painstakingly taken from[8] Agatha and James about the finding of the bottle.

1. subi une effraction
2. un Bill Wong qui avait l'air épuisé
3. les lieux
4. lors de ses rondes
5. signe de cambriolage
6. flic
7. jette le doute
8. on enregistra minutieusement les déclarations d'

'They analysed the one we eventually[1] found and it contains traces of a tranquillizer[2]. We have checked with the local doctor and it would amaze you in this enlightened day and age[3] how many women are on tranquillizers,' said Bill. 'Now I have something to say to both of you. The police at times seem very slow and plodding[4], but it's a safer way of doing things than having amateurs running around stirring things up[5]. Please do not interfere again.'

'If we had not interfered, as you put it,' said Agatha hotly[6], 'you would have gone on thinking Paul Bladen's death was an accident.'

'And Mrs Josephs might still be alive. Leave it to us, Agatha.'

After the police had gone, James said reluctantly[7], 'It seems we're not exactly popular[8].'

'Yes, I suppose we'd better drop it[9].' Agatha looked reluctant. 'Perhaps I should think about some gardening.'

'Your lawn at the front could do with treatment[10],' said James. 'Come and I'll show you what I mean.'

Agatha was first out of her front door. She glanced down the lane and saw Freda Huntingdon standing on James's doorstep and retreated so quickly she bumped into him.

'I've changed my mind,' she said, slamming the door and leading the way back to the kitchen. 'Have another cup of coffee and I'll tell you about it.'

'Now,' she began when they were seated, 'the way I look at it is this.'

Her doorbell rang, sharp and peremptory.

'Aren't you going to answer that?' he asked.

1. finalement
2. calmant
3. en cette époque éclairée où nous vivons
4. procéder lentement et laborieusement
5. semant la pagaille
6. avec véhémence
7. à regret
8. en vogue
9. qu'on ferait mieux de laisser tomber
10. Un peu de soin ne ferait pas de mal à votre pelouse de devant

1. jeta un coup d'œil dans le judas
2. Un vendeur de doubles vitrages
3. insistants
4. retentit à nouveau, stridente
5. grimaça
6. Comment alors nous traiter d'importuns
7. L'une des dames qu'il a plaquées
8. rente
9. retraite de militaire
10. les critères
11. Où exactement
12. le peu de temps qu'a duré le cabinet véto
13. Les oreilles aux aguets d'Agatha
14. insonorisé
15. qu'elle n'entendait presque jamais rien

'I suppose so.' Agatha got reluctantly to her feet. She peered through the spyhole[1]. Freda was standing on the step. Agatha returned to the kitchen and sat down.

'Double-glazing salesman[2],' she said. 'They're so pushy[3]. Not worth answering the door.'

The bell shrilled again[4] and Agatha winced[5]. 'I'll go,' said James, rising.

'No, sit down, please. I think we should go to Leamington and question Miss Mabbs. How can that be called interfering[6]? Just a few questions. If we knew more about what Paul Bladen was like, then we might know what lies behind his death. After all, what makes someone kill?'

'Passion,' said James. 'One of his jilted ladies[7].'

'Or money,' said Agatha, thinking of her unfortunate experience in London.

But James, secure in the comfort of a private income[8] and an army pension[9], shook his head. 'He hadn't much to leave, not by today's standards[10].'

The doorbell rang again.

'No,' said Agatha sharply. 'Just wait and whoever it is will go away. Whereabouts[11] in Leamington does Miss Mabbs live?'

He took out a notebook and flipped the pages. 'Here we are. Miss Cheryl Mabbs, aged twenty-three, employed for only the short time the surgery lasted[12] in Carsely, lives at 43, Blackbird Street, Royal Leamington Spa.'

Agatha's straining ears[13] could not hear anything from outside, but then the cottage was so insulated,[14] she hardly ever did[15]. 'I'll just go upstairs and put some make-up on,' she said, 'and then we'll go. If that doorbell rings again, ignore it.'

Upstairs, she peered out of her bedroom window and saw with satisfaction the slim retreating figure[1] of Freda.

She put on a little make-up, not too much or he might be frightened off again, sprayed some Rive Gauche over herself, and went back downstairs. She fed the cats, and as the day was not particularly cold, let them out into the back garden.

'Why don't you get a cat door?' asked James.

'I've had a few scares before[2],' said Agatha, 'and when I think of a cat door, I think of a small burglar[3], writhing his way through it[4] like a snake.'

'That doesn't happen. Tell you what,' said James, feeling obscurely that he had to make amends[5] for deserting his post the night before, 'buy one and I'll fix it for you.'

Agatha beamed at him[6]. How domestic they were becoming[7]. A simple wedding in Carsely Church. Too old to wear white. Perhaps a silk suit and a pretty hat. Honeymoon somewhere exotic. 'Famous Detective Agatha Raisin Weds,' that's what the local headlines[8] would say.

James looked at her uneasily[9]. Her small eyes had an odd glazed look[10]. 'Are you feeling all right?' he asked. 'You look just the way I feel when I have indigestion.'

'I'm all right,' said Agatha, returning to earth with a bump[11]. 'Let's go.'

Leamington, or Royal Leamington Spa, to give it the full title which few people hardly ever use, was a relatively short drive[12] and they arrived there in under an hour.

The day had become grey and overcast[13], but unusually mild. Although in the centre of the country, Agatha thought Leamington had the air

1. silhouette

2. déjà eu quelques frayeurs

3. cambrioleur

4. s'y faufilant

5. qu'il lui fallait se racheter

6. lui fit un grand sourire

7. Quel vrai petit ménage ils devenaient

8. manchettes des journaux locaux

9. avec inquiétude

10. curieux aspect vitreux

11. de retour sur terre un peu brutalement

12. trajet relativement court en voiture

13. couvert

of a seaside town like Eastbourne or Brighton and kept expecting to turn a corner and see the sea.

James, to her irritation, said he wanted to view the public gardens before they started any detective work. Agatha stumped along angrily beside him while he enthused over[1] plants and blossom. She was obscurely aware[2] she was jealous of the scenery[3] and wished some of his raptures[4] could be directed at her. She glanced at him sideways. He was strolling easily along with his hands in his pockets, at peace with the world. She wondered what he thought about her. She wondered what he thought about anything. Why wasn't he married? Was he gay? And yet look at the way he had left that splendid clue to go running after a stupid bitch[5] like Freda Huntingdon.

He was staring up in dazed wonder at[6] the cascading blossoms of a cherry tree when Agatha suddenly snapped[7], 'Are we going to commune with nature all day, or are we going to get on with it[8]?' He gave her a glance, half-rueful[9], half-amused, and all at once Agatha had a picture of him escorting some woman who would share his enthusiasm for the scenery, who would know all these county names he had talked about at that old manor house, and felt bullying and coarse-grained[10].

'All right,' said James amiably, 'let's go.'

He took out a small street map and consulted it. 'We can walk,' he said. 'It's not far.'

They set off. 'Where does she work?' asked Agatha. 'Oh, and how did you find out about her?'

'I don't know where she works, but I got her address from Peter Rice in Mircester. She isn't a veterinary nurse, simply a sort of receptionist.'

Agatha began to wonder if they were ever going to get there, James's idea of 'not far' not being

1. s'extasiait devant
2. consciente
3. décor
4. ravissements
5. garce
6. contemplait, émerveillé,
7. dit d'un ton sec
8. est-ce qu'on avance
9. mi-chagrin
10. se sentit agressive et fruste

her own. But they finally arrived at a long street of shops with flats above them. The shops had probably always been shops. The buildings were Georgian and run down[1], with cracked stucco[2] and grimy fronts[3] dating from the days before the Clean Air Act[4], when soot fell on everything[5].

It was six o'clock. Most of the little shops were closed and the street was quiet. Agatha could remember the days when a street such as this would resound with the cries of children: children playing hopscotch[6], children playing ball, children playing cowboys and Indians. Now they were probably all indoors watching television, videos, or playing computer games. Sad.

Number 43 turned out to be[7] a staircase between two shops leading to flats above. At the top of the staircase was a battered[8] wooden door and beside it a row of bells with names on cards beside each bell. There was no Mabbs listed[9].

'Must have the wrong address,' said James.

'I didn't walk all this way for nothing,' said Agatha impatiently, for[10] her feet were sore[11]. She pressed the nearest bell.

After a few moments the door was opened by a thin, anaemic-looking girl with blonde hair gelled up into spikes[12]. 'Wotyerwant?[13]' she asked.

'Miss Cheryl Mabbs,' said Agatha.

'She's on bell 4,' said the girl, 'but you won't find her in[14]. She and Jerry has gone out.'

'Where?' asked James.

'How should I know, mate[15]? They usually has fish an' chips and goes to the disco.'

'Where is this disco?' James smiled at the girl, who smiled back.

1. délabrés
2. un crépi fissuré
3. des façades crasseuses
4. [loi promulguée en 1956 à la suite d'un terrible épisode de smog londonien]
5. du temps où la suie se déposait partout
6. à la marelle
7. s'avéra être
8. fatiguée
9. Le nom de Mabbs n'était pas inscrit
10. car
11. douloureux
12. coiffés en pointes avec du gel
13. [= What do you want ?]
14. chez elle
15. mon pote

'Not your style,' she said. 'It's down the road. Rave On Disco. Can't miss it[1]. Wait till later and you'll hear the noise.'

'Well, that's that[2],' said James as they emerged out into the street again.

'No, it's not.' Agatha looked up at him. 'We could have a bite to eat and then go to the disco ourselves.'

He shied slightly[3] and looked off into the middle distance. 'I really think I would rather go home, Agatha. As the young lady there pointed out, discos are not my style.'

Agatha glared at him[4]. 'Hardly mine either[5],' she said, feeling her feet throb[6].

He stood there, looking down at her in polite embarrassment and obviously waiting for her to give in[7].

'Dinner and think about it?' suggested Agatha.

'I suppose I am hungry. It's a bit early for dinner. We'll find a pub.'

Over drinks[8], followed later by a modest dinner in an Indian restaurant, Agatha reflected that the more time she spent with James, the less she seemed to find out about him. He seemed to have an endless fund[9] of impersonal topics[10] to talk about, from politics to gardening, but what he really felt or thought about anything, he did not say.

But he agreed to try the disco.

Back along Blackbird Street they went. They heard the thud, thud, thud[11] of the disco music as they approached.

The disco was called Rave On[12] and was a club, but they got inside easily after paying a modest entrance fee[13]. 'Enjoy yourself, Grandma,' said the bouncer[14] to Agatha, who glared at him and said,

1. Pouvez pas le rater
2. ben voilà
3. eut un léger mouvement de recul
4. le regarda furieuse
5. Pas vraiment le mien non plus
6. sentant ses pieds l'élancer
7. qu'elle renonce
8. Devant un verre
9. fonds inépuisable
10. de sujets
11. boum, boum, boum
12. Délirez
13. prix d'entrée
14. videur

'Get stuffed[1],' and then realized that James's face had taken on that shuttered look[2] again.

Inside it was full of bodies writhing under strobe lights[3]. Following closely behind James[4], Agatha shouldered her way[5] to a black plastic-padded bar in the corner.

James ordered a mineral water for Agatha because she was driving and a whisky and water for himself. 'How much is that?' he shouted at the barman, a white-faced youth[6] with a pinched, spotty face[7].

'On the house, officer,' said the barman.

'We are not police officers.'

'In that case, pay up, guv[8]. Four pound for every drink. Eight quid, squire[9].'

'Do you know Cheryl Mabbs?' asked James. 'We're friends of hers.'

He pointed. 'Over there in that booth[10], her wiff the orange-and-pink 'air.[11]'

Through the stabbing[12] strobe lights and shifting gyrating bodies[13], they could make out a gleam of orange and pink in a far corner.

'Drink up[14],' said James and tossed his back[15].

'I'll leave mine,' shouted Agatha above the din[16]. 'I never did like gnat's piss anyway[17].'

His eyes had that blank look[18] which Agatha had come to interpret as a sign of disapproval. But he said, 'We'd better dance our way over[19]. Less conspicuous[20].'

He joined the gyrating figures, cheerfully waving his arms in the air and dancing like a dervish[21]. Agatha tried to follow suit[22] but felt ridiculous. Teenagers were stopping their own dancing to cheer James on[23].

Inconspicuous, thought Agatha with a groan. The whole damn place is looking at us.

1. Va te faire voir
2. air impénétrable
3. un éclairage stroboscopique
4. Talonnant James
5. se fraya un chemin
6. jeune homme
7. boutonneux et les traits tirés
8. faut payer, m'sieur
9. Huit balles, monsieur
10. box
11. celle qu'a les ch'veux orange et rose
12. lancinantes
13. les corps mouvants et tournoyants
14. Finissez votre verre
15. avala le sien
16. vacarme
17. la pisse d'âne, de toute façon
18. air absent
19. On ferait mieux d'y aller en dansant
20. Moins voyant
21. derviche tourneur
22. d'en faire autant
23. encourager James

A few more whirls and turns[1] and James came to a stop at Cheryl's booth, wildly applauded by the customers.

It was a different Miss Mabbs from the quiet, pallid girl in the white coat Agatha had first seen at the vet's. Her hair was sprayed[2] pink and orange and arranged in what Agatha could only think of as tufts[3]. She wore a black leather jacket with studs[4] over a yellow T-shirt with some slogan on it that Agatha could not read in the gloom[5]. Beside her was a leather-jacketed young man with a face like a tipsy fox[6].

'Miss Mabbs!' cried Agatha. 'We've been looking for you.'

'Who the hell are you?' said the girl and picked up her drink, which was of as vile[7] a colour as her hair, nudged aside[8] the little paper umbrella on the top with her nose[9] and took a sip of it through a straw.

'I am Agatha Raisin,' said Agatha, thrusting out her hand.

'So what?' mumbled Cheryl.

'I met you at the vet's in Carsely. I came along with my pussy.'

'Took your pussy along[10], did you?' demanded Cheryl's escort with a cackle[11]. 'Any luck?[12]'

Cheryl sniggered[13].

'Look here,' said James in the authoritative tones of the upper class, 'can we go somewhere quiet where we can talk?'

'Sod off[14],' said Cheryl, but the young man put a hand on her arm. His foxy[15] eyes glinted up at[16] James. 'What's it worth to us?[17]'

'A tenner[18] and a drink,' said James.

'Okay,' he said. 'Come on, Cher.'

1. tours et pirouettes
2. laqué de
3. des houppes
4. cloutée
5. pénombre
6. renard éméché
7. horrible
8. écarta
9. du bout du nez
10. T'as amené ta chatte
11. gloussement
12. Ça a marché ?
13. ricana
14. Va te faire foutre
15. rusés
16. pétillèrent en regardant
17. Et qu'est-ce qu'on y gagne ?
18. billet de 10

They were soon all seated in a quiet dingy pub, perhaps one of the few left in Britain without a slot-machine[1] or juke-box or piped music[2]. A few old men sat around in corners. The bar smelt of must[3] and old beer and old men.

'What do you want to know?' asked Cheryl Mabbs.

'About Paul Bladen,' said Agatha eagerly[4]. 'It now seems he was murdered.'

Interest showed in her face for the first time. 'And I thought nothing exciting would ever happen in that dump of a village[5]. Me, I prefer the more cosmopolitan life, like[6],' she stated, as if Leamington Spa were Paris. 'Who done it?'

'That's what we want to find out,' said James. 'Any ideas?'

She scowled[7] horribly and took a hearty swig at[8] her glass of vodka and Red Bull. 'Could be anyone,' she said finally.

'There's Mrs Josephs as well,' said Agatha and told of that murder.

'I told him trouble would come when he destroyed[9] her old cat,' said Cheryl. 'He didn't like cats, and that's a fact[10]. Hated the beasts. But he sweet-talked those old dears in the village a treat[11]. Always taking one or the other of them out for dinner.'

'Why?' asked Agatha.

'Why else?' countered Cheryl. 'After their money, I suppose. I mean, what other reason could there be?'

'And why would he want their money?' demanded James, flashing a sympathetic look at Agatha, who was now outscowling[12] Cheryl. 'I mean, he left a fair bit[13].'

1. machine à sous
2. musique d'ambiance
3. la moisissure
4. vivement
5. bled pourri
6. genre, voyez
7. fronça les sourcils
8. bonne lampée de
9. a tué
10. y a pas de doute
11. cajolait un max toutes ces vieilles chéries du village
12. fronçait maintenant les sourcils encore plus fort que
13. un bon paquet

1. avait un faible pour
2. les ai surpris en pleine action

'It was an impression, that's all. He was keen on[1] that Freda Huntingdon. I caught them hard at it[2].'

'Where?' demanded Agatha with a triumphant look at James.

3. à mon avis
4. Bien sûr il a dû passer la pommade à
5. lui rendait la vie difficile avec cette histoire de chat
6. C'est tout

'Right on the examining table. Her skirt was up around her ears and his trousers were down round his ankles. Laugh! I nearly died. But the others? Holding hands and taking them out for dinner was about as far as he got, I reckon[3]. Course he had to soft-soap[4] Mrs Josephs, didn't he? I mean, she was making things hot for him over that cat[5]. Then there was that funny old creature, Webster. That's it[6].'

Agatha's scowl came back. She estimated that Josephine Webster, she who ran the dried-flower shop, was probably younger than herself.

'None of these ladies is really old,' she protested.

7. me paraissent avoir 102 ans
8. cruauté de la jeunesse
9. Est-ce qu'il batifolait également
10. l'annonce

Cheryl shrugged. 'All look like a hundred and two to me[7],' she said with all the callousness of youth[8].

'Did he get up to any of this philandering[9] in Mircester?' asked James.

'Didn't know him then,' replied Cheryl. 'Saw the ad[10] for a vet's receptionist and got the job.'

'So what are you doing now?'

11. Un chenil
12. Sont meilleurs que les gens, y a pas photo

'Kennels[11]. Out Warwick way.' Cheryl's face suddenly softened. 'I like animals. B'etter'n people any day[12].'

13. ce déplaisant duo
14. en baisait une

'So all we got out of that unlovely pair[13],' said James as they drove back to Carsely, 'was much as we supposed. He was charming the ladies of Carsely ...'

'And screwing one[14],' said Agatha with a grin.

'I must confess I was very surprised to hear that about Freda,' he said stiffly[1]. 'Do you think our Miss Mabbs could have been making it up[2]?'

'Not for a moment,' said Agatha gleefully[3].

'Oh, well, I suppose we should now concentrate on Miss Webster. Then there's Mrs Mason to see. Who was the other one you saw at the funeral?'

'Harriet Parr.'

'We'll see them all tomorrow,' said James. 'But better not let Bill Wong know what we're doing.'

'And yet,' said Agatha, 'I can't help feeling that the clue to the whole thing lies with[4] his ex-wife. She must know more about him than anyone. And who was the woman who answered the phone that night I called and said she was his wife? I'll bet that was our Mrs Skirt-up-to-Her-Eyeballs[5], Freda Huntingdon.'

'Can we please drop the subject of Freda?' he said. Agatha glanced sideways at him as they approached the orange lights of a roundabout[6]. His face looked grim[7].

Damn Freda, thought Agatha bitterly, pressed her foot harder on the accelerator and sent the car racing homewards through the night.

'Do you think there is a Mr Parr?' asked James as he and Agatha strolled through the village the next day to renew their investigation.

'I shouldn't think so[8]. There are an awful lot of widows about. Men don't live that long[9].'

'Probably only the married ones,' said James.

He put his hands in his pockets and began to whistle something complicated – probably Bach or some old bore like that[10], thought Agatha.

Mrs Harriet Parr lived in a modern bungalow on the outskirts[11] of the village. When they reached

1. l'air pincé
2. l'inventer
3. allègrement
4. se trouve chez
5. Madame Jupe-par-dessus-tête
6. rond-point
7. sévère
8. À mon avis, non
9. aussi vieux
10. un vieux raseur du même acabit
11. à la périphérie

the gate, Agatha said suddenly, 'This is a waste[1] of time.'

'Why?'

'I don't remember meeting a Mrs Parr at the vicarage, and if she wasn't there to overhear[2] what Mrs Josephs said to me, how can she have anything to do with it?'

'Perhaps Mrs Josephs was going about saying the same thing earlier.'

'Oh, well, let's get on with it[3].'

Mrs Parr answered the door herself. Agatha began by saying they hadn't met, but she and Mr Lacey would like to ask her a few questions, and soon they found themselves in a comfortable living-room. Agatha counted six cats. There was something claustrophobic about seeing so many cats in one room. She felt obscurely that at least some of them ought to be outside.

Mrs Parr was a small woman with curly black hair and an oddly old-fashioned sort of hourglass figure[4]. Agatha decided she was probably wearing a corset. She had hard red cheeks and a small pinched mouth which when she spoke revealed pointed teeth.

It was some time before[5] Agatha could get down to questioning her[6] because she and James had to be introduced to each cat in turn. Then Mrs Parr fussed over[7] James, asking him if he were comfortable, plumping cushions at his back[8], before rushing off to fetch tea and 'some of my special scones'.

'No Mr Parr,' whispered Agatha.

'Might be out at work,' said James.

Mrs Parr came back with a loaded tray[9]. After tea had been poured[10] and the lightness[11] of

1. perte
2. surprendre
3. allons-y
4. taille de guêpe curieusement démodée
5. Un certain temps s'écoula avant qu'
6. puisse commencer à la questionner
7. fut aux petits soins avec
8. arrangeant des coussins dans son dos
9. plateau bien rempli
10. versé
11. légèreté de la pâte

scones admired, Agatha said, 'Actually[1], we're really interested in finding out about Paul Bladen.'

Mrs Parr's cup rattled against[2] the saucer. 'Poor Paul,' she said. She put cup and saucer down and dabbed at her[3] eyes with a crumpled tissue[4]. 'So young and so brave.'

'Brave?'

'He was going to found[5] a veterinary hospital. He had such dreams. He said he could only talk to me. I was the only one with enough imagination to share[6] his vision.'

Then they heard the front door open. 'My husband,' whispered Mrs Parr. 'Don't …'

The door of the living-room opened and a tall thin middle-aged man with a grey face and a prominent Adam's apple bobbing over a rigid shirt collar[7] came in.

'People from the village, dear,' said Mrs Parr. 'Mrs Raisin and Mr Lacey. They both live in Lilac Lane. They've just been admiring my scones.'

'What brought you here?' asked Mr Parr bluntly[8].

'We've just started asking a few questions about Paul Bladen – you know, the vet that was found dead.'

'Get out of here,' hissed[9] Mr Parr. He held the door wide open. 'Out!'

'We were only –' said Agatha, but that was as far as she got.

'Get out!' he shouted at the top of his voice[10] this time, his thin tired face working with rage[11]. 'Never come here again. Leave us alone.'

'I am very sorry we upset you so much,' said James politely as he and Agatha edged past the infuriated husband[12].

'Fuck off, you upper-class twat[13],' yelled Mr Parr and spat full in James's face[14].

1. En fait
2. cliqueta contre
3. se tamponna les
4. mouchoir en papier chiffonné
5. fonder
6. partager
7. allant et venand sur un col de chemise rigide
8. sans ménagement
9. siffla
10. à pleins poumons
11. grimaçant de fureur
12. se faufilaient à côté du mari furieux
13. Fous le camp, connard de la haute
14. il cracha au visage de James

There was a horrified silence, punctuated[1] only by the sound of Mrs Parr's weeping[2]. James slowly cleaned his face with a handkerchief. Mr Parr was now trembling and looking appalled at[3] the enormity of his own behaviour.

James put his large hands on Mr Parr's shoulders and shook him backwards and forwards.

He punctuated each shake[4] by saying, 'Don't … ever … do … that … to … me … again.'

Then he abruptly released him[5] and strode out, with Agatha at his heels.

'We're really stirring up mud, Agatha,' he sighed. He looked back at the neat bungalow. 'You know, sometimes when I was coming home on leave[6], I would look out at little houses like that from the train and imagine secure and cosy lives. What awful emotional dramas lurk[7] behind the façades of all the houses called comfortable names like Mon Repos and Shangri-La, what breeding grounds[8] for murder.'

'Oh, it's quite a lively place, the country[9],' said Agatha cheerfully. 'I feel we're getting somewhere[10]. Mrs Parr must have been having a fling with[11] Bladen. Let's try Josephine Webster.'

'Perhaps before we get to her, we should call on Freda Huntingdon.'

'What? That floozy[12]? How can you bear to look at that slut[13] without blushing?' demanded Agatha.

He stopped and looked down at her, leaning back, hands in his pockets and rocking slightly on his heels. A faint gleam of malice[14] shone in his eyes. 'On the contrary, Agatha, I find the idea of a Freda Huntingdon with her skirt around her ears quite delectable.'

Agatha walked on. Well, they would call on Freda because Agatha was suddenly sure, had a

1. ponctué
2. les larmes
3. consterné par
4. secousse
5. le lâcha
6. en permission
7. se cachent
8. viviers
9. très animé, à la campagne
10. qu'on avance
11. a dû avoir une aventure avec
12. pouffiasse
13. salope
14. méchanceté

sudden gut feeling[1] that Freda was the murderer. She, Agatha Raisin, would prove it. Freda would be dragged off by the police. She would be sentenced to life imprisonment. She would be locked away from society and James would never set eyes on her again.

'Why are you racing along?' demanded James plaintively from somewhere behind her. 'I thought you weren't all that keen on seeing the woman[2].'

'I've decided that after all I do want to visit dear Freda,' snapped Agatha.

Droon's Cottage, which Freda had bought, was at the back of the village on a rise[3]. It was a Georgian cottage with a splendid wisteria[4] hanging over the Regency doorway, its purple blooms just beginning to show.

'The bell doesn't work,' said James and Agatha scowled horribly at this sign of his knowledge of the workings[5] of Freda's house.

The door was opened by Doris Simpson, who cleaned for[6] Agatha.

'What are you doing here?' demanded Agatha, who felt that this excellent cleaning woman was her sole property[7], although Doris only came one day a week now.

'I does[8] for Mrs Huntingdon, Agatha,' said Doris, and Agatha thought that Doris should at least have addressed her as 'Mrs Raisin' in front of James.

'Is she in?' asked James.

'No, James, her's up at[9] Lord Pendlebury's. Got a horse and he's keeping it in his stables for her. Oh, and Bert thanks you for the loan[10] of the books.'

'We'll go up to Pendlebury's and have a word with her there,' said James.

1. soudain l'intuition

2. que vous ne teniez pas tellement à la voir

3. hauteur

4. glycine

5. fonctionnement

6. faisait le ménage chez

7. propriété exclusive

8. [= work]

9. elle est partie chez

10. prêt

'I didn't know you knew Bert and Doris Simpson,' said Agatha.

'I sometimes have a drink with them in the Red Lion. Should we walk to Pendlebury's? It's a fine day.'

'Oh, all right,' said Agatha ungraciously[1], thinking, trust Freda to ingratiate herself with[2] the aristocracy.

She was cursing[3] her middle-aged feet by the time they reached Eastwold Park. She was wearing a low-heeled pair of black suede shoes which up until that day[4] had appeared a miracle of comfort. But shoes which had only been worn around the house and for a short walk from the car to the shops had developed hard ridges and bumps[5] on the inside, of which she had previously been unaware[6].

As they approached the door of the mansion[7], Agatha felt her working-class soul cringing[8].

This was intensified by a smell of baked beans[9] coming from the kitchen, which vividly brought back memories of the shabby[10] streets of Birmingham: squalling babies[11], large belligerent[12] women, and a small Agatha who nursed a dream[13] of one day having a home in the Cotswolds. The food of the poor, remembered Agatha, had always seemed to be tinned baked beans or fish and chips.

Mrs Arthur opened the door. 'He's got company,' she said. 'He's over at the stables.'

'We'll find him there,' said James.

Agatha limped[14] after him towards the stables.

Freda and Lord Pendlebury were standing outside, talking. Freda was wearing a tweed hacking jacket[15], jodhpurs and new riding-boots. She

1. de mauvaise grâce
2. faites confiance à Freda pour s'attirer les faveurs de
3. maudissait
4. jusqu'ici
5. avaient vu se développer des plis et des bosses
6. qu'elles n'avait pas encore remarqués
7. belle maison
8. se hérisser son poil de prolétaire
9. haricots-tomate
10. misérables
11. les pleurs des bébés
12. agressives
13. nourrissait le rêve
14. boitilla
15. veste d'équitation en tweed

looked as if she had stepped out of a glossy advertisement[1] in *Country Life*.

'James!' she cried when she saw him and she ran forward and kissed him on the cheek. Agatha wished she had not come. Lord Pendlebury sloped over[2]. 'What's this, young man? I was just enjoying the company of this pretty lady before you came along,' and he gave Freda a doting look[3]. Then he saw Agatha. 'Good God!' he exclaimed. 'It's that woman back again.'

Freda giggled[4] and hung on James's arm, smiling up at him.

'We've been asking questions about Paul Bladen's death,' said Agatha, harshly and loudly. 'We gather you were having it off with him[5].'

'Really!' Freda looked at Agatha with distaste and then her eyes appealed silently to the two gentlemen for help.

'Go away, you horrible woman. Shoo[6]!' said Lord Pendlebury.

'Too blunt[7], Agatha,' murmured James. 'Why don't you go home and leave this to me? I'll call in on you later.'

Face red, Agatha wheeled round[8] and stalked off[9]. She could feel them all looking at her. Why had she been so blunt? Damn Freda!

James would probably drop the investigation and all because of that floozy.

Her feet hurt and her heart hurt and she was glad to get home to the undemanding affections[10] of her cats.

She felt she should forget about James and go and ask Josephine Webster a few questions. The phone rang.

To her outrage[11] and amazement, she recognized Jack Pomfret's voice. 'Look, Agatha,' he

1. publicité sur papier glacé

2. vint nonchalamment vers eux

3. lança à Freda un regard énamouré

4. riait bêtement

5. Apparemment vous couchiez avec lui

6. Ouste

7. Trop direct

8. pivota

9. partit d'un pas raide

10. retrouver l'affection peu exigeante

11. indignation

wheedled[1]. 'Okay, I went about things the wrong way[2]. Yes, you guessed it. I went bust[3] in Spain. But I've got a nice little earner lined up[4] and ...'

Agatha dropped the phone. She found she was trembling with outrage. How *dare* he[5]! She felt almost frightened that he should persist in trying to get money out of her. Think of something else. Think of Josephine Webster. And then there was Mrs Mason. She had been at the funeral.

But somehow[6] she was too upset to think clearly. She thought about pouring herself a drink and then decided against it. She was not going to end up one of those people who poured themselves a drink the minute anything upset them[7]. So she switched on the television and stared blindly[8] at an American soap[9], gradually feeling herself relax.

An hour later, when her doorbell went[10], she jumped nervously, almost frightened that Jack Pomfret had pursued her to the country. But it was James who stood on the doorstep. 'Sorry about that,' he said. 'But you were too blunt. Freda knows you don't like her and so she is not going to take kindly to being questioned by you[11].'

'So did you get anything at all out of her?' asked Agatha.

'When I got rid of the doting Pendlebury, I had a talk with her. She says she had a bit of a fling[12] with Bladen, but that was all. She pointed out, rightly, that she's free and single[13] and can do what she likes. She was quite open about the whole business.'

'But why in the surgery?' demanded Agatha. 'They've both got the privacy of homes and beds. Doesn't that suggest passion rather than a casual affair[14] to you?'

'Well,' he said awkwardly[15], 'Freda's quite a girl.'

1. dit-il d'une voix cajoleuse
2. je ne m'y suis pas pris comme il faut
3. ai fait faillite
4. une jolie petite affaire en vue
5. Comment osait-il
6. bizarrement
7. dès que quelque chose les contrariait
8. sans le voir
9. feuilleton
10. sonna
11. n'acceptera pas facilement que ce soit vous qui l'interrogiez
12. une aventure
13. célibataire
14. simple passade
15. d'un air gêné

'Middle-aged woman, rather.'

'Let's not quarrel about Freda. I don't think there's anything there to worry about. Let's try Josephine Webster.'

Glad of an excuse to be with him again and get away from the phone, Agatha set off with him to Josephine Webster's shop. It was not a proper shop[1]. It was a terraced house[2] on the main street and she used what would normally have been the living-room to display her wares[3]. The shop was dark and heavy with[4] the ginger[5] and cinnamon smells[6] of herbal soaps and perfumes. Bunches of dried flowers hung from the beamed ceiling[7]. Straw hats ornamented with dried flowers hung on the walls.

Neat[8] Miss Webster was sitting at a desk in the corner of this room, doing accounts[9].

Determined to be more tactful, Agatha bought a cake of sandalwood soap[10], talked about the Carsely Ladies' Society, the weather, and then finally got around to the[11] subject of Paul Bladen.

'A most unfortunate death,' said Miss Webster, peering at Agatha over a pair of gold-rimmed spectacles[12]. 'Such a sad accident.'

James stepped in[13]. 'But now, in view of[14] Mrs Josephs' murder, the police are beginning to think that someone might have murdered Paul Bladen.'

'That's ridiculous. I can't believe that.'

'There's a mobile police unit being set up outside the village,' said James, 'and I don't think it's all because of Mrs Josephs.'

Her face had a pinched, closed look. 'I am very busy. If you do not wish to buy anything else, please leave.'

'But you must have been very close[15] to Paul Bladen,' pursued Agatha. 'I saw you at his funeral.'

1. une vraie boutique
2. maison mitoyenne
3. pour exposer ses articles
4. sentait fortement
5. gingembre
6. la cannelle
7. plafond à poutres apparentes
8. La très soignée
9. ses comptes
10. pain de savon au bois de santal
11. en vint au
12. en regardant Agatha par-dessus ses lunettes cerclées d'or
13. intervint
14. étant donné
15. proche

'I was there to pay my respects, although I did not like him,' she said. 'Us[1] village people went to pay our respects. Outsiders like you no doubt went along out of[2] vulgar curiosity, and if you take my advice, leave investigations to the police.'

'So that's us, with a flea in both ears[3],' commented James outside. 'All we seem to be getting are insults. What about Mrs Mason?'

'At least we'll get a welcome there,' said Agatha. 'She lives on the council estate[4].'

'How are your feet?'

'Fine now. I changed my shoes.'

Mrs Mason indeed gave them a warm welcome. More tea and scones. Gossip about the village. But Agatha began to shift[5] nervously. A big murder investigation was taking place in the village. Surely it was odd that Mrs Mason should not mention that.

'Lot of police around,' ventured[6] Agatha.

'Yes, poor Mrs Josephs. I find it hard to believe. I think she took her own life. She was so upset[7] about her cat.'

'That was a wicked thing of Bladen to do[8],' put in James. 'Of course, the police now think he was murdered.'

There was a long silence while Mrs Mason stared at him, her matronly figure rigid[9]. 'That's ridiculous,' she said at last. 'No one would kill Mr Bladen.'

'Why?'

'He wasn't the kind of person who gets murdered. He was a man of purpose and vision[10]. A kind man.'

'Not very kind to kill Mrs Josephs' cat.'

'That was a *mercy* killing[11]. He told me the old cat was in *agony*[12].'

1. Nous autres
2. par pure
3. Et voilà, c'est la deuxième qui nous envoie balader
4. dans un logement social
5. à s'agiter
6. risqua
7. si triste
8. cruel de la part de Bladen
9. raidissant sa taille plutôt enrobée
10. résolu et plein de discernement
11. une euthanasie, pour mettre fin à ses souffrances
12. souffrait le martyre

Agatha leaned forward[1]. 'Just think for a moment, Mrs Mason, just suppose someone had murdered Paul Bladen. Can't you think of any reason why?'

'No, I really can't. I wouldn't get involved in[2] all this, Mrs Raisin. I really wouldn't. It's not decent. Perhaps it's the way people go on in the city, but …'

'But don't you even want to know who killed Mrs Josephs?'

'Yes, but that's a job for the police.'

They couldn't get anything else out of her and retreated to Agatha's cottage.

'I would like to have a go at that ex-wife, Mrs Bladen, one more time[3].' said Agatha. 'But no doubt she would just slam the door in our faces[4].'

'You know,' said James, 'we could go back and see Bunty Vere-Dedsworth at the manor house. She might help us in getting Greta Bladen to talk.'

'Then let's go,' said Agatha eagerly, frightened that if they waited in Carsely any longer, Freda would arrive on the doorstep.

1. se pencha en avant

2. Je ne me mêlerais pas de

3. faire une nouvelle tentative auprès de son ex, Mrs Bladen

4. nous claquerait la porte au nez

Chapter Seven

They were just about to leave when the phone rang. Agatha started[1] and looked at it as if it were a hissing snake. Was it Freda? Or was it Bill Wong asking them to mind their own business and leave the investigation to the police? He had always had a nasty way of knowing[2] what she was up to[3].

She picked up the receiver and gave a tentative[4] 'Hello.'

'Look here, Agatha,' said Jack Pomfret's voice sternly[5]. 'This is ridiculous. I –'

'Go away and leave me alone!' she screamed and banged down the receiver.

Then she stood and wiped her moist[6] palms on her skirt. 'He's mad,' she muttered. 'I could kill him.'

'Who? Are you all right, Agatha?'

She shook her head as if to clear it and gave a sigh. 'Someone I used to know. He's trying to con money out of me[7]. He starts a new business. I pay. He knows I found out he was trying to cheat me[8]. But he's insane. He keeps phoning. I feel humiliated. I feel threatened.'

The phone rang again and Agatha jumped.

'Allow me,' he said. He picked up the receiver and listened. Then he said in glacial tones, 'This is Agatha's husband speaking. I handle[9] all her financial affairs. One more call from you and I will

1. sursauta
2. façon désagréable de savoir
3. fricotait
4. hésitant
5. avec sévérité
6. moites
7. de me soutirer de l'argent
8. me rouler
9. m'occupe de

suggest to the police that they take a close look at[1] your business transactions.'

James looked at the receiver before putting it down and smiled.

'What did he say?' demanded Agatha.

'He gave a frightened squawk[2] and rang off[3]. You won't be hearing from him again.'

'Why are you so sure of that?'

'Because, my dear Agatha, it's an old-fashioned world, however tough and independent women have become. He now thinks he has an irate[4] husband to deal with. Come along. You look too rattled[5] to drive.'

As she climbed into his car, Agatha felt a warm glow[6] permeating her body[7]. He had said he was her husband! Oh, somehow she must tell Freda Huntingdon that!

The day was blustery[8], with great cloud shadows racing across the fields, where new corn rippled in the fleeting sunlight[9]. Agatha's heart sang. And then her voice sang, 'Oh, what a beautiful morning.'

'It's afternoon,' said James. He switched on the radio, a pointed rebuke[10], and Agatha sank back into silence.

The manor house looked as it had done before, calm and benign[11], part of the landscape rather than some building thrust upon it.

'So you're back,' said Bunty, looking pleased. 'I was just going to have some coffee.'

'We need your help,' said James when they were all seated in the comfortable kitchen.

He succinctly outlined[12] all that had happened and explained they were sure that Greta Bladen could help them.

1. regardent de près
2. a laissé échapper un couic d'effroi
3. a raccroché
4. fâché
5. secouée
6. onde de chaleur
7. se répandre en elle
8. Ce jour-là le vent soufflait en bourrasques
9. le blé encore vert ondulait dans la lumière intermittente du soleil
10. reproche sans équivoque
11. affable
12. donna un aperçu rapide

Bunty listened carefully, her eyes bright with interest.

'As I told you before, I know Greta,' she said. 'We all know each other in this little village. I'll phone her and ask her to come up.'

She went off and came back shortly to say that Greta was on her way. 'You had better let me do the talking,' said Bunty. 'She can be prickly[1].'

And prickly was what Greta looked as she entered the kitchen and stopped short[2] at the sight of Agatha and James.

'Now you can't run away from people asking questions about Paul's death,' said Bunty firmly. 'You didn't like the man, but surely you don't want a murderer to be left to roam the Cotswolds in peace[3]. Sit down, Greta, and have coffee. You see, we all feel that if we knew a bit more about Paul Bladen, then we might be able to guess which of the suspects might have done it.'

'Including me,' said Greta bitterly, but she sat down and shrugged off[4] her short coat.

'Well, it's a dreary[5] story,' she said. 'As you probably realize, I was ten years older than Paul when I met him. He was working as a vet in Leamington Spa where I lived. I had a dog then I was devoted to[6], the way only the unloved can become devoted to animals.'

Agatha, who had been thinking of her cats, stared down into her coffee cup.

'I took my dog to the vet for some shots. Paul was charming. I could not believe my luck when he asked me out[7]. My parents had died and left me a house and a comfortable amount of money. It was what the romances call a whirlwind courtship[8]. Shortly after we were married, I found my dog dead one morning. The animal had been fit

1. irascible
2. stoppa net
3. laisser un meurtrier se promener en liberté dans les Cotswolds
4. se débarrassa de
5. triste
6. que j'aimais beaucoup
7. m'a invitée à dîner
8. une cour éclair

and healthy[1] the day before. Paul was all sympathy and did an autopsy. He said the dog had died of heart failure[2]. Only in later years did I suspect he had poisoned it. Strange in a vet, but he had a hatred of dogs and cats[3]. He told me about his dream of a veterinary hospital. He said he would name it after me. I gave him a considerable amount of money to get started.

'During the following year, he regaled me with stories of the plot of land[4] he had bought and how the builders had started work. I was excited and asked to see it, but he said he wanted it to be a surprise. I said, "At least tell me where it is," and he said Chimley Road on the outskirts of Mircester. He started to come home very late. He said he was always going over to the building site[5] when he finished work. Then he said we were moving to Mircester to be near the new hospital. He did not ask me for money. He said he had a house all ready but I was to promise not to go near Chimley Road until he was ready to surprise me.'

Greta sighed. 'I was so much in love with him. That was until I met his partner, Peter Rice, at a party. I had known Peter before, by the way[6]. We were old friends. So I thought it all right to ask him if they would still run the surgery[7] when the new veterinary hospital was opened.

'He asked me, "What veterinary hospital?" I told him. He gave me a pitying[8] look and said why didn't I go out to Chimley Road and have a look. Alarmed, I set off the next day. It was a long row of terraced houses. No building site.

'I taxed Paul with it[9]. He began to say that things hadn't worked out there[10], so the building site was in Leamington, and when I didn't believe him, he finally came out with the truth. He was

1. en très bonne forme
2. un arrêt cardiaque
3. les chiens et les chats en horreur
4. ne cessa de me parler du terrain
5. chantier de construction
6. soit dit en passant
7. cabinet de consultation
8. compatissant
9. Je pris Paul à partie à ce sujet
10. là-bas ça n'avait pas marché

1. joueur invétéré
2. est devenu mauvais
3. vieille bique
4. rompre

a gambler, a dedicated gambler[1]. Not only had he spent all the money I had given him in gambling but he needed more to pay his debts. I refused. He grew ugly[2]. He told me he had only married an old bat[3] like me for my money. Yes, I could have killed him then. But I wanted free of him[4] and so I made him agree to a separation and subsequent divorce. If he did not agree, I said, I would tell Peter Rice all about him.'

5. leur extorquait de l'argent

'So,' said James, 'one of his ladies could have murdered him because he conned money out of them[5].'

'Surely that's hardly a reason for murder,' protested Bunty.

'Oh, yes, it is,' said Agatha, thinking of Jack Pomfret.

'So now you've got what you want from me,' said Greta in a tired voice, 'may I go?'

'Of course, my dear,' said Bunty 'But you must realize how essential it is to find out who did this terrible thing.'

6. sans souffrir

Greta stood up. 'Why? Why is it so important? He died painlessly[6]. He was cruel and useless.'

'But there is the murder of Mrs Josephs,' said Agatha quietly. 'You must have read about that.'

'Yes, but what's that got to do with Paul?'

'She said she was going to tell me all about him,' said Agatha, 'and the next day she was dead.'

7. en signe de perplexité
8. n'a rien à voir avec

Greta shook her head in bewilderment[7]. 'I cannot bring myself to believe that Paul's death was anything other than an accident. I don't know this Josephs woman – I mean I didn't know her. Possibly her death is unrelated[8].' Her voice shook. 'I've done what I can for you. Please don't trouble me again.'

There was a long silence after she had left. Then, 'Poor woman,' said Bunty.

'Perhaps.' Agatha laced her fingers tightly round the coffee mug[1]. 'On the other hand, she surely had the most reason to kill Paul. She would know about Immobilon. Perhaps she would have access to Adrenalin, if he had left any of his drugs behind when he left her.'

'You're forgetting about the break-in[2] at the surgery,' James pointed out.

'The police seem to think that might have been done *after* Mrs Josephs's death.'

'So many women. So many suspects,' mourned[3] James. 'But we have taken up enough of your time, Bunty.'

They thanked her and left.

'We've got one thing,' said Agatha, as they drove off. 'Money, not passion, seems to be at the bottom of things. Look, Jack Pomfret didn't get any money out of me, right? But the very[4] fact that he tried to trick me[5], the fact that he has the gall[6] to phone me up makes me want to murder him, gives me a mad hatred[7] and fear of him. Can you understand that?'

'Yes, I think so. If any of these women, I mean any of our suspects, apart from Greta, paid up[8], there would be a motive. We could go to Mircester and ask Peter Rice what happened to Paul Bladen's deposit book[9].'

Agatha agreed, delighted at an opportunity of more time in his company.

The evening surgery at the vet's in Mircester was just closing. Peter Rice greeted them this time amiably enough but scoffed[10] when they asked if he had any of Paul Bladen's bank-books[11].

1. enserra étroitement de ses doigts la tasse de café
2. cambriolage
3. déplora
4. simple
5. me rouler
6. culot
7. haine
8. est passée à la caisse
9. livret de dépôt
10. se gaussa
11. livrets d'épargne

'I cleared[1] all his papers out and made a bonfire of them[2],' he said. 'I've put the house up for sale. I could hardly sell it with all his junk[3] around. I asked Greta if she wanted anything but she didn't, so I gave his clothes to charity and the contents of the house are being sold with it.'

'Which was his bank?' asked James.

'The Cotswold and Gloucester. But bank managers don't reveal anything about their customers' accounts[4], even when they're dead, as far as I know[5].'

'You didn't happen to notice if Paul had received any large sums from women recently?' asked Agatha.

He gave a jolly laugh. 'He was hardly young enough to be a toy boy[6]. The lawyers will only pass over to me what is left after their bill[7] and the funeral costs have been settled[8]. I'm afraid his banking affairs have gone to the grave with him[9]. But why do you ask? Hadn't been ripping you off, had he?[10]'

'Just curious,' said Agatha. 'I mean it is odd, now that it's turned out someone murdered Mrs Josephs[11]. I mean, it definitely makes Paul Bladen's death look like murder.'

'Not to me,' said Peter. 'Pendlebury asked me to do that operation and I said I would never touch Immobilon again.'

'Let's get something to eat,' suggested James when they had left the surgery.

They chose a nearby pub – but not the one where Agatha had ruined[12] the hand basin – and began to discuss the suspects, or rather, Agatha discussed the suspects while a preoccupied James frowned into his beer[13].

1. J'ai viré
2. avec j'ai fait un grand feu
3. bazar
4. les comptes de leurs clients
5. à ma connaissance
6. gigolo
7. que leurs honoraires
8. auront été réglés
9. n'aient été enterrées avec lui
10. Il ne vous escroquait pas, si ?
11. qu'il s'avère que Mrs Joseph a été tuée
12. démoli
13. fixait sa bière en fronçant les sourcils

'I don't believe you've been listening to a word I've been saying,' said Agatha crossly.

'I've been half-listening. The fact is I've been thinking about committing a crime.'

'You?'

'Yes. I've been thinking about breaking[1] into the Cotswold and Gloucester Bank.'

'But that's impossible. There'll be sophisticated burglar alarms[2] and laser beams[3] and pressure pads[4] and God knows what else.'

'Perhaps not. Let's finish our food and drink and go and take a look at it.'

The bank was a converted shop in a side street where old Tudor buildings with overhanging eaves[5] crowded out[6] the night sky above.

'Burglar alarm of course,' said James. 'We'll take a look round the back if we can get there.'

They found a lane which ran along the back of a row of shops and the bank. There were a series of lock-ups[7], garages, and tall wooden fences, all having a closed, impregnable[8] air.

James counted along. This is the back of the bank,' he said, 'what used to be the garden. Surely they wouldn't wire up[9] this wooden door in the wall.'

He took a small wallet[10] of credit cards out of his pocket. Agatha bit back[11] the impatient remark she was about to make – that apart from in the movies, she had never seen anyone open a lock with a credit card. He selected one.

Agatha turned away and looked along the lane, which was lit with sodium lamps, making everything look unreal, and, she thought more practically[12], probably making her lips look purple.

1. entrer par effraction
2. systèmes d'alarme
3. des rayons laser
4. tapis de contact avec alarme
5. des avant-toits en saillie
6. cachaient
7. remises
8. inaccessible
9. ne raccorderaient pas
10. portefeuille
11. ravala
12. pensa-t-elle avec plus de réalisme

There was a click and she swung round. The door in the wall was standing open. 'Amazing,' said Agatha.

'Let's get inside before someone sees us,' whispered James.

Agatha followed him in. He closed the door behind them and took out a pencil torch[1]. 'You've done this before,' accused Agatha.

He didn't reply but led the way up[2] a narrow path between two strips of lawn. 'Look,' he murmured, 'there's a kitchen at the back.'

'What does a bank want a kitchen for?'

'Make tea for the staff[3]. Left over from[4] when it used to be a shop. Now, let me see …'

The thin beam[5] of the torch flicked up and down[6] the building. 'I don't see any sign of an alarm here,' he said. 'I'm going to have a go[7]. Be prepared to make a run for it[8].'

'But we might not hear any alarm,' said Agatha in an agony of nerves[9]. 'It might just ring inside the police station[10].'

'Where's your sense of adventure?' he mocked.

He took out the card again. Agatha prayed that he would not be able to get the door open. She imagined police cars swooping up the lane[11], police with loud-hailers[12]; the reproachful eyes of Bill Wong. But all she heard was James's voice saying softly, 'It's open. Come on.'

Now Agatha's heart was hammering so hard[13], she felt sure it could be heard for miles. The kitchen door closed behind them, the torch beam flickered rapidly to right and left. James opened a door leading out of the kitchen and led the way through.

They found themselves in a square room full of desks and computers. 'The office,' said James,

1. lampe stylo
2. ouvrit la voie en suivant
3. le personnel
4. Un reste de
5. faisceau
6. balayait de haut en bas
7. faire une tentative
8. Soyez prête à déguerpir
9. les nerfs à vif
10. commissariat
11. débarquant en trombe
12. des haut-parleurs
13. cognait si fort

'which is all we need. Just as well. Look at that door over there. That's the one into the bank proper[1], where the money is.'

Agatha shivered[2]. There was an alarm box over the door and a steady red light glared down on them like an infuriated eye[3].

'Now,' he said, 'make yourself comfortable. This might take some time. There are no windows in this room except for that one through to the main bank, which is just as well, for the light from the computer screen could have been spotted[4] from outside.'

Agatha sat down in a dark corner and waited, too frightened to watch what he was doing, although she was aware of[5] a computer screen[6] flickering into life[7] and the soft sound of drawers[8] being opened and shut.

It had been a long day and extreme fear had the effect of making Agatha feel sleepy. Her eyes closed.

She awoke with him shaking her shoulder and cried, 'We've been caught! The police!'

'Shhh! I've found his account,' hissed[9] James.

'Good. Can we get out of here?'

'Yes, I've taken notes. Quietly now.'

As Agatha finally followed him down the garden path, she felt sure there must be people living above the adjoining shops[10], people who were staring down at the two figures in the garden and reaching for[11] their telephones, but when she shot one frightened look back[12], everything was as dark and silent as before.

Only when they were safely outside did she realize that fear was affecting her physically. 'I must find a Ladies'[13] … quick,' she gasped[14].

'Are you feeling sick?'

1. celle qui mène à la banque proprement dite
2. frissonna
3. œil furibond
4. repérée
5. perçut
6. écran d'ordinateur
7. qui se mettait en marche en clignotant
8. tiroirs
9. siffla
10. boutiques voisines
11. tendant la main vers
12. jeta en arrière un coup d'œil apeuré
13. des toilettes
14. dit-elle, haletante

1. faire pipi
2. J'en ai jusqu'aux yeux
3. maudit
4. grossièreté

'No, I've got to *pee*[1],' said Agatha. 'There's a tide of pee rising up to my eyeballs[2].'

'We'll go back to the pub,' he said. 'It isn't far.'

Agatha cursed[3] her own crudity[4]. But she almost ran back to the pub.

5. enchantée
6. lui était passée

'Now what?' she asked, elated[5] because her fright was over[6] and she had used the services of the pub's toilet.

'Don't you want to know what I found out?'

'Oh, yes.'

'Listen to this. In the short time Paul Bladen was in Carsely, he had deposits in his account: one of twenty thousand pounds, one of fifteen thousand, then nine thousand, one of four thousand, five deposits of five thousand, and one for five hundred. That's apart from his pay.'

'Who paid him?'

7. C'est là le hic

'There's the rub[7]. Didn't say. I've been thinking. I would like to get inside that house of his. We could do it tonight.'

8. [= gentlemen]

'Last orders, please, ladies and gennelmen[8]. If you please,' called the barman.

'As late as that!' exclaimed Agatha. 'Well, we could start out tomorrow early and –'

'No, tonight.' He looked at Agatha's cherry-red coat. 'We need some dark clothes.'

9. libéré
10. tout seul
11. tâtonnèrent
12. en empoignant

What monster is this I have unleashed[9]? thought Agatha, looking at his animated face. She could tell him to go on his own[10]. And yet, there would be all the excitement of the adventure, which might lead to … They fumbled around[11] in the dark of Paul Bladen's house. 'What's that?' he cried, clutching hold of[12] Agatha. 'Nothing,' he murmured, still holding her. 'Your perfume smells divine. Oh, Agatha!' And he bent his lips to hers.

'Agatha! Stop day-dreaming[1] and let's get on,' said James sharply and Agatha blinked the rosy vision away[2], obscurely irritated that he had snapped her out of it[3] before he had kissed her.

Back at her cottage, Agatha changed into a pair of black slacks[4] and a black sweater[5]. She wondered whether he meant her to blacken her face[6]. Better wait and see.

He rang her bell at one in the morning. He too was wearing a black sweater and black trousers. 'We'll be causing no end of a scandal[7],' he said cheerfully. 'I only hope no one sees me calling on you at this hour of the night,' and Agatha thought of Freda and fervently hoped that someone had.

James, who had been drinking mineral water during their last visit to the pub, elected to[8] drive again. Agatha snuggled down[9] in the passenger seat and dreamt they were racing off on their honeymoon.

'Just to be on the safe side[10],' said James, 'we'll park a street away and walk.'

Paul Bladen's house stood quiet and shuttered[11] in a road of Victorian villas. Agatha remembered her last visit and was glad now she had run away.

James looked up and down the quiet street, which was lined with[12] cherry trees in full bloom. A breeze blew down the street and blossom cascaded about them. 'Isn't it sad,' mourned James, 'that such beauty should be so fleeting[13]?'

'Too true,' said Agatha edgily[14]. 'But if you stand here for much longer admiring the blossom, then someone's going to see us.'

He gave a little sigh and Agatha wondered whether he were wishing he was with someone who could share his love of beauty.

1. de rêvasser
2. clignant des yeux, écarta sa vision béate
3. qu'il l'ait forcée à se ressaisir
4. mit un pantalon noir
5. pull
6. s'il comptait lui noircir le visage
7. un énorme scandale
8. choisit de
9. se pelotonna
10. Pour plus de sûreté
11. tous volets fermés
12. bordée de
13. éphémère
14. nerveusement

'I think as there is no one around, we should go straight up to the front door,' he whispered. 'There's a dark porch and once we're there, we'll be pretty much shielded[1].'

'Why bother about dark clothes if we're not going to sneak around the back[2]?' asked Agatha.

'Because it might take me a bit of time to get the door open, and so long as we are dressed in black, there's less chance of us being noticed from the street by any passer-by[3].'

When they were in the shelter of the porch, he flicked the beam[4] of his pencil torch at the door and then switched it off. 'Yale lock[5],' he said with satisfaction. 'Lovely stained-glass panel[6] on the door. I wonder if Peter Rice knows you can get money these days for Victorian stained glass.'

'Get on with it,' said Agatha, looking nervously over her shoulder.

And then they heard the sound of slow footsteps coming along the street and stiffened[7].

'Stand very still[8] in the corner and turn your face away from the street and don't move,' hissed James.

They froze[9].

The footsteps came nearer, stopping every once in a while[10]. 'Come on, Spot,' said a man's voice irritably. Someone walking the[11] dog.

Agatha could feel sweat trickling down[12] her face.

And then, to her horror, she heard the light patter of paws[13] behind her and then a dog sniffing at her ankles[14] and the sound of the owner[15] walking up the garden path.

'Come out of there,' cried the owner sharply. Please God, prayed Agatha, get me out of this one[16] and I'll never be bad again.

1. à peu près à l'abri
2. nous ne nous faufilons pas par l'arrière
3. un passant
4. dirigea le faisceau
5. serrure Yale
6. vitrail
7. se raidirent
8. sans bouger
9. s'immobilisèrent
10. de temps en temps
11. qui promenait son
12. la sueur ruissellant sur
13. un léger bruit de pattes
14. qui lui renifla les chevilles
15. propriétaire du chien
16. tirez-moi d'affaire cette fois-ci

The dog pattered off[1]. 'I'm putting you on the leash[2] now,' said the owner's voice. This was followed by a metallic click and then those footsteps slowly retreated out of the garden and off down the street.

'Whew[3]!' said Agatha. 'That was close[4]. We should have pretended to be a courting couple[5],' she added hopefully. 'Then, if he'd seen us, he would have sheered off[6].'

'On the contrary,' said James, 'nothing infuriates the suburbanite[7] more than the sight of a couple snogging[8] on someone else's property.' He took out a bunch of thin metal implements[9].

'Where did you get those?' asked Agatha. 'You're not a retired burglar, are you?'

'Chap in the[10] regiment. Now, keep quiet while I get to work.'

Agatha stood and fidgeted[11]. She hoped the much-advertised deodorant she had put on was working. He tried one implement after the other until there was a soft click.

A moment later, Agatha stood in the hall where she had panicked before Paul Bladen. 'Now,' said James in a normal voice, 'there's a good bit of light coming from the street lamps outside and the curtains aren't closed. So we search around for some sort of study or a desk.'

Agatha opened a door in the hall. 'I'll try this side,' she said. 'You try the other.'

She could dimly[12] see that the windows of the room she found herself in looked out over the back garden to a railway track[13]. She moved cautiously around in the darkness, feeling with her fingers for a desk[14]. It seemed to be the sitting-room – sofa, coffee-table, easy chairs[15]. Suddenly, with a roar, a late-night passenger train

1. s'éloigna en trottinant
2. te mets ta laisse
3. Ouf
4. On l'a échappé belle
5. couple d'amoureux
6. aurait décampé
7. banlieusard
8. se bécotant
9. trousseau de fins outils en métal
10. Un copain du
11. se tortilla sur place
12. confusément
13. donnaient, au-delà du jardin, sur une voie ferrée
14. cherchant à tâtons un bureau
15. des fauteuils

heading for[1] Oxford rumbled along[2] the track at the end of the garden and then crawled to a stop[3]. Agatha crouched down[4] on the floor. The lights from the carriages shone straight into the room. There were a few people sitting reading books or just staring out into space. Then, with a wheeze[5], the train crawled on[6], slowly gathered speed, and roared off[7] into the night.

Agatha got up and made her way with trembling legs to the door, fell over something and crashed down, swearing loudly.

James came in and said impatiently, 'Try to keep it quiet, Agatha. I've found the study. Follow me. Other side of the hall.'

'It's all right. I haven't hurt myself,' said Agatha sarcastically. 'I knocked something over[8].'

The torch stabbed down[9]. A canterbury[10] lay on its side, papers and magazines spilled across[11] the floor. 'You'd think Rice would have thrown these away,' complained James, picking them up and putting them back after he had righted[12] the canterbury. 'Hardly add to the value of the house.'

They crept across[13] the hall and into the study. James approached a desk by the window and gently slid open[14] the drawers. 'Nothing here,' he mumbled. 'Maybe lower down[15].' He slid out a bottom drawer and then his searching fingers found something at the back of it. He drew out a file[16]. 'Come out to the hall so I can flash the torch on this.'

In the hall, the thin beam of light showed bank-books and a deposit book and bank statements[17] tucked[18] into the cardboard file. 'May as well get out of here and take this home,' said James.

'Won't it be missed[19]?' asked Agatha.

1. en direction d'
2. s'approcha en grondant sur
3. ralentit et s'arrêta
4. s'accroupit
5. dans un sifflement
6. repartit à petite vitesse
7. s'éloigna en grondant
8. J'ai renversé quelque chose
9. pointa vers le bas
10. meuble de rangement [à partitions]
11. répandus sur
12. redressé
13. traversèrent lentement
14. ouvrit doucement
15. plus bas
16. dossier
17. des relevés de compte
18. glissés
19. Ils ne vont pas chercher où le dossier est passé

'No. Rice said he had burnt all the papers. This was jammed at the back of the[1] bottom drawer. He must have missed it[2].'

Agatha, delighted to be outside again and once more in the fresh air, tripped gaily forward down[3] the garden path and fell headlong over[4] something. There was a curse[5] from Agatha, a yelp of canine pain[6], and then that dratted[7] voice calling, 'Spot!'

The dog pattered off to its master. James helped Agatha to her feet[8].

'What's going on there?' came the dog owner's voice.

They walked to the garden gate. A man stood under the street light, holding a small white dog, his face pinched with suspicion. 'Did you kick my dog?' he demanded wrathfully[9].

'My wife tripped over[10] your dog in the dark,' said James coldly.

'Is that so?[11] And what are you doing in there at this time of night?' asked the dog owner.

'I do not see it is any business of yours[12], but my wife and I were looking at our new home. We have just put in an offer for this house and so I would like to take this opportunity of telling you that you ought to keep that animal of yours on a leash and stop it straying over[13] private property. Come, Agatha.'

Agatha, all too conscious of how odd they must look[14] in their black clothes[15], edged past[16] the dog owner with a weak smile.

She could feel his suspicious eyes boring into their backs[17] at they walked to the car.

'Let's get home,' said James. 'I'm dying to have a look at those bank statements. What a horrible man. What sort of man goes wandering around[18]

1. coincé à l'arrière du

2. le rater

3. s'engagea gaiement sur

4. de tout son long sur

5. juron

6. le glapissement de douleur d'un chien

7. fichue

8. à se relever

9. rageusement

10. a trébuché

11. Ah bon ?

12. Je ne pense pas que ça vous regarde

13. de vagabonder dans

14. parfaitement consciente de la bizarrerie de leur accoutrement

15. tout noir

16. passa discrètement devant

17. leur transperçant le dos

18. se promène dans

the streets with his dog at this time of night? Probably a sex maniac.'

Agatha giggled. 'He's probably just a respectable suburban insomniac, or his dog's incontinent and he is now wondering what kind of people decided to view a house in the dead of night[1].'

'It's all your fault,' said James. 'You should look where you're going.'

'How was I to[2] know the damn dog would be there?' retorted[3] Agatha.

'I don't know. You never seem to have anything sensible on your feet[4], always limping about[5] and falling over things.'

'Are we having our first quarrel?' asked Agatha sweetly.

There was a long silence. Then he said, 'I am sorry. I was a bit strung up[6]. Shouldn't take it out on you[7]. The fact is, I'm not used to burglary.'

'You're forgiven.'

'It was not an apology,' he said, 'simply an explanation.'

'Then why did you say you were sorry?'

They bickered[8] the whole way home but neither of them could bring themselves to stalk off to[9] their respective residences until that file was examined.

They went into James's house. He lit the fire, which was already set. He sat down in an armchair on one side of the fire and Agatha took the armchair opposite.

'Ah, here's the deposit book,' he said. 'Good heavens!'

'What? What have you found?'

'A cheque from Freda was paid in – twenty thousand pounds.'

1. en pleine nuit
2. pouvais-je
3. rétorqua
4. n'êtes jamais chaussée correctement
5. à boitiller
6. à cran
7. Je ne devrais pas m'en prendre à vous
8. se chamaillèrent
9. ne pouvait se résoudre à regagner

'Women's Lib[1],' chortled[2] Agatha maliciously[3]. 'Not often the woman pays the man.'

'The others are, let me see: fifteen thousand pounds from Mrs Josephs, nine thousand from Miss Webster, five thousand from Mrs Parr, four more deposits of five thousand, all from Freda, and five hundred from Miss Simms. Oh, and four thousand from Mrs Mason.'

'Freda!' Agatha looked triumphant. 'Do you realize the payments to Bladen come to[4] forty thousand pounds? Now any woman cheated out of[5] that amount of money would feel like[6] murder.'

He looked uncomfortable[7]. 'I know Freda pretty well. She seems to be awfully rich …'

'No one's that rich[8],' put in Agatha.

He stretched[9] and yawned[10]. 'I'm tired. Better leave it for tonight. Should we turn this lot over to[11] the police tomorrow?'

Agatha looked horrified. 'And have to explain how we came by it[12]?'

'We could say we were viewing the house.'

'What! At two in the morning? And the estate agents would point out that we never approached them.'

'All right,' said James, 'we'll tackle[13] these women tomorrow. You had best leave Freda to me.'

Agatha thought furiously about how she might be able to dissuade him from seeing Freda alone, but decided to sleep on it[14].

But as it turned out[15], she was the one to tackle Freda after all.

She struggled from[16] a deep sleep the following morning with the sound of her own doorbell ringing in her ears.

1. L'émancipation des femmes
2. pouffa
3. méchamment
4. s'élèvent à
5. grugée de
6. aurait des envies de
7. mal à l'aise
8. n'a autant d'argent
9. s'étira
10. bâilla
11. remettre le tout à
12. nous nous le sommes procuré
13. interrogerons
14. d'y réfléchir jusqu'au lendemain
15. en fin de compte
16. émergea d'

She pulled on a dressing-gown and thrust her feet into slippers and went to answer the door. Freda stood there, her noisy dog cradled[1] in her arm. 'James here?' she asked brightly. 'I can't get any reply at his house.'

'No,' said Agatha, 'but come in and keep that dog of yours away from my cats.'

'Yes, I think I want a word with you.' Freda followed Agatha through to the kitchen. Agatha caught a glimpse of herself[2] in the hall mirror: tousled hair[3], unmade-up face[4]. Freda was as cool and fragile as a figure in a Fragonard painting. She sat down at the kitchen table, put her dog on the floor, and crossed her long legs. Agatha opened the back door and let her cats out into the garden.

'You've been running all over the place[5] with James,' said Freda. 'He's a bit of a softy[6]. You shouldn't take advantage of[7] his good nature[8].'

'And just what's that supposed to mean?'

'He has been plagued[9] by every old bat in the village, has he not? I warned him[10] that these frightening menopausal women often get the wrong idea[11]. Give him a break[12].'

'Listen, you murderess,' hissed Agatha, 'just because you let Paul Bladen screw you[13] on the surgery table doesn't make you Cleopatra. Besides, you had to pay for that, did you not? Forty thousand pounds, to be exact.'

The doorbell rang and Freda was up like a shot[14] and running to answer it, her dog yapping at her heels. Agatha followed in time to see Freda throw herself weeping into James's arms, sobbing[15], 'This dreadful woman. She's accusing me of murder.'

1. tenu tendrement
2. s'entrevit
3. les cheveux ébouriffés
4. pas maquillée
5. par monts et par vaux
6. trop bonne pâte
7. profiter de
8. bon caractère
9. harcelé
10. l'avais prévenu
11. se méprennent
12. Lâchez-lui les baskets
13. vous baiser
14. se leva comme un ressort
15. en sanglots

'Now, then,' he said, 'no one's accusing you of anything.' He detached himself from her grasp[1]. He looked at Agatha. 'Did you ask her about the money?'

Freda let out a gasp. 'You have no right to poke about[2] my private affairs. I shall tell the police.' She ran out of the door and down the lane, with her dog scurrying at her heels[3].

'What did you say, Agatha?' demanded James.

'She started by insulting me. She said …' Agatha bit her lip. She did not want to put the idea into James's head that she was one of those menopausal women with fantasies[4]. 'Anyway, she was vile[5]. So I taxed her[6] about the money. Then you rang the bell and she went to answer it.'

'Damn. You'd better get dressed, Agatha, and we'd best go and look at that house of Bladen's officially and then take the file along to Bill Wong, as if we've just found it[7].'

As they drove to Mircester, Agatha said suddenly, 'Was Bladen blackmailing them[8]? I mean, all payments are relative. Five hundred pounds from Miss Simms, well, that's a fortune for her.'

'Yes, but she's single[9] and so is Miss Webster, and Freda is a widow. Freda seemed quite unfazed by the[10] fact we found out she had been having an affair[11] with Bladen, so how could he blackmail her?'

At the estate agent's[12], instead of giving them the keys, a young girl called Wendy said she would accompany them. She was a cheerful Sloane Ranger type[13] and talked non-stop to Agatha and James as they walked around the rooms of the house wondering how to get rid of her so that they could pretend to[14] find the file. At last James said, 'We would like to be alone to have a private

1. étreinte
2. vous mêlez de
3. courant sur ses talons
4. qui se faisaient des idées
5. ignoble
6. l'ai interpellée
7. on venait de le trouver
8. Est-ce que Bladen les faisait chanter
9. célibataire
10. indifférente au
11. liaison
12. agence immobilière
13. BCBG joyeuse
14. puissent faire semblant de

discussion,' and to Agatha's relief, Wendy said, 'Right ho[1], drop the keys back at the office when you're finished,' and shot off[2].

They decided to have a thorough search of[3] the house in the hope of finding letters or documents, but there was nothing. Out in the back garden there was an old oil drum with holes banged in its sides[4] which had obviously been used for burning garden rubbish. James poked[5] moodily[6] at the contents with a stick. 'This is where Rice burnt the papers,' he said, 'but we're out of luck. He did a thorough job[7]. Not even an edge of paper left uncharred and legible[8]. Oh, well, let's go and see Bill Wong.'

At police headquarters, Bill Wong studied the bank papers and deposit book and then looked up at them, his eyes shrewd[9]. 'A man phoned in a report in the middle of the night that two people dressed in black were in Paul Bladen's house and told him they had bought it. That wouldn't have been you pair, now would it[10]?'

'Us?' exclaimed James. 'Had it been us[11] and had we found this file, then we would have brought it straight along[12].'

'I wonder[13]. You must stop interfering. Yes, I know. I'm grateful for this and these women will all be interviewed – by the police. If I find you have been continuing with your amateur investigations, then I will really have to inquire more closely into[14] the identities of that couple who were seen at Bladen's last night. Do I make myself clear?'

'Yes, very,' said Agatha huffily[15].

'So that's all the thanks we get,' she complained as James drove them back to Carsely.

1. OK d'accord
2. partit sur-le-champ
3. consciencieusement fouiller
4. baril de pétrole percé de trous
5. piqua
6. avec morosité
7. a fait ça soigneusement
8. épargné par les flammes et lisible
9. l'œil malin
10. vous deux, par hasard
11. Si ça avait été nous,
12. on vous l'aurait apporté tout de suite
13. Je me demande
14. chercher de plus près
15. sèchement

'I'm relieved[1] in a way,' said James. 'Oh, well, back to that writing.'

There was a long silence. Then Agatha said, 'I have to pay my subscription[2] to the Carsely Ladies' Society and that means calling on Miss Simms. Like to come along? I mean, Bill can't stop us asking a few questions in a neighbourly way[3]. Dammit[4], he can't stop us talking to the villagers at all!'

'And how's he to know?' said James. 'I mean, everyone calls on everyone else in Carsely.'

'Miss Simms will be at work until this evening,' said Agatha. 'Let's try Mrs Mason first.'

1. soulagé

2. cotisation

3. de façon amicale

4. Bon sang

Chapter Eight

It was one of those typically English days. Steady rain drummed down[1] and fallen cherry blossom bobbed along[2] in the rivulets[3] running between the old cobbles[4] in Lilac Lane. They had fortified themselves with coffee and sandwiches, and with a lack of enthusiasm that the one would not admit to the other[5], Agatha and James set out to speak to Mrs Mason again.

Mrs Mason was so welcoming, so obviously thought they had come on a social call[6], that it was hard to get down to brass tacks[7]. 'And you must have some more of my famous scones, Mr Lacey,' said Mrs Mason. 'And that's *real* strawberry jam, not shop-bought. Soon be strawberry season again. I do hope this nasty weather clears up, don't you?' She looked at James archly[8]. 'You and Mrs Raisin are quite the talk of the village. I was saying to the vicar the other day that we would soon be hearing the banns read[9].'

James looked at her in blank horror[10] and nearly forgot why they had come. 'Mrs Mason,' began Agatha, 'we really don't want to distress you further[11], but we would like to know why you gave Mr Bladen such a large sum of money.'

Mrs Mason blinked rapidly[12]. 'That is really none of your business.' Agatha glanced around the

1. tombait en tambourinant
2. flottaient le long
3. petits ruisseaux
4. pavés
5. qu'ils ne s'avouaient pas l'un à l'autre
6. lui faisaient une visite de courtoisie
7. d'en venir aux choses sérieuses
8. d'un air malicieux
9. les bans seraient bientôt publiés
10. avec une expression d'horreur hébétée
11. tourmenter plus longtemps
12. cilla

living-room. Four thousand pounds was an awful lot of money for such as Mrs Mason to part with[1].

'We came to warn you[2] that the police are about to make it their business[3],' said James.

'Then I shall speak to the police when they arrive. But how did you find out?'

'Agatha and I were looking around Paul Bladen's house, which is up for sale[4], and we happened to come across his old bank statements and deposit book. We did give them to the police.'

Mrs Mason studied James, her eyes suddenly sharp. 'So you and Mrs Raisin were looking at a house together. Well, well, romance does seem to be in the air. Quite cheering[5], really. It shows one is never too old.'

And that, as she had planned, had the desired effect of driving James to his feet and towards the door.

Agatha gloomily followed him out. James climbed into the car without holding the door open for her and stared moodily at the rain trickling down the windscreen[6]. Agatha got into the passenger seat.

'Damn all gossiping women[7],' said James, striking the steering wheel. 'You, me, it's bloody ridiculous.'

'Yes, a laugh a minute[8],' said Agatha drily, although her heart was sore[9]. 'She only said that to get rid of you[10], and get rid of you it did[11].'

His face lightened. 'Oh, that was the reason. How naïve of me.'

'You are really over-sensitive on the subject,' said Agatha. 'It's my belief that you think every woman you come across is pursuing you.'

He gave an awkward laugh. 'Let's try the Webster female[12].'

1. à céder pour quelqu'un comme Mrs Mason
2. vous prévenir
3. va très bientôt considérer que ça les regarde
4. mise en vente
5. réjouissant
6. pare-brise
7. les commères
8. qu'est-ce qu'on rigole
9. douloureux
10. se débarrasser de vous
11. et ça a marché
12. la Webster

1. se disputait avec
2. trempés
3. marchander
4. chez les antiquaires
5. Ah bon ?
6. engagèrent une
7. entreprendre
8. d'un ton hargneux
9. pleins aux as
10. a économisé
11. tenir leurs comptes
12. les étrangers
13. prêts à les arnaquer
14. cria-t-elle d'une voix perçante
15. une ménagère chassant des chats à coups de balai

Josephine Webster was arguing with[1] a couple of rain-washed[2] American tourists who were trying to haggle over the price of[3] a dried-flower arrangement. 'The price is marked on it,' said Miss Webster, exasperated. 'This is not a bazaar.'

'You can haggle over the price of things in antique shops[4],' said James to the Americans in a kindly voice, 'but most other places you're expected to pay the price marked.'

'Is that a fact?[5]'

The American man and woman fell into[6] amiable conversation with James about their visit, Miss Webster returned to her desk, and Agatha stared out of the window at the main street. She had no desire to tackle[7] Miss Webster while these tourists were in the shop.

'I've no time for Americans,' said Miss Webster waspishly[8] when the couple had left. 'Always complaining.'

'It's not their fault,' said James. 'They feel they have to protect themselves. A lot of people think American tourists are made of money[9]. Now that couple saved[10] all their lives for this one trip. They have to budget[11] very carefully, and they've probably been told back home that all foreigners[12] are out to cheat them[13].'

'But we're not foreigners,' said Miss Webster. 'We're British.'

James smiled. 'Talking about money, we wondered why you had paid such a large sum of money to Paul Bladen.'

Miss Webster's face went white and then red. 'Get out of here,' she called shrilly[14]. 'Get out!' She picked up a bunch of assorted dried flowers and waved it at them like a housewife shooing cats out with her broom[15].

'We're not getting anywhere[1],' said James gloomily after he and Agatha had retreated out of the shop. 'Do you want to see Mrs Parr again?'

1. On n'avance pas

'So long as[2] that husband of hers is not around,' said Agatha.

2. Du moment que

But Mrs Parr did not open the door to them. The curtain twitched[3] and they saw the quick blur of a face[4] behind the glass, but the front door stayed resolutely shut.

3. remua

4. ils entrevirent un visage indistinct

'We're running out of people[5],' said James. 'Perhaps I should try Freda. If I went on my own[6] –'

5. Les troupes s'amenuisent

6. tout seul

'No,' said Agatha quickly. 'Why don't we try Miss Mabbs again? Say we know these women were paying him. Ask her some more questions.'

'Oh, all right. But I don't want to have to wait until that disco opens up.'

'We can find her where she works. She said it was a kennels[7] "out Warwick way". I'll look up the Yellow Pages before we go.'

7. un chenil

At last, armed with the name of a kennels situated between Leamington Spa and Warwick, they set off.

The rain was slowly easing off[8], to be replaced with[9] pale-yellow sunlight.

8. se calmait lentement

9. laissant place à un

They found the kennels easily enough. Dogs were barking, dogs were howling piteously[10], and the wet air smelled of damp dog.

10. piteusement

They went into the office, which was housed in a timber hut[11], and asked for Cheryl Mabbs.

11. baraque en bois

The man behind the desk looked up sharply[12]. 'Friends of hers?'

12. attentivement

'Yes,' said James.

He stood up. He was a small, thickset[13] man with grey hair and rimless spectacles[14]. 'Then you know exactly where to find her,' he said. 'Get out.'

13. trapu

14. des lunettes à monture invisible

'If we knew where to find her,' said James, 'we wouldn't be here asking for her. Does she work here, or doesn't she?'

Agatha had a sudden flash of inspiration. She edged in front of[1] James and said mildly[2], 'I am afraid we have misled you[3], but we do not like to go around announcing who we are. We are social workers[4].'

'Oh.' He sat down suddenly. 'Why didn't you say so? Although you still make me feel angry. I had a recommendation from you lot[5] that she was on the straight[6].'

Agatha affected an air of weariness[7], although her heart was beating hard. 'What has she done this time?'

'Not told you yet, have they? Pah! That's bureaucracy for you. The whole of England is top-heavy with idiotic pen-pushers[8]. She broke into the drugs cabinet[9], that's what she did.'

'Did you have Adrenalin in there?' asked James eagerly.

'Yes, of course, but the fact is she would have been better off raiding[10] a doctor's or chemist's unless she wants to prevent hard pad and distemper[11]. I called the police right away and they went to her digs[12] and found the stuff. Or what was left of it. She had been flogging pills around[13] some disco in Leamington, claiming they were a new sort of happy pill. I think the youth[14] of Leamington can consider themselves well and truly wormed[15] by now.'

James and Agatha were both dying to know what Cheryl Mabbs's record had been[16], but then, as supposed social workers, they were supposed to know.

1. se glissa devant
2. doucement
3. Pardon de vous avoir induit en erreur
4. travailleurs sociaux
5. de vous autres
6. comme quoi elle avait décroché
7. lassitude
8. regorge de gratte-papier imbéciles
9. a pris dans l'armoire à pharmacie
10. aurait mieux fait de faire une descente chez
11. l'hyperkératose et la maladie de Carré
12. piaule
13. refourguait des pilules à proximité d'un
14. les jeunes
15. radicalement vermifugés
16. quels étaient les antécédents de Cheryl Mabbs

'She's a silly girl,' said the man. 'I'm Bob Picks, by the way. She was a wizard[1] with animals. Why did she want to go and smash up[2] her career? Young people these days, I ask you.'

They left him, still shaking his head over the iniquities of youth.

'So,' said Agatha outside, 'that's where the Adrenalin could have come from. Damn! We can't ask the police, or word might get to Bill Wong[3] that we're still asking questions.'

'So many suspects,' mourned[4] James. 'Tell you what, let's try her digs. She might be out on bail[5], or that unlovely boyfriend of hers might be there.'

Agatha nodded, although she felt suddenly depressed. She could not help remembering how horrified and shocked he had been at any suggestion of a romance between herself and him. The sun struck down[6], lighting up the grey patches in his black hair and showing the strong lines down the side of his nose. In that moment, he did not look nearly so handsome as he usually did and Agatha took small comfort from that.

They drove to Blackbird Street and parked outside the door to the flats where Miss Mabbs lived.

They walked up the stairs and pressed the right bell this time. They waited a long time and then heard the sound of someone approaching the door. It opened an inch[7]. 'Oh, it's you,' said Jerry, Miss Mabbs's boyfriend. 'Wot[8] you want?'

'Where's Miss Mabbs?'

'In the slammer[9].'

'Can we come in? We'd like to ask you a few questions.'

The door opened wider and his foxy face stared at them. 'Cost you[10].'

James sighed. 'A tenner, like last time.'

1. savait y faire
2. a-t-il fallu qu'elle bousille
3. Bill Wong pourrait apprendre
4. déplora
5. a peut-être été libérée sous caution
6. Un rayon de soleil apparut
7. s'entrouvrit de quelques centimètres
8. [= What]
9. En taule
10. Faut payer

'Done[1]. Not here. Meet you down the pub. The Fevvers.'

'The what?' asked James as they walked down and out into the street.

'He meant the Feathers,' said Agatha.

'The old men's pub. That's where we went last time. I'm fed up with[2] mineral water. I'll try tomato juice this time.'

The pub looked the same, tired and dusty. Dust motes swam in shafts of sunlight[3] striking through the windows. An old man slumbered over[4] his beer in a corner.

James ordered a tomato juice for himself and a gin and tonic for Agatha.

Time passed while they discussed the suspects in the case in a desultory way[5]. Agatha would have liked to debate the possibility that Freda was the murderess. After all, she had paid out the biggest amount of money. But James's face went rigid at the very mention of Freda's name[6].

James ordered[7] another round of drinks and carried them back to the table. 'I don't think our young friend is coming,' he said. 'Maybe we'd better go back and try again.'

At that moment the pub door opened and six youths came in. Black leather and jeans, shaven heads[8], mean pinched faces[9]. The leader saw them and jerked his head at the others[10].

'Trouble[11],' said James.

'I don't like your face,' said the leader. A bicycle chain hung from one tattooed hand. 'And I'm going to rearrange it.' Agatha looked round wildly for help. The barman had disappeared, the old man slept on[12].

James threw back his head and shouted, '*Help! Help! Murder!*' It was a terrible shout,

1. Conclu
2. J'en ai assez de
3. Des grains de poussière dansaient dans les rayons de lumière
4. sommeillait le nez sur
5. d'une façon décousue
6. à la seule mention de Freda
7. commanda
8. crâne rasé
9. visages mauvais, aux traits tirés
10. rameuta les autres d'un sec signe de tête
11. Voilà les ennuis
12. dormait toujours

deafening[1] and shocking, a bellow[2]. It was as if he had thrown a hand grenade into the group. They darted for[3] the door and crashed out[4], colliding with one another[5], while James's terrible shouts went on and on. The old man woke up and stared at him in amazement.

'It's all right,' said Agatha, white-faced. 'They've gone.'

James smiled at her. 'Nothing like a good scream for help, I always say. Let's go and sort out[6] young Jerry.'

'What's it got to do with him? Oh, you think he knows Cheryl Mabbs did the murders and he's sent along[7] his friends to silence us.'

'Romantic idea. But I think young Jerry phoned his friends and told them that there was some rich jerk[8] in the pub with a fistful of tenners for the taking[9]. I just can't wait to see him again.'

Once more they stood outside the shabby door and once more James pressed the bell. 'Who is it?' came Jerry's cautious voice.

'Got the money outer that twat[10],' said James in a gruff[11] voice.

The door opened wide. Jerry saw them and tried to slam[12] the door, but James shouldered his way in[13]. He slapped Jerry hard on one side of his head and then on the other. Then, holding him by the scruff of the neck[14], he said, 'Your flat. Time we had a talk.'

'Don't hurt me,' squeaked[15] Jerry. 'I ain't done nothink[16].'

'Where is it? Which door is yours?' demanded James.

Jerry pointed to an open door. James pushed him inside. 'Now, before I really get to work on

1. assourdissant
2. beuglement
3. se précipitèrent vers
4. sortirent en trombe
5. au point de se rentrer dedans
6. Allons nous occuper du
7. a envoyé
8. connard
9. poignée de billets de 10 bons à prendre
10. J'lui ai tiré son pognon, à c'pauv' mec
11. rauque
12. claquer
13. rentra d'un coup d'épaule
14. peau du cou
15. couina
16. [= I haven't done anything]

you, why did you send your friends to beat us up[1]?'

'I dinnet[2].'

There was a one-bar heater[3] burning in front of an empty fireplace. James twisted Jerry's arm behind his back and then thrust his face down towards the bar of the heater. 'Speak up while you've still got a face left.'

'Okay, I'll tell you.'

James pushed Jerry down into a chair and stood over him. 'I phoned up Sid and said to tell the boys there was good pickings off[4] a couple in the Fevvers, that's all. See, I don't know nuffink[5] about Cheryl. No, don't,' he shouted as James loomed over him[6]. 'I'm telling you the truff[7], s'welp me God[8]. It was her idear to steal the drugs from the kennels. Get a bit of cash. She says them hopheads[9] at the disco would buy anythink. Honest[10].'

His voice went on and on, pleading and explaining. It turned out he had not known Cheryl when she was working in Carsely.

James finally turned away in disgust.

Outside, Agatha looked nervously up and down the street. 'We should call the cops[11],' she said.

'I wouldn't do that.' James unlocked the car door. 'It might all come out[12]. In fact, we'd better get out of here in case that chap at the kennels has found out we're impostors.'

When they got back to Carsely, James said, 'I'll make us a snack and then we'll tackle Miss Simms.'

Agatha brightened. 'I'll go to my place, feed the cats and then let them out. They've been locked up most of the day.'

The cats gave her a rapturous welcome[13]. Agatha sat down suddenly and watched them while

1. nous tabasser
2. [= I did not]
3. radiateur à résistance unique
4. qu'il y avait du blé à se faire sur
5. [= nothing]
6. se tenait au-dessus de lui, menaçant
7. [= truth]
8. [so help me God]
9. que les camés
10. J'vous jure
11. flics
12. Tout pourrait être découvert
13. accueil enthousiaste

they fed. She felt weak and shaky and on the point of crying. She had had a bad fright[1] in the pub. Bill Wong was right. She should leave this sort of business to the police. But if she dropped the investigations, then James would drop *her* and go back to his writing.

She let the cats out into the garden and stood for a moment watching them frolicking about[2] and then went along to James's cottage.

'I've set our meal in the kitchen,' he said when he answered the door. 'Come through.'

Agatha looked eagerly[3] around the kitchen. It was cheerful and warm. A large bowl of daffodils[4] stood on the windowsill[5]. There was a square scrubbed table in the middle and some elegant ladder-backed chairs[6]. Supper consisted of cold ham and an excellent salad with a cold bottle of white Mâcon.

Agatha studied him covertly[7] as he ate with the absorbed attention he gave to everything and everyone except herself. 'It's time,' he said finally, pushing away his plate, 'for us to separately write down everything we know about everyone. Whoever killed Paul Bladen and Mrs Josephs did both killings in panic or rage and on the spur of the moment[8]. But first, let's see what we can get out of Miss Simms.'

Miss Simms lived on the council estate near Mrs Parr. She answered the door to them and said cheerfully, 'Just finished bathing the kids. I'll be with you in a minute.'

'I didn't know she had children,' whispered Agatha when they were alone.

'Must be a single parent[9],' said James. 'Quite common these days.'

1. belle frousse
2. folâtrer
3. avec curiosité
4. jonquilles
5. rebord de la fenêtre
6. chaises à dossier en échelle
7. à la dérobée
8. sur un coup de tête
9. mère célibataire

The living-room was a mess of discarded toys and picture books[1]. An old television set flickered in one corner. The furniture was of the kind bought on the pay-up plan[2], which grew old and shabby[3] before the final payment was made.

Miss Simms came tittuping back in on[4] the ridiculously high heels she always wore.

'Drink?' she offered.

James and Agatha both shook their heads. Agatha looked at James and James looked at Agatha and it was Agatha who said, 'We happen to know you paid Paul Bladen five hundred pounds. Why?'

'I don't think that's very nice. I don't really,' complained Miss Simms. 'What's it got to do with you, anyway?'

Agatha sighed. 'We just want to know who killed Paul Bladen and Mrs Josephs. We feel if we knew why you gave him the money, it might help. The others gave him thousands and thousands, but they won't talk.'

Her gaze sharpened[5]. 'There were others?'

Agatha nodded.

Miss Simms sighed and sat back on the low sofa and crossed her legs, her skirt rucked up to show an edge of scarlet lace knicker[6]. How little I really know about the people in this village, thought Agatha. I didn't even know Miss Simms had children. It's the car, that's what. People in villages have become mobile and so they're less curious about their fellows[7]. And television. And yet it's funny how people go on and on about the good old days when they had to make their own entertainment[8]. If it was so great, why did they all rush out to buy television sets[9] as soon as they could?

Miss Simms's voice broke into her thoughts. 'I may as well tell you, only it makes me so mad;

1. un fatras de jouets abandonnés et de livres d'images
2. à crédit
3. râpés [meubles]
4. revint en faisant résonner
5. Son regard se fit plus perçant
6. remonant en plis et laissant voir un bout de culotte en dentelle écarlate
7. semblables
8. se divertir par eux-mêmes
9. des téléviseurs

like when I think of the way that bastard[1] tricked me. He took me out to a posh[2] restaurant in Broadway. He told me all about this veterinary hospital he hoped to start. He said if I gave him some money, he would call it after me[3]. He said he would get Prince Charles to open it[4]. I drank too much and well, things got a bit passionate that night and before I knew what was what[5], I'd written him out a cheque for everything I'd got in the Post Office savings[6]. After a bit when he didn't come round again, I got worried. Not nice to be dropped like that. I asked him about the hospital and he said he was too busy to talk about it. I asked for my money back and he got nasty[7] and said I had given it to him of my own free will[8]. I felt such a fool. I work over at a computer place in Evesham. I pay a chunk out of my wages[9] to pay for child care for the kids[10]. I told Mrs Bloxby. She said I should pray to God for guidance[11] and so I did and do you know what?'

'No, what?' asked James.

'The very next day[12] God sent me a new gentleman friend[13] with a nice job in soft furnishings[14] and he pays me an allowance, like[15].'

'You'll be getting married soon,' said James.

She laughed. 'He's married, which suits me[16]. Don't like having a man underfoot all the time[17].'

'Does Mrs Bloxby know the outcome[18] of your prayers?' asked Agatha curiously.

'Ooh, yes. She said as how God moves in mysterious ways[19].'

The vicar's wife, reflected Agatha, was always the soul of tact[20].

'I was so mad with that Paul Bladen, I could've killed him,' said Miss Simms. 'But I didn't, and so good luck to whoever did.'

1. salaud
2. restaurant chic
3. il lui donnerait mon nom
4. demanderait au prince Charles de l'inaugurer
5. avant même de m'en rendre compte
6. du montant de mes économies à la Poste
7. mauvais
8. en toute liberté
9. Je donne une bonne part de mon salaire
10. pour payer la garde des enfants
11. pour que Dieu me guide
12. Dès le lendemain,
13. petit ami
14. tissus d'ameublement
15. il me verse une sorte d'alloc
16. me va très bien
17. sans arrêt dans les pattes
18. résultat
19. que les voies du Seigneur étaient impénétrables
20. le tact personnifié

'But there's Mrs Josephs.'

Miss Simms looked sad. 'Forgot about her. Old duck she was.[1] What about a drink now?'

Both cheerfully accepted now that there was no danger of their being thrown out and Miss Simms produced an excellent bottle of malt whisky supplied by her gentleman friend. Agatha paid her membership fee[2] for the Carsely Ladies' Society and Miss Simms entered it carefully in a ledger[3].

'So are you pair going to get spliced?[4]' she said cheerfully.

James put down his glass. 'No danger of that,' he said evenly[5]. 'I am a confirmed bachelor.'

Miss Simms laughed. 'Wouldn't be too sure about that. When our Mrs Raisin sets her mind to something[6], there's no stopping her[7]. Mrs Harvey in the shop was only saying the other day that we would be hearing wedding bells soon.'

'She must have been talking about someone else,' said Agatha, pink with embarrassment.

When they had said goodbye to Miss Simms and walked outside, there was a constraint between them[8]. Agatha felt quite tired and weepy.

'I think I'd better go home to bed,' she said in a small voice quite unlike her usual robust tones.

'Don't look so upset[9],' he said in a kind voice. 'They'll go on talking about us, and when nothing happens, the gossip will die away[10].'

But I want something to happen, wailed[11] Agatha's heart, and to her horror a large tear slipped out of one eye and ran down her nose.

'You've had a rotten day[12],' said James. 'Tell you what, we'll walk to the Red Lion and I'll get you a stiff nightcap[13].'

Agatha gave him a watery[14] smile.

1. Quel chou elle était !
2. cotisation
3. l'enregistra soigneusement dans son classeur
4. Et vous deux, alors, vous allez vous marier ?
5. d'un ton égal
6. a une idée en tête
7. impossible de l'arrêter
8. une certaine gêne régnait entre eux
9. si atteinte
10. les cancans s'arrêteront
11. gémit
12. une journée pourrie
13. un dernier verre bien tassé
14. larmoyant

The pub was blessedly quiet[1], only a few of the regulars[2] standing at the bar. They carried their drinks over to a table by the fire.

And then Freda walked into the pub with a man. She was wearing a pale-green tailored suit[3] and a white silk blouse[4] and looked as cool and fresh as a salad. Her companion was a florid-faced[5] middle-aged man with silver hair, dressed in a blazer and flannels[6]. They ordered drinks. Freda half-turned her head and saw James and Agatha. She whispered something to her escort[7], who let out a great braying haw-haw-haw of a laugh[8] and stared at them insolently.

Agatha noticed James's face was wearing a blank look and that his body was tense. Please God, let him not be jealous, she prayed, at the same time wondering why she kept praying to a God in whom she did not quite believe.

'I think I am tired,' said James abruptly.

They left together and walked silently home. Agatha gave him a sad goodnight and went to her own cottage. At least the cats would be glad to see her.

She unlocked the door and stepped inside, switching on the hall light as she did so[9].

There was a square white envelope lying on the doormat[10]. She opened it up. It contained one sheet of paper with a simple typed message.

'Stop poking[11] your nose into things that don't concern you or you will never see your cats again.'

Agatha let out a whimper of fear[12]. She ran through to the kitchen and opened the back door. 'Hodge, Boswell,' she called, but all was darkness and silence. She switched on the back outside lights. The square of garden lay before her. No cats.

1. par chance, était très calme
2. habitués
3. tailleur sur mesure
4. chemisier
5. rougeaud
6. pantalon de flanelle
7. cavalier
8. un grand braiment en guise de rire
9. en même temps
10. paillasson
11. de fourrer
12. couinement de frayeur

She went inside and picked up the telephone and phoned the police.

The windows of James's bedroom overlooked[1] the front of his cottage. He undressed and climbed into bed and switched out the light. Just as he was about to close his eyes, a blue light flickered up and over his ceiling[2] and he could hear the sound of a car sweeping past in the lane outside.

He switched on the light again and scrambled back into his clothes[3]. As he stepped out of his own front door, another police car arrived.

He ran to Agatha's cottage, hoping she was all right, worried that by encouraging her to go on this murder hunt[4], he might have endangered her.

PC Griggs was standing on duty[5] on the doorstep. 'You can step inside, Mr Lacey,' he said. 'She'll need some help.'

'What happened?'

'Someone stole her cats.'

James was so relieved that Agatha was not hurt that he nearly said, 'Is that all?' but bit the remark back in time[6].

Agatha's sitting-room seemed full of policemen, plainclothes[7] and uniformed.

Bill Wong looked up as James came in. He had an arm around Agatha's shoulders, an Agatha who was sobbing[8] quietly. Agatha had never thought of herself as a cat lover. In fact, she sometimes regretted the responsibility of looking after the pair. But now all she could think of was that they had either been slaughtered[9] or were locked up somewhere, being mistreated and frightened.

'You'd best sit down and tell us everything you did today,' said Bill. 'Agatha's in no state to give us

1. donnaient sur
2. se mit à clignoter au plafond
3. se rhabilla à la va-vite
4. chasse à l'homme
5. montait la garde
6. ravala à temps la remarque
7. en civil
8. sanglotait
9. abattus

a coherent account[1]. Begin at the beginning and go on to the end and don't leave anything out[2].'

The only thing that James left out was that they had both pretended to be social workers. In a flat voice, he described the interviews they had conducted, the trip to Leamington, the finding out about Cheryl Mabbs's theft of the drugs including Adrenalin, and the attacks in the pub.

He then fell silent, waiting for a lecture[3], but Bill said, 'We'll have this all typed up and get you to sign it tomorrow. We'll need to interview everyone in Lilac Lane and see if they saw anyone or heard a car while you were both in the pub.'

He turned to Agatha and gently questioned her again, taking notes of his own while she confirmed James's story.

James ambled off to[4] the kitchen and made some coffee. Men were dusting[5] Agatha's front door for fingerprints, examining the road outside for tyre tracks[6], picking over[7] the front garden. He sat down at the kitchen table, listening to the murmur of voices in the other room and reflecting that he had initially retired to the country for peace and quiet.

At last he rose and went back to his own house and dug out a sleeping-bag, put his pyjamas, toothbrush, and shaving-kit in a bag and returned to Agatha's cottage.

Bill and the others were just leaving. 'I'll sleep downstairs here tonight,' said James, and Bill nodded.

Mrs Bloxby, the vicar's wife, was sitting with Agatha when he went into the sitting-room. 'That nice Mr Wong phoned me,' said Mrs Bloxby. 'What a terrible business. Agatha should not be left alone.'

1. compte rendu
2. n'omettez rien
3. réprimande
4. se dirigea d'un pas tranquille vers
5. poudraient
6. à la recherche d'empreintes de pneus
7. passant au peigne fin

'She won't be,' said James. 'I'm sleeping down here. Don't cry, Agatha. Cats are great survivors[1].'

'If they're still alive,' sobbed Agatha.

'I'm glad you are staying, Mr Lacey,' said Mrs Bloxby. 'But phone me if you need any help.'

James saw her out[2] and then returned to Agatha. 'Off to bed with you[3],' he said gently, 'and I'll bring you something to make you sleep.'

Agatha scrubbed her eyes and trailed up[4] the stairs. Part of her mind told her that such a short time ago she would have believed any sacrifice was worth getting James[5] to stay under her roof and look after her[6], but the rest of her mind cried out for[7] her lost pets.

After she was in bed, the door opened and James came in carrying a tray. 'Whisky and hot water and a couple of aspirin,' he said. 'I'll be downstairs. Drink up.' He sat on the edge of the bed and held the glass to her lips and waited until she had swallowed the aspirin.

After he had left, Agatha lay awake, tears trickling out of the corners of her eyes. Everyone seemed sinister[8] to her now, even James. What did she know of him? A man arrived in a village and claimed to be[9] a retired colonel and everyone took him at face value[10]. And yet, Bunty knew his family, and she, Agatha, had met his sister a year ago. But how formidable[11], how terrifying he had been when he had been slapping the miserable Jerry around. Ruthless[12], that was the word for it.

Slowly she drifted off to sleep, plagued with nightmares[13]. Freda was torturing the cats and laughing while James looked on; Bill Wong invited her to dinner and served up the cats, roasted on a tray; and Miss Webster was sitting efficient-

1. ont un instinct de survie très développé
2. la raccompagna jusqu'à la porte
3. Et maintenant au lit
4. se traîna pour monter
5. aurait été prête à n'importe quel sacrifice pour que James
6. reste sous son toit et s'occupe d'elle
7. réclamait
8. menaçant
9. se prétendait
10. le croyait sur parole
11. redoutable
12. Impitoyable
13. s'assoupit dans un sommeil peuplé de cauchemars

ly at her desk, with Agatha's two cats, stuffed and mounted[1], in front of her.

Agatha awoke in the morning. Sunlight was streaming into[2] the room, there was a smell of coffee and the hum[3] of voices from downstairs. She looked at the clock beside the bed. Ten in the morning!

She washed and dressed and went downstairs. Her kitchen was full of women: most of them members of the Carsely Ladies' Society, Mrs Harvey from the general store, and Mrs Dunbridge, the butcher's wife, all being served coffee by James.

They surrounded her as she came in, murmuring sympathy[4]. Her kitchen counter[5] was loaded with gifts of cake and jam and flowers. Even Miss Simms was there. 'Took the day off[6] from work,' she said.

'That's very kind of you,' said Agatha, '*but* I don't know what you can do.'

'Mr Lacey has had a very good idea,' said Mrs Bloxby. 'We're organizing a search. Your cats may have been dumped off[7] somewhere in the village, so we are all going out on a house-to-house hunt[8]. You sit quietly here with Mr Lacey and we'll report[9] if we find anything.'

Agatha abruptly left the room and went up to the bathroom and cried her eyes out[10]. All her life she had forged on[11], pushy[12] and determined to get to the top of the public relations profession, all her life she had been alone. All this friendship and help made her feel weak[13].

When she went back downstairs, red-eyed but composed[14], only James and Mrs Parr were left.

'Mrs Parr has just been telling me much the same story as Miss Simms,' said James. 'Bladen

1. empaillés et sur monture
2. inondait
3. bourdonnement
4. des paroles de sympathie
5. plan de travail
6. un jour de congé
7. abandonnés
8. allons tous partir à leur recherche, maison par maison
9. vous tiendrons au courant
10. pleura comme une Madeleine
11. était allée de l'avant
12. ambitieuse
13. faible
14. plus calme

told her about the veterinary hospital and said he would name it after her. Her husband found out about the missing money and hit the roof[1].'

'I suppose I might have done the same thing,' said Agatha slowly, remembering that dinner at the Greek restaurant. 'He told me about his plans and I said I would contribute[2] something, but I was thinking of a cheque for twenty pounds. And he was all ready to go to bed with me but I panicked and ran away. Did you have an affair with him, Mrs Parr?'

She shook her head. 'I wouldn't have done. That wasn't how he tricked me. I was so flattered by him because he said I was the only woman who understood him. I am not very happy in my marriage and he made me feel attractive[3]. I should have told you before, but I felt such a fool. I was still a bit in love with him when he died, but after the funeral my mind cleared up[4] and I could see what he had done.'

'Mrs Mason was telling me the same thing while you were upstairs, Agatha,' said James, 'He was a compulsive gambler[5], Mrs Parr, and that's why he needed the money.'

'That's odd,' said Agatha. 'He didn't spend any of it. I mean, what he got out of the ladies of Carsely was still in his account[6].'

'I'll go off and join the search,' said Mrs Parr. 'The least I can do[7].'

'Thanks for all this, James,' said Agatha, when they were alone. Her eyes filled with tears again.

'Now, now, the time for crying is over. Let's sit down and discuss what we know. Instead of thinking that, say[8], Freda must have done it because she paid out the most money, what we should be

1. a piqué une crise
2. donnerais
3. me donnait le sentiment d'être séduisante
4. mes idées se sont clarifiées
5. joueur invétéré
6. sur son compte en banque
7. C'est le moins que je puisse faire
8. par exemple

looking for is someone with the *character* to do such a thing,'

'Who can say what anyone will do when they're goaded[1]?'

'You wouldn't kill anyone, Agatha, now would you[2]?'

Except Freda, thought Agatha.

'What we should do,' he went on, 'is make a list of suspects and then divide it up[3] and follow each one and see what she does during the day and who she sees and if there is anything suspicious about her behaviour. Now, the women who gave money to Bladen were Mrs Parr, Mrs Mason, Freda, Miss Webster, Mrs Josephs and Miss Simms. Then we have to take into account Paul's ex-wife, Greta. Also, there is one side of the case we have not been looking at. Bladen was killed up at Lord Pendlebury's stables. Bob Arthur found the body and came running out, saying, "Looks like someone's done fer him." Why should he say that? Why not think it a heart attack or something? There's another interesting thing I noticed about Bladen's bank statements. There were no major withdrawals[4], so he must have had cash to pay for all his food and entertaining[5]. How did he pay the bill[6] at the Greek restaurant?'

'Cash.'

'Right. So what about Mrs Arthur? There's a thought[7].'

'It gets worse and worse[8],' said Agatha. 'Where do we begin?'

'I'll begin with Freda. No, don't scowl[9]. My motives are pure detection[10]. You start by watching Mrs Parr.'

'Oh, come on! That woman couldn't hurt a fly[11].'

1. ce que quiconque ferait s'il était provoqué
2. allons
3. se les répartir
4. de retraits importants
5. les dîners offerts
6. l'addition
7. C'est une idée, tiens
8. De pire en pire
9. ne faites pas la tête
10. L'investigation est ma seule motivation
11. ne ferait pas de mal à une mouche

'She's terrified of that husband of hers. Bladen might have known that. She may yet not be telling us all. He could have been blackmailing her. Give you something to do. You want your cats back[1], don't you?'

Agatha winced[2].

'Anyway, I'll get moving on my side and we'll meet up here, say, at six o'clock this evening. Nothing like action to beat the blues[3], Agatha.'

Agatha went numbly about the kitchen[4] after he had left, stacking away[5] the various gifts in cupboards. Apart from cakes and pots of jam there was a large bunch of dried flowers, but they could hardly be from Miss Webster[6]. Agatha shoved them in a vase and went upstairs to put on the make-up she had wept off.

She was on her way out when she stopped in the hall. The back of the front door was still covered in fingerprint dust. A gleam of sunlight lit up a tiny[7] coloured object sticking among the coarse coconut matting[8] of the doormat. She bent down and looked at it and then picked it out. Puzzled[9], she turned it this way and that[10]. Then her face cleared. It was a tiny dried petal. It must have fallen off that bouquet of flowers that someone had brought. She flicked it from her fingers[11] and then opened the door.

Then she froze[12].

Suddenly it was the night before and she was lifting the envelope from the doormat and opening it, taking out the letter, smoothing it out[13]. Surely a flicker of something small and bright had drifted down[14].

1. récupérer vos chats
2. fit la grimace
3. pour combattre la déprime
4. resta hébétée à s'affairer dans la cuisine
5. empilant
6. ce n'était certainement pas Miss Webster qui l'avait apporté
7. tout petit
8. grosses fibres de coco
9. Intriguée
10. et retourna
11. s'en débarrassa d'une pichenette
12. s'immobilisa
13. la défroissant
14. quelque chose de petit et de brillant en était tombé en miroitant

Chapter Nine

Agatha felt weird and strange[1] as she walked numbly out[2] into the bright sunlight. Two policemen were asking questions at the other cottages in Lilac Lane. People waved and called to her as she went past but she did not hear them.

Agatha Raisin was no longer thinking about who had murdered the vet or Mrs Josephs, all she wanted was her cats back.

As she approached Josephine Webster's shop, she saw a white hand twisting the card[3] on the door round from 'Open' to 'Closed'. Of course, half-day in the village. With such a search going on, if Miss Webster had the cats, then she wouldn't have them in the shop or in her flat above it.

Agatha returned home and got into her car. She parked a little way away from the shop and waited, not noticing[4] people passing up and down the main street, intent only on[5] Josephine Webster.

And then Miss Webster came out, neat and trim[6] as ever, and got into her car, which was parked outside the shop. She drove off. Grimly[7], Agatha followed. Miss Webster drove down into Moreton-in-Marsh and turned along the Fosse. Agatha let a car get between her and her quarry[8] and followed. Miss Webster headed for[9] Mircester, her little red car sailing up and over[10] the Cotswold hills on the old Roman road which ran straight as an arrow.

1. toute drôle
2. lorsqu'elle sortit, hébétée,
3. panonceau
4. ne prêtant aucune attention à
5. concentrée uniquement sur
6. impeccable
7. D'un air sombre
8. proie
9. se dirigea vers
10. sillonnant

Agatha followed her into a multi-storey carpark[1], parked a little bit away and waited until Miss Webster got out and locked her car, then got out of her own.

Josephine Webster went first to Boots, the chemist's, tried various perfume samples[2], and then bought a bottle. From there, she went to a dress boutique. The day was unseasonably chilly[3] and Agatha shivered[4] as she waited outside. At last, she risked a peek[5] through the shop window. Miss Webster was turning this way and that before a mirror, wearing a low-cut[6] red dress. She said something to the assistant and disappeared back into a changing room. After ten minutes, she came out of the shop, carrying a carrier-bag[7]. From there, she went to a lingerie shop and Agatha again froze and fidgeted[8] outside until Miss Webster appeared carrying a carrier-bag with the lingerie shop's name on it.

When she walked on, followed by Agatha, and turned in at the tall Georgian portico[9] of the public library, Agatha was beginning to despair. It was all so innocent. Fear for her cats had tricked[10] her memory. That little petal had probably fallen off the bouquet that morning. But the doggedness[11], the single-mindedness[12], and the tenacity that had made her successful in business took over[13]. She waited outside for half an hour and then cautiously walked inside. No sign of Miss Webster.

Had she seen her and escaped out of a back door? In her frantic[14] search to find a way out of the back of the library, Agatha nearly ran into Josephine Webster, who was sitting in a leather chair in one of the bays[15], calmly reading, her shopping bags beside her.

1. garage à plusieurs niveaux
2. échantillons
3. anormalement frais pour la saison
4. frissonnait
5. coup d'œil
6. décolletée
7. sac de courses
8. trépigna
9. porche
10. joué un tour à
11. obstination
12. détermination
13. prirent le dessus
14. effrénée
15. devant l'un des bow-windows

Agatha picked the next bay, took a book at random[1] from the shelves and pretended to read. Her stomach rumbled[2]. She should eat something, but she dare not risk leaving the library.

After two hours, a rustle of bags[3] in the next bay warned her[4] that her quarry was about to depart.

She waited a few moments and then cautiously got up and poked her head round the bay[5]. Josephine Webster was disappearing in the direction of the exit. Agatha followed, heart beating hard again now that the pursuit was back on[6].

Miss Webster tripped gaily along[7], as if she hadn't a care in the world[8]. She turned in at the door of Mircester's Palace Hotel.

Agatha, hovering at[9] the entrance, saw her head up a passage at the side of the reception under a sign which said 'Rest Rooms[10]'.

She bought a newspaper from a kiosk in the foyer[11], sat down in an armchair and barricaded herself behind it, lowering it from time to time to make sure Miss Webster had not escaped.

After a full hour, Agatha saw Miss Webster emerge. She was wearing the new dress and was heavily made up. She had obviously left her bags and coat in the cloak-room[12]. Agatha jerked up[13] the newspaper as Miss Webster crossed the foyer in a cloud of scent and lowered it again in time to see her going into the bar.

Feeling stiff and hungry, Agatha threw aside the newspaper and looked cautiously round the door of the bar and then jerked her head back[14].

Miss Webster was sitting talking to Peter Rice, ugly red-haired[15] Peter Rice, Bladen's partner[16]. He must have entered the hotel and gone into the bar when Agatha's whole attention was focused on watching for Josephine Webster.

1. au hasard
2. gargouillait
3. bruissement de sacs
4. l'avertit
5. passa la tête vers le bow-window
6. reprenait
7. marchait gaiement
8. pas le moindre souci
9. indécise devant
10. Toilettes
11. hall d'accueil
12. vestiaire
13. releva brusquement
14. rejeta vivement la tête en arrière
15. le laideron roux
16. l'associé

She sat down again in the foyer, her mind working furiously. It could be an innocent meeting. Yes, wait a bit. Miss Webster had a cat. She could have taken the cat for treatment to Mircester and struck up a friendship[1] with Peter Rice. No harm in that. But … Greta Bladen had said something about Peter Rice being an old friend.

She looked about her. There was a sign pointing to the hotel restaurant. She walked along to it. The staff were just setting up[2] the tables for the evening meal, but the maître d'hôtel was there. Agatha asked him if a Mr Rice had made a booking for dinner. He checked. Yes, Mr Rice had booked a table for two. For eight o'clock. Agatha glanced at her watch. Only six thirty. They wouldn't leave the hotel. Somehow[3], she had to see Greta Bladen before returning to the hotel to keep a watch on them[4].

She stopped at a phone-box on the road to the car-park and phoned James, but there was no reply. She drove off, praying that Greta would be at home.

Greta answered the door and frowned[5] when she saw her visitor was Agatha.

'I must speak to you,' pleaded Agatha. 'You see, I've been threatened[6]. Someone stole my cats to stop me investigating and I think I might know who that someone might be.'

Greta sighed but held open the door. 'Come in. I don't quite grasp[7] what you are saying. Do you mean someone is trying to stop you investigating Paul's death?'

'Yes.'

'Well, I haven't got your cats.'

'Could you tell me what you know about Peter Rice?'

1. se lier d'amitié avec
2. dressaient
3. D'une façon ou d'une autre
4. les surveiller
5. fronça les sourcils
6. menacée
7. Je ne comprends pas très bien

'Peter? Oh, he can't have anything to do with it. I've known Peter for ages[1].'

'Tell me about him anyway.'

'I don't know very much. He lived a couple of doors away from me in Leamington in the old days[2]. We were friends, played tennis together, but never anything romantic. I mean, I never thought any man would look at me that way, and so I was glad of Peter's company. Then Paul came along.

'I thought Peter would be delighted that I had found happiness at last, but he threw a very ugly scene[3]. He said he had been going to ask me to marry *him*. I was so much in love with Paul that somehow that made me callous[4]. It was only old Peter behaving in a most odd way. The next time I saw him he apologized for his behaviour and said he was moving to Mircester.'

'And you never saw him again?' prompted[5] Agatha.

'Well, I did, of course. I met him when Paul went into partnership with him and, as I told you, it was Peter who suggested I check out the site of this supposed veterinary hospital. I told him long afterwards how I had been cheated[6]. After my divorce, we went out for dinner a couple of times, but there was nothing there and I really don't think there ever was anything there.'

'Then how do you explain the scene when you told him you were going to marry Paul?'

'Oh, that. I think Peter is the kind who would have been jealous if any close[7] friend, male or female, got married. He was a very solitary man. Come to think of it[8], I suppose I was the only friend he had in Leamington.'

1. depuis des lustres
2. autrefois
3. m'a fait une scène épouvantable
4. dure
5. relança
6. bernée
7. proche
8. Réflexion faite

'Why did he decide to open the surgery in Carsely?' asked Agatha. 'I mean, there are lots of villages closer to Mircester, and larger ones, too.'

'Let me think. He said something about that when I met him one day in the square. He said, "I'm finding that ex of yours something useful to do. I think it's better we work apart. I've told him to start up a surgery in Carsely. Keep him out of my hair[1]." I said, "Why Carsely?" and he said that some friend of his who had a shop there said it was a good place for business.'

'Josephine Webster,' said Agatha. 'So that's the connection. And I think I know where my cats are.'

She got up to leave. She looked wild-eyed[2] and her face was working[3].

'If you suspect anyone of anything,' said Greta, 'go to the police.'

Agatha merely snorted[4] and went out to her car.

She thought furiously on the road to Mircester. Josephine Webster could have tipped off[5] Peter Rice about Mrs Josephs. She could have been in the pub to hear Freda telling everyone about the discovery of that bottle and warned Rice, or she could have removed the bottle herself.

Agatha flicked a glance at the dashboard[6] of her car. Eight o'clock. Peter Rice would just be sitting down to dinner.

She drove straight to the veterinary surgery and parked outside. She got out and took a tyre-iron[7] out of the car. The surgery was a low building set at the back of a small car-park. A light was burning over the door. Agatha moved to the side of the building, which was in darkness but with enough light for her to make out[8] a glass-paned side door. She had no time or expertise[9] to emulate[10] James

1. Ça le tiendra éloigné de moi
2. avait l'air paniquée
3. le visage crispé de tics
4. se contenta de grogner
5. informé
6. jeta un coup d'œil au tableau de bord
7. démonte-pneu
8. distinguer
9. compétence
10. pour imiter

Lacey's burglary techniques. She smashed a pane of glass in the door with the tyre-iron. A volley[1] of hysterical barks greeted her ears[2]. Grimly ignoring them, she tugged out[3] the remaining glass with her gloved hands[4], reached in[5] and unlocked the door.

Eyes glittered at her in the darkness and somewhere among the barks and yelps[6] she heard several plaintive miaows[7].

'In for a penny, in for a pound[8],' muttered Agatha and switched on the light.

'Shhh!' she whispered desperately to the cages of animals. Her eyes ranged along them[9]. And there, together in a cage, were Hodge and Boswell.

With a glad cry, she undid the latch[10] and opened the cage.

The barking and yowling[11] suddenly died abruptly. Agatha, reaching in to get her cats, was aware of a heavy air of menace. She heard a soft footfall[12] and turned around.

Josephine Webster smiled up at the waiter as he pulled out her chair for her in the restaurant. Peter Rice sat down opposite. The maître d' bowed over them[13] and presented menus and made suggestions.

When their order[14] had been taken by one of his minions[15], he gathered up[16] the huge leather-bound menus and then suddenly said, 'Will the other lady be joining you?'

'What other lady?' demanded Peter Rice, and Miss Webster giggled and said, 'One of your harem, Peter?'

'A lady came in earlier and asked if you had booked a table for this evening.'

'What did she look like?' asked the vet.

1. charivari
2. lui parvint
3. retira
4. de ses mains gantées
5. glissa le bras
6. aboiements et jappements
7. miaulements
8. Quand le vin est tiré il faut le boire
9. Du regard elle les passa en revue
10. loquet
11. miaulements de douleur
12. bruit de pas
13. Le maître d'hôtel s'inclina très bas
14. commande
15. grouillots
16. rassembla

'Middle-aged, straight brown hair, expensively cut, quite smart clothes.'

'No, she won't be joining us,' said Peter. 'Hold my order[1]. I've got to do something in the surgery. Give Miss Webster a drink and look after her until I get back.'

James Lacey was worried. He had called at Agatha's cottage several times without getting a reply. He had not been able to get much more out of Freda. Her friend with the silver hair stayed with her all the time, and James could not manage to get a word with her in private.

He decided to pass the time until Agatha's return trying to write his book, but instead he found himself writing about the case. He wrote on and then gave[2] an exclamation, took out one character[3] and tried to fit the evidence he had to it[4].

He was roused from[5] his efforts by the doorbell. Bill Wong stood there with Inspector Wilkes. 'Where's Agatha?' asked Bill.

'Isn't she back? We were supposed to meet at six. Isn't her car there?'

'No, I'm getting worried. We'll need to ask around and see if anyone saw her leaving the village.'

'I'll go out and try to find her myself,' said James. 'Here, take a look at my notes, Bill, and see if you come to the same conclusion.'

James went straight to Josephine Webster's shop. It was in darkness, as was the flat above, and he got no reply to his banging and knocking[6]. A head popped out of a window next to the flat above the shop and a man's voice said, 'Ain't no use[7] you ringing and banging, fit to wake the dead[8]. Her[9] goes to Mircester on half-day.'

1. Mettez ma commande en attente
2. poussa
3. personnage
4. de lui accoler les indices dont il disposait
5. tiré de
6. quand il tambourina à la porte
7. Ça sert à rien
8. à réveiller les morts
9. [= She]

James went back and got his car and told Bill he thought Agatha might be in Mircester. He suddenly knew where Agatha had gone and prayed he would not be too late.

Agatha slowly straightened up.

Peter Rice stood in the doorway, looking at her. She was aware again of the strength of that body which supported[1] the disproportionately small head. She had left the tyre-iron lying beside the shattered door[2]. Her eyes flew this way and that[3], seeking a weapon[4].

'Don't even think of it,' he said. He produced[5] a small automatic pistol from his pocket. 'Through to the examining room[6], Mrs Raisin,' he said. 'We won't be disturbed there.'

Even though she felt weak with fear, even though she felt her bladder was about to give[7], Agatha gave the door of the cage with her cats in it a kick as she passed and tried to send them telepathic messages to escape. Rice switched off the lights in the room with Agatha's cats and the other animals and switched on the lights in the small examining room.

Keeping the pistol trained on[8] Agatha, he asked, 'How did you know it was me?'

'I didn't really,' said Agatha. 'But I guessed Josephine Webster had been the one to take the cats and leave that note. I followed her and saw her with you. You can't shoot me. The police will find my body and they'll know it was you.'

'Mrs Raisin, you broke into[9] my surgery. I saw the light and a figure[10] inside who rose, I thought, as if to attack me. I shot you. I was defending my life and property.'

1. soutenait

2. posé à côté de la porte brisée

3. furetaient

4. cherchant une arme

5. sortit

6. Direction le cabinet de consultation

7. sa vessie était sur le point de céder

8. braqué sur

9. êtes entrée par effraction dans

10. silhouette

'I left a note, saying where I would be,' said Agatha.

He studied her for a few moments and then smiled. 'No, you didn't, or that Lacey fellow would be here. Anyway …' He raised the pistol an inch.

'It was because of Greta, wasn't it?' said Agatha.

'In a way. But I didn't think of killing him then. I didn't even think of it when she told me how he had been cheating her. No, it was when he started cheating me, ah, then I began to get really angry. That famous veterinary hospital of his. So good for conning[1] gullible[2] women. We had a receptionist here, a nice girl. Paul got his claws into her[3]. She was to persuade the customers to pay cash as much as possible and pass the money to him. Did she get a cut of it[4]? Of course not. All was to go to that hospital which, of course, was to be named after the receptionist. I had taken a long fishing holiday. This is a wealthy practice[5]. I had hired[6] a young vet to stand in for me[7] when I was away and to work with Paul because Paul mostly handled[8] all the cases of horses and farm animals. When I came back, I remarked that trade had dropped by a considerable amount[9]. I suspected the temporary vet, but then one day I was talking to one of the customers in the square and we were complaining about taxes and business taxes in general. "I suppose," says she, "that's why you want so much money in cash. To avoid tax. The girl always asks for it." Of course I got hold of[10] the girl and she broke down and said she had only been stealing for the greater good[11], namely[12] the founding of that fictitious[13] hospital. I sacked[14] the girl but not Paul. Oh, no. He was going to have to pay me back. But I wanted him out of my hair[15]. Josephine said Carsely was a good place, and so

1. Si commode pour escroquer
2. crédules
3. la tenait sous son emprise
4. A-t-elle touché sa part
5. Mon cabinet marche très bien
6. engagé
7. pour me remplacer
8. s'occupait de
9. les affaires avaient considérablement chuté
10. j'ai interrogé
11. pour la bonne cause
12. à savoir
13. fictif
14. J'ai renvoyé
15. je ne le voulais plus dans mes pattes

I told him to set up a business there and trick the ladies with his stories if he liked, but every penny was to come to me, and just in case anything happened to him, I got him to make out his will in my favour[1]. I said unless he paid me back in full, I would go to the police.'

Agatha stayed rigid, seeing out of the corner of her eye that her cats had slid into[2] the room beside her.

'I still wouldn't have killed him. But one of the women he tricked was Miss Josephine Webster, whom I had come to love. She came to me, crying and sobbing[3], and told me the whole story. I knew he was up at Pendlebury's. I was going to curse him[4], sack him[5], punch him on the nose, that was all. The stables were empty apart from Paul. I saw him with the syringe, I knew what was in it, what the operation was and something took over[6] and the next thing I knew[7] he was dead. I slipped off[8] without anyone seeing me. I thought I was safe. I was furious when I realized he had taken a double mortgage[9] out on that house, so instead of gaining by his death, I lost. Josephine and I were going to announce our engagement[10] after the fuss had died down[11]. She knew what I had done. Then that Josephs woman came here. She said Paul had tricked her and she was going to tell the police the truth. She said Paul had told her that I had encouraged him to dupe the women out of money. I promised to pay her back. Then I panicked when Josephine phoned me and told me that you, you Nosy-Parking bitch[12], were about to hear all from Mrs Josephs. Josephine told me she suffered from diabetes. But still I didn't mean to do it if she saw sense[13]. I tried to give her the money back, but the silly old bat[14] wouldn't take it[15]. She said she was

1. je l'ai obligé à rédiger son testament en ma faveur
2. s'étaient glissés dans
3. pleurant à gros sanglots
4. l'injurier
5. le virer
6. m'a envahi
7. l'instant d'après,
8. suis sorti discrètement
9. hypothèque
10. nos fiançailles
11. une fois l'agitation retombée
12. sale fouineuse
13. entendait raison
14. vieille chouette
15. n'en a pas voulu

going to the police after talking to you. I jabbed the Adrenalin into her[1]. The minute she was dead, I went into a blind panic[2]. I dragged her upstairs in the hope that when she was found dead in the bathroom, they would think it suicide or accident. I chucked the empty bottle out of the car window, as if by getting rid of it, I had got rid of the stain of murder[3]. But you had to interfere again, you and that Lacey. "Take her cats," said Josephine. "That'll shut her up[4]." What a mess. What a bloody mess[5]. But I'm going to marry Josephine, and nothing's going to stop me.'

Hodge jumped up on the examining table and sat looking from one to the other.

Agatha could suddenly smell her own fear, rank and bitter[6], and so could the cat. Its tail puffed up like a squirrel's[7].

'So, Mrs Raisin, I need to get this over with. I advise you to stand still and take what's coming to you[8].'

His finger began to squeeze the trigger[9]. Agatha dived[10] under the table as a shot rang harmlessly above her head.

One beefy[11] hand dragged her out from under the table. Panting[12], he threw her against the wall. Hodge flew straight into his face, clawing and spitting[13]. In his panic, the vet tried to shoot the cat off his face[14] but the shot went wild[15], smashing into a cabinet of bottles.

Agatha tried to drive[16] the examining table into his stomach as he tore the cat from his face and flung it across the room. She had seen people in films doing that, but it was bolted to the floor[17]. She dived to the side as he fired again, wrenched her ankle[18] and fell on the floor.

1. lui ai injecté l'adrénaline
2. j'ai été pris de panique
3. la souillure du meurtre
4. Ça la fera taire
5. Quel sacré bordel
6. écœurante, tenace
7. Sa queue s'hérissa de poils comme celle d'un écureuil
8. d'accepter ce qui vous arrive
9. à presser la gâchette
10. plongea
11. musclée
12. Haletant
13. griffant et crachant
14. de se débarrasser du chat d'un coup de pistolet
15. le tir s'égara
16. de lui envoyer
17. elle était fixée au sol
18. se tordit la cheville

She shut her eyes. This was it. Death at last. And suddenly Bill Wong's voice like a voice from heaven said, 'Give me the gun, Mr Rice.'

There was another shot and a cry from Bill. Agatha screamed, 'Oh, no!' and then felt strong hands tugging at her[1] and James Lacey's voice in her ear, saying, 'It's all right, Agatha. Don't look. Rice has shot himself. Don't look. Come with me. Keep your head turned away.'

Agatha rose, clinging to him, and buried her face in the rough tweed of his jacket.

Three hours later Agatha, bathed and wrapped in her dressing-gown[2], sat in her sitting-room with the cats on her lap, being fussed over by James[3].

'Bill Wong will be calling on us[4],' he said. 'Is he grateful to us for having solved two murders for him? Not a bit of it[5].'

'Us?' demanded Agatha. 'I was the one who found out about Rice.'

'I had more or less come to the same conclusion,' said James, 'although it took me some time to guess Josephine Webster was involved. What put you on to her?[6]'

Agatha told him about finding that shred[7] of dried petal on the doormat.

'But you should have come to me,' exclaimed James, 'or told Bill Wong.'

'I only thought of the cats,' said Agatha. 'Funny, isn't it? I thought my heart would break when they were taken, but here they are, purring away[8], two animals to be cared for and fed, and now they just seem like an everyday nuisance[9].'

'Though from what you say, Hodge saved your life,' James pointed out. 'I wonder if they got

1. des mains puissantes la tirer
2. emmitouflée dans son peignoir
3. et un James aux petits soins pour elle
4. va passer nous voir
5. Pas le moins du monde
6. Qu'est-ce qui vous a mise sur sa piste ?
7. petit bout
8. ronronnant à tout-va
9. souci quotidien

Josephine Webster. I wonder if she was still sitting there in the hotel restaurant waiting. Bill and his boss went right there while we had to go to the police station and make endless statements.'

'So you had worked it all out yourself[1]?' said Agatha.

He threw another log on the fire and sat down. 'Once I had written down what everyone had done and said, Peter Rice seemed the obvious suspect. He was strong enough to have dragged Mrs Josephs up the stairs, he knew where Bladen would be on the day he was murdered, he knew about the operation on that horse. One always thinks of murderers as planning everything scientifically, but in Rice's case it was all panic[2] and then luck. All he had to do was sit tight[3] and let Mrs Josephs make her accusations to the police. The police wouldn't have thought the philandering and conning tactics of Paul Bladen[4] had anything to do with Peter Rice. I think it was our nosing around[5] that rattled him so badly[6].'

'Don't say that,' pleaded Agatha. 'That means we are both directly responsible for Mrs Josephs's death.'

'Well, he would probably have panicked anyway.'

The doorbell rang. 'That'll be Bill[7],' said James, 'come to read us the riot act[8].'

Bill was on his own. 'An off-duty call[9],' he said, sinking down wearily[10] on the sofa beside Agatha. 'Yes, we got Webster. It must have seemed a lifetime[11] to you, Agatha, when he was trying to kill you, but there she was, drinking martinis, just where he had left her.

'She denied the whole thing[12], but when we took her to the station[13] and then told her that

1. aviez élucidé toute l'affaire de vous-même
2. que de l'affolement
3. ne pas bouger
4. que les agissements du coureur de jupons et arnaqueur Paul Bladen
5. que c'est notre façon de fureter partout
6. qui l'a salement déstabilisé
7. Ça doit être Bill
8. qui vient nous passer un savon
9. visite en dehors du service
10. avec lassitude
11. éternité
12. a nié en bloc
13. commissariat

Rice had confessed everything to you, she broke down. Cruel thing to say, but we hadn't yet told her he was dead.

'She had been having an affair with Rice for a few months, up until Paul Bladen arrived in Carsely. Before her affair with Rice, she had been a virgin. Think of that, in this day and age.[1] I think her affair with Rice made her feel like a femme fatale, and so, when it seemed that Bladen was courting her as well, it went right to her silly head[2]. That snowy evening you were supposed to meet him in Evesham, that was the evening she went to his house and gave him the cheque. So the grateful Bladen took her to bed. Even if it hadn't been snowing, he probably wouldn't have turned up to meet you, Agatha. She was the one who answered the phone to you.

'But Bladen was up to his old tricks[3]. He asked her for more money and she grew alarmed and said she could not afford any more. So he lost interest in her, and the repentant[4] Miss Webster went back to the arms of Peter Rice and told him all about Bladen. So, to Rice, history was repeating itself. He had, I gather from what you said in your statement, Agatha, been deeply in love with Greta. Paul had taken her away. Now Paul was doing the same thing with Josephine. But what put you on to them?'

'I found a dried-up flower petal on the doormat,' said Agatha proudly, 'and realized it had probably fallen out of the note about the cats, and so I knew dried flowers meant Josephine Webster.'

Bill looked puzzled[5]. 'We wouldn't have missed anything like that[6].'

1. Vous imaginez, à notre époque !

2. ça lui est carrément monté à la tête, cette bécasse

3. recommençait ses vieilles combines

4. contrite

5. perplexe

6. n'aurions pas laissé passer un pareil détail

'That's what I thought,' said James. 'Someone brought you a bouquet of dried flowers, Agatha, the morning after, so it probably fell from that.'

'Why should you be looking closely[1] at the doormat?' exclaimed Agatha, exasperated. 'Your men were searching *outside*, where whoever[2] delivered the letter had stood, as well as all over the back garden, because whoever took the cats must have got into the garden by the lane which runs between mine and James's garden. They wouldn't bother about the doormat.'

'I think you'll find it came from the bouquet after all, Agatha. You made a lucky guess[3], and a near-fatal one for you[4]. I'm not going to lecture you[5] tonight on the folly of amateurs interfering. Goodness,' he laughed, 'I suppose it's a case of rank amateurs setting out to catch a rank amateur[6].'

Agatha glared[7].

'Anyway, I'm glad it's all over. I'm off on a special training course[8], so I won't see you for a few weeks.' Bill stood up. 'Has the doctor seen you, Agatha?'

She shook her head.

'You'd best see him tomorrow. You're going to be a wreck when reaction sets in[9].'

'I'll be all right,' said Agatha, giving James an adoring look[10].

He returned it with a startled one[11] and then stood up and said, 'Do you want me to get Mrs Bloxby to stay with you, Agatha?'

'No,' she said, disappointed that he was not volunteering to fetch his sleeping-bag. 'I'll be all right after a good night's sleep.'

After they had left, Agatha rose and went up to bed, the two cats trotting after her. She smiled

1. de près
2. celui
3. avez deviné juste mais par hasard
4. cela a failli vous être fatal
5. vous sermonner
6. un exemple de parfaits amateurs décidés à attraper un parfait amateur
7. eut l'air furieuse
8. Je pars faire une formation spéciale
9. vous effondrer quand viendra le contre-coup
10. regard enamouré
11. répondit par un regard inquiet

before she drifted off to sleep. It was all over. She had survived. She felt great. No need to see any doctor. It would take more than one murderer to get Agatha Raisin down[1]!

1. abattre Agatha Raisin

Chapter Ten

The next few days were glorious for Agatha, despite the fact that James had sent her a note saying he was shutting himself up to write for a few weeks.

So many people came to call to hear about how Agatha had solved the murders of Paul Bladen and Mrs Josephs, and Agatha stitched away at[1] her story, embroidering[2] the details, so that by the time she gave a talk to the Carsely Ladies' Society, it had become a real blood-and-thunder[3] adventure.

'How exciting you make it all seem,' said Mrs Bloxby after Agatha's talk. 'But do be careful. It can take a little time for reality to set in[4], and then you might suffer badly.'

'I was not lying[5],' said Agatha hotly[6].

'No, of course you weren't,' said Mrs Bloxby. 'I particularly liked that bit when you said to Peter Rice, "Shoot me if you dare, you evil fiend[7]." '

'Oh, well,' muttered Agatha, shuffling her feet[8] and avoiding the steady gaze[9] of the vicar's wife, 'a bit of poetic licence is allowed, I think.'

Mrs Bloxby smiled and held out a plate. 'Have a slice of seed cake[10].'

From that moment, Agatha began to feel extremely uncomfortable[11]. Her version of events, which had become a highly coloured adventure

1. peaufinait
2. enjolivant
3. mélodramatique
4. reprenne ses droits
5. ne mentais pas
6. avec véhémence
7. monstre malfaisant
8. en piétinant
9. regard posé
10. gâteau aux graines de carvi
11. mal à l'aise

story, had indeed come to seem like reality. As she walked back from the vicarage, she noticed how *dark* the village seemed and how the light near the bus shelter had gone out again.

The lilac trees were all out[1] in Lilac Lane, whispering in the night wind, nodding their plumed heads[2] as if gossiping[3] about Agatha as she scurried[4] homewards[5] underneath[6], thinking that the smell of their flowers reminded her of funerals.

She went inside. The cats did not come to meet her and she let out a whimper[7] of fear and ran to the kitchen. They were curled up together[8] in their basket in front of the stove, happy in each other's company, fast asleep and not caring about one frightened mistress who wanted them to wake up and keep her company.

She reached out a hand to switch on the electric kettle and all the lights went out.

In blind terror, she stumbled round the kitchen[9], searching for a torch[10], until some sane[11] voice in her mind told her it was only another of the village's frequent power cuts[12]. Forcing herself to be calm, she remembered she had candles in the kitchen drawer, found one and lit it with her cigarette lighter[13]. She held it up and found a candlestick[14]. May as well go to bed, she thought.

This was how they had gone to bed in the old days when the cottage was built, people walking up this very staircasc[15] with the shadows leaping before them in the wavering candle-flame[16]. So many generations. So many dead. Just think how many had gasped out their last breath[17] in this very bedroom. Her dressing-gown at the back of the door looked like a hanged man[18]. Faces stared at her out of the pretty flowered wallpaper. She was in a cold sweat[19].

1. tous en fleurs
2. inclinant leurs têtes empanachées
3. comme s'ils cancanaient
4. se hâtait
5. pour rentrer chez elle
6. sous leurs frondaisons
7. geignement
8. pelotonnés l'un contre l'autre
9. marcha à tâtons dans la cuisine
10. lampe électrique
11. raisonnable
12. coupures d'électricité
13. briquet
14. bougeoir
15. escalier précisément
16. les ombres dansant devant eux dans le vacillement de la flamme
17. avaient rendu leur dernier soupir
18. avait l'air d'un pendu
19. avait des sueurs froides

She forced herself to make her way downstairs to the phone in the hall. She put the candle on the floor, sat down on the floor herself, cradled the phone in her lap[1] and dialled James Lacey's number.

His voice when he answered sounded brisk and efficient[2]. 'James,' said Agatha, 'can you come along?'

'I'm writing hard[3]. Is it important?'

'James, I'm frightened.'

'What's happened?'

'Nothing. It's just that that reaction everyone's been warning me about has set in.'

'Don't worry,' he said. 'Help is on its way[4].'

Agatha stayed where she was. Her fear had gone now that he was coming, but she decided she had better remain looking as frightened as she had been. Perhaps she might throw herself into his arms. Perhaps he would hold her close[5], and say, 'Agatha, let's give all those gossips a treat[6] and get married.' Perhaps he would kiss her. What would that be like?

This rosy fantasy[7] went on until she realized that a considerable amount of time had passed. Of course, he was probably packing his pyjamas and shaving-kit, but still[8] …

The doorbell rang, making her jump. Yes, she would throw herself into his arms.

Mrs Bloxby said gently, 'Now, now, Mrs Raisin. I knew this would happen.'

Agatha opened her eyes and backed off in confusion[9].

She had seen a dark figure[10] on the step and had taken it to be James.

1. installa le téléphone sur ses genoux
2. sonnait clair, efficace
3. Je suis en plein travail d'écriture
4. Les secours arrivent
5. la serrerait dans ses bras
6. faisons plaisir à toutes ces commères
7. rêve tout en rose
8. tout de même
9. recula, en pleine confusion
10. silhouette

The vicar's wife was carrying an overnight bag[1]. 'Mr Lacey phoned me and I came as quick as I could. The doctor's on his way.'

Feeling almost ill with disappointment, Agatha allowed Mrs Bloxby to lead her to the kitchen. The lights came on again. Everything was normal.

By the time a sedated[2] Agatha was in bed, the doctor had left, and Mrs Bloxby was sleeping in the spare room[3], she could only reflect woozily[4] that James was a beast[5] and a bastard[6].

Agatha spent a long and miserable time of panics and nightmares, glad of callers[7] during the day, glad of the members of the Carsely Ladies' Society, who took it in turns[8] to sleep in her spare room during the night. Not one woman mentioned James Lacey and Agatha's heart was sore with rejection[9].

And then her fears ebbed away[10] and her mood was improved with long sunny days.

In such a small village it was inevitable that she should meet James again. He smiled at her in a kindly way[11] and asked after her health[12], he said writing was coming easily and he was working hard. He said they must have lunch sometime, that very English remark which usually means absolutely nothing. Agatha looked at him with bitter hurt in her bearlike eyes[13] but replied politely and coolly, thinking they were almost like a couple who had once had an affair[14], regretted now on one side.

And then one morning, as lunchtime was approaching, Agatha's doorbell rang. She no longer rushed to it expecting to see James. Bill Wong stood on the step.

1. sac de voyage
2. sous sédatif
3. chambre d'amis
4. se dire, l'esprit dans les choux
5. chameau
6. salopard
7. visiteurs
8. se relayaient
9. souffrait d'être rejeté
10. refluèrent
11. avec gentillesse
12. s'enquit de sa santé
13. lui lança un regard meurtri de ses yeux de nounours
14. liaison

'Oh, it's you,' said Agatha. 'You must have been back from that course[1] ages ago.'

'I was,' said Bill, 'but another case came up which involved liaising with[2] the Yorkshire police, so I've been travelling a bit. Aren't you going to ask me in[3]?'

'Of course. We can have coffee in the garden.'

'Lacey around[4]?' he asked as he followed her through the house.

'No,' said Agatha bleakly[5]. 'In fact, apart from little talks like "How are you" and "Isn't the weather great" over the grocery counter, I haven't really seen him.'

'Odd, that. I thought the pair of you were as thick as thieves[6].'

'Well, we're not,' snapped Agatha. She had bought a new garden table and chairs. 'Sit down, Bill. I was just going to get a bite to eat. Cold chicken and salad suit you?'

'Anything. Your garden could do with some flowers[7]. Give you an interest[8].'

'I suppose. I'll get the food.'

Over lunch, Bill told her about the case he was working on and then they finally got around to[9] discussing the case of Peter Rice.

'It's odd,' said Bill, 'when you think of the pair of them, Rice and Webster. Hardly[10] Romeo and Juliet to look at, but there was passion there, real passion. Take one man who feels he's too ugly to get a woman and one virgin and that's an explosive mixture. When Rice found out she'd been sleeping with Bladen, it must have nearly broken his heart. History repeating itself. First Greta, then Josephine. But Josephine is back in his arms again. She's not shocked he's killed Bladen. Now they

1. formation
2. nécessitait d'être en liaison avec
3. me faire entrer
4. est-il dans les parages
5. d'un air sombre
6. comme larrons en foire
7. Quelques fleurs dans votre jardin ne seraient pas de trop
8. Ça vous ferait une occupation
9. en vinrent à
10. Pas vraiment

are bound even more closely by the crime[1] and still more after the death of poor Mrs Josephs.'

He looked about him. 'You wouldn't think when you drive through one of these pretty Cotswold villages how much terror and passion and anger can lurk[2] beneath the beams[3] of these old cottages. You know, Agatha, Lacey's an odd bird[4]. Some of these army chaps are. He's only in his fifties, not dead old for these days[5].'

'Thank you,' said Agatha drily.

'If he'd been married, he might be an easier mark[6], but these army bachelors, well, it's as if they've come out of the monastery. Play it cool and he'll come around.'

'I have no interest in him,' said Agatha evenly[7].

'I think you have too much interest in him and that's what frightened him off,' said Bill.

'Oh, really, so young and so wise[8]. What's *your* love life like?'

'Pretty good. You know the Safeways supermarket in Mircester?'

'Yes.'

'There's a pretty girl called Sandra works at the check-out[9]. We've been dating[10].'

'That's nice,' said Agatha, who felt obscurely jealous.

'So I'd better go. Keep away from murders, Agatha!'

After he had left, Agatha drove down to the Batsford Garden Centre at the bottom of Bourton-on-the-Hill and looked at flowers and plants. They also had full-grown trees. Instant garden[11], that was the answer. But just a little to start. Something for the borders[12] round the grass[13] at the back and a hanging basket of flowers for the front of the cottage. She bought some Busy Lizzies[14]

1. le crime les a beaucoup rapprochés
2. se dissimuler
3. poutres
4. un drôle de coco
5. pas si vieux de nos jours
6. une proie plus facile
7. d'une voix uniforme
8. plein de sagesse
9. à la caisse
10. Je sors avec elle
11. Le jardin instantané
12. plates-bandes
13. pelouse
14. impatiens

and pansies[1] and decided she would get started by planting them.

The work was relaxing and the cats played about her in the sunlight and she was so absorbed in her work that it took her some time to realize her doorbell was ringing.

If only it would be ...

But Agatha recoiled a step[2] when she opened the door. Freda Huntingdon stood there.

'What do you want?' asked Agatha crossly[3].

'To bury the hatchet[4],' said Freda. 'Come along to the pub. I feel like getting plastered[5]. I'm sick of men.'

Curiosity warred with distaste[6] in Agatha's mind and curiosity won.

'What's happened?'

'Come to the pub and I'll tell you.'

Only the idea that it might have something to do with James drove Agatha into accompanying[7] Freda.

Freda bought them both large gins and they sat down.

'I'm thinking of selling up,' said Freda. 'Nothing's gone right since I came here.'

'You mean Bladen?'

'That and other things. You see, George, my husband, was much older than me, but oodles of money[8]. We used to travel a lot, go to exotic places. But George kept a strict eye on me and I used to think of all the freedom I'd have if he dropped dead and left me the money.

'Well, he did. I had a couple of unfortunate affairs, and so I thought to hell with it[9]; I'll move to the Cotswolds, get myself a dinky[10] cottage and look around for another husband. I got my eye on Lacey. Sorry I was such a bitch[11], but I

1. des pensées
2. recula d'un pas
3. avec humeur
4. Enterrer la hache de guerre
5. J'ai envie de prendre une cuite
6. et le dégoût bataillèrent
7. incita Agatha à accompagner
8. blindé de fric
9. au diable tout ça
10. mignonnet
11. une vraie garce

really fancied him[1], but not a hope there. That business with Bladen threw me[2]. I really believed he was head over heels in love with[3] me. I really believed all that rubbish[4] about that hospital. When George was alive, I thought I was the clever, worldly, shrewd one[5], but it was George who had the brains[6]. Then Tony came along. That chap you saw me with in the pub. No Adonis, but good business, Gloucester way[7]. His wife called on me yesterday. His wife! And he swore he was a widower.' Freda snivelled dismally[8]. 'I'm just a stupid old tart[9].'

'You need another big gin,' said Agatha, ever practical.

James Lacey read over again what he had written and groaned. Thanks to his experiences in the Bladen case, he had thought he would write a mystery story[10]. How easily the words had come. How rapidly the thousands of little green words had built up on the screen of his computer. But it was as if a mist had cleared. He was looking down at pages of total rubbish[11].

The windows of his cottage were all open because it was a hot day. From next door, he could hear the sound of voices and the clink[12] of glasses and china. He went out into his garden and peered over the hedge[13]. Bill Wong and Agatha were sitting having lunch and absorbed in conversation. He wished he could go and join them, but he had been cool to[14] Agatha, had snubbed her, and now he had cut himself off[15].

He returned to the house and pottered about miserably[16]. Later he heard Bill leave and shortly after that, he saw Agatha driving off.

1. il me plaisait vraiment
2. m'a perturbée
3. follement amoureux de
4. toutes ces fadaises
5. c'était moi qui étais intelligente, avisée, futée
6. le cerveau
7. à l'échelle de Gloucester
8. pleurnicha lamentablement
9. allumeuse
10. roman à suspense
11. complètement nulles
12. tintement
13. jeta un œil par-dessus la haie
14. distant avec
15. par sa faute les liens étaient rompus
16. s'affaira pitoyablement

He went back out into his garden in the afternoon and began to weed the flower-beds[1]. He heard movement from Agatha's garden and once more looked over. She was planting a row of pansies. He was sure she didn't know anything about gardening. If he hadn't been so stupid, he could have strolled over for a chat[2]. But really! All those women expecting him to propose[3]! And Agatha herself, the way she had looked at him.

But on the other hand, she had nearly been killed. He had misread[4] her looks before. It was all the fault of that bloody captain's wife in Cyprus[5]. He should never have had an affair with her. What a scandal that had been. She had pursued him, flirted with *him*, but when the scandal had broken, he was the guilty party[6], the beast that had seduced her and tried to take her away from her noble and gallant[7] husband.

He settled down to read a detective story by Reginald Hill and found it depressingly good.

In the evening, he heard the sound of noisy singing coming along the lane.

Puzzled, he went out and stood in the evening air on his doorstep.

Lurching along the lane[8], arms about each other[9], singing, 'I Did It My Way', came Agatha and Freda Huntingdon.

When they came abreast of him[10], they stopped singing. Freda hiccuped[11] and said, 'Men!' and Agatha Raisin grinned[12] and gave James Lacey the victory sign[13], but the wrong way round[14].

James retreated inside[15] and banged the door as, laughing and shouting, the unlikely pair[16] went on their way.

1. désherber les plates-bandes
2. aller lui faire un brin de causette
3. s'attendant à ce qu'il les demande en mariage
4. mal interprété
5. Chypre
6. le coupable
7. vaillant
8. Remontant la ruelle en titubant
9. se tenant par la taille
10. à sa hauteur
11. eut un hoquet
12. eut un grand sourire
13. fit à James le V de la victoire
14. à l'envers
15. se replia à l'intérieur
16. l'improbable duo

La collection Yes you can!

Les faux débutants

Linwood Barclay	*Broken Promise*
M. C. Beaton	*Agatha Raisin and the Quiche of Death*
M. C. Beaton	*Agatha Raisin and the Vicious Vet*
Harlan Coben	*The Stranger*
Michael Connelly	*The Black Box*
Michael Connelly	*The Burning Room*
Michael Connelly	*The Drop*
Michael Connelly	*The Wrong Side of Goodbye*
Ken Follett	*The Modigliani Scandal*
Mary Higgins Clark	*A Cry in the Night*
Mary Higgins Clark	*A Stranger is Watching*
Mary Higgins Clark	*Loves Music, Loves to Dance*
Mary Higgins Clark	*Where are the Children?*
Anthony Horowitz	*The House of Silk*
Ian Rankin	*Knots & Crosses*
Nicholas Sparks	*Message in a Bottle*

Les intermédiaires

Harlan Coben	*Caught*
Harlan Coben	*Play Dead*
Harlan Coben	*Stay Close*
Harlan Coben	*Tell No One*
Harlan Coben	*The Woods*
Ken Follett	*Paper Money*
Anthony Horowitz	*Moriarty*
P. D. James	*A Mind to Murder*
P. D. James	*Death Comes to Pemberley*
Douglas Kennedy	*The Big Picture*
Stephen King	*Finders Keepers*

Stephen King *The Green Mile*

John le Carré *A Most Wanted Man*

Yann Martel *Life of Pi*

Les avancés

Paul Auster *Leviathan*

Paul Auster *Oracle Night*

Julian Barnes *The Sense of an Ending*

Michael Cunningham *By Nightfall*

Michael Cunningham *The Hours*

Helen Fielding *Bridget Jones's Diary*

Helen Fielding *Bridget Jones: The Edge of Reason*

Elizabeth George *A Great Deliverance*

Stephen King *Dolores Claiborne*

Stephen King *Misery*

Les classiques

Jane Austen *Pride and Prejudice*

G. K. Chesterton *The Innocence of Father Brown*

Arthur Conan Doyle *The Hound of the Baskervilles*

Francis Scott Fitzgerald *Tender is the Night*

Francis Scott Fitzgerald *The Great Gatsby*

Washington Irving, Arthur Conan Doyle, Edgar Allan Poe *The Legend of Sleepy Hollow and Other Scary Stories*

George Orwell *Animal Farm*

Edgar Allan Poe *The Fall of the House of Usher and Other Stories*

Mary Shelley *Frankenstein*

Bram Stoker *Dracula*

Edith Wharton *The Age of Innocence*

Oscar Wilde *The Importance of Being Earnest*

Oscar Wilde *The Picture of Dorian Gray*

Virginia Woolf *To the Lighthouse*

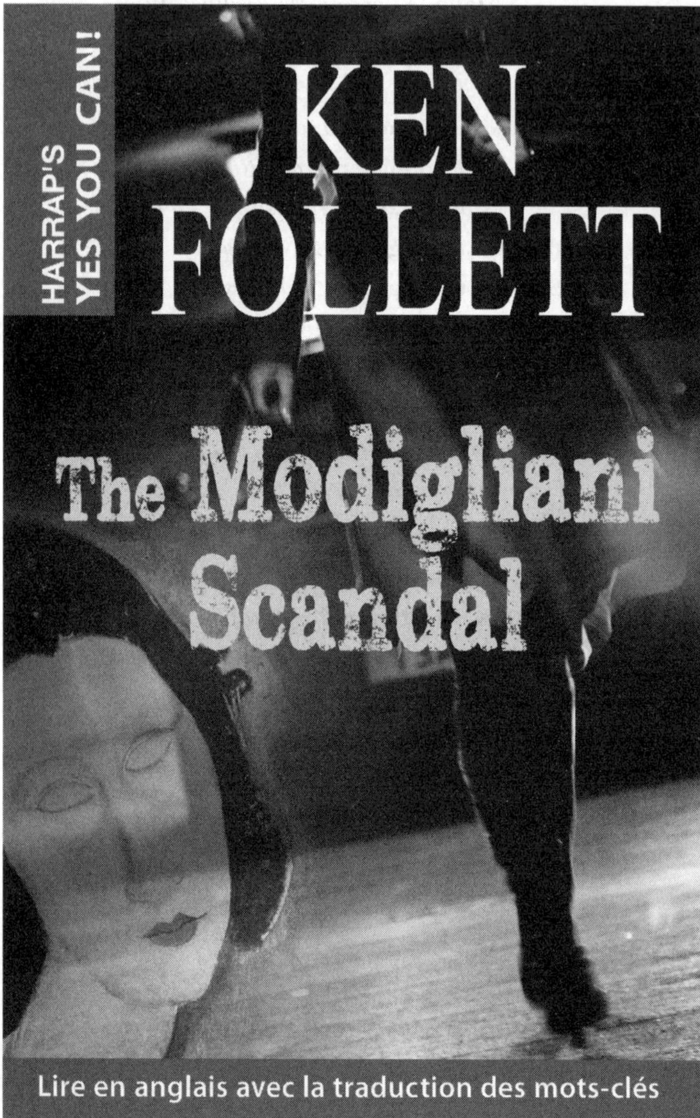
HARRAP'S
YES YOU CAN!
KEN
FOLLETT
The Modigliani
Scandal
Lire en anglais avec la traduction des mots-clés

HARRAP'S
YES YOU CAN!
M.C.
BEATON
Texte intégral en VO
Pour lire en anglais avec la traduction des mots-clés

PAPIER À BASE DE
FIBRES CERTIFIÉES

HARRAP s'engage pour l'environnement en réduisant l'empreinte carbone de ses livres. Celle de cet exemplaire est de :
700 g éq. CO_2
Rendez-vous sur www.larousse-durable.fr

Imprimer en Italie par Grafica Veneta
Dépôt légal : février 2020
324542-02/11049529 - février 2022